MW00780521

PLAYING WITH LIES

HOLLOW POINT

RILEY EDWARDS

BE A REBEL
Riley Edwards Romance

Hollow Point

Playing with Lies

100% HUMAN CREATED

Cover design: Lori Jackson Designs

Written by: Riley Edwards

Published by: Riley Edwards/Rebels Romance

Edited by: Kendall Black

Proofreader: Julie Deaton

Book Name: Playing with Lies

Paperback ISBN: 978-1-951567-55-2

First edition: December 26, 2023

To my family - my team – my tribe.
This is for you.

CONTENTS

1

I WASN'T GOING CRAZY.

I knew I wasn't.

Last week I thought I was, then I thought maybe I was being paranoid due to a lack of nutrition and stress. One of my many, *many* toxic traits—I was an overachiever who thrived on a deadline. In other words, I was a classic procrastinator who lied about thriving under pressure so I wouldn't feel bad about myself. I mean, who likes to work themselves sick? Anyway, there I was, working myself to the bone as my deadline loomed (something I always did) not eating and living off coffee; therefore, being paranoid wasn't a stretch.

But after I'd hit my deadline, I'd made up for my lack of nourishment and refueled. So, now I was properly fed and hydrated and I knew I wasn't going crazy.

Someone was following me.

But I had no proof. I hadn't actually seen anyone. I could just *feel* them. Like eyes were on me as I walked to my car after work. Or when I was at the grocery store, it felt like someone was watching me. Or when I left the gym. It was a tinge of awareness.

But I wasn't going crazy and right then, as I was making my way across the parking lot of Balls Deep, I knew someone was there in the shadows. All the fine hairs on the back of my neck were tingling. I picked up my pace. I needed to get inside of the pool hall where my friends were waiting for me. Or I should say Wren, my boss, was waiting for me. The rest of the people I was meeting were her friends. I was just the tag-along.

I yanked open the heavy door and was immediately assaulted with rock music and the sound of balls slapping together. I took a moment to glance around the crowded space, noting once again how much I loved the dark navy-blue walls and wood accents. When I got around to remodeling my kitchen and dining room, I was totally stealing Matt's designer's ideas.

Side note: Matt Kessler and his wife Chelsea owned the bar. Chelsea ran Balls Deep. Matt worked for a company called Triple Canopy. Wren had told me the company specialized in tactical training and security. She'd also told me they were highly sought after and were known as the best security company in Georgia and the surrounding states. I'd thought about talking to Hadley Walker, one of the women Wren had introduced me to. Her father along with three of his Army buddies had started Triple Canopy. They'd since retired and now their children ran the place. Hadley was married to Brady and from what I gathered from Wren he was one of the head honchos at Triple Canopy. However, being the best in the state meant they'd be expensive. I could dip into my rainy-day fund, but seeing as I wasn't positive-*positive* someone was actually following me I wasn't sure spending my life savings was the smart thing to do.

Though if I was right and someone was stalking me I might not have a life to enjoy my savings.

My musings about how much my life was worth—that was, if I wasn't being delusional due to permanent nervous system damage from my caffeine intake—were cut short when I spotted him.

Dalton Neary.

Much to my very logical father's dismay, I'd taken after my mother. Not that my dad didn't adore my mom; he totally did and he showed it and that further cemented my fanciful notions. My dad said I lived with my head in the clouds. He wasn't totally right. Most of the time I lived in the real world. I had a job, I was a homeowner, I was responsible with my money. Fiscal independence, that was what my dad had taught me, the part of me that'd come from him. But the rest, I was all Mom. She'd filled my head with all things kismet and soulmates. To hold out for my Prince Charming. Through her I'd learned that my Prince Charming wouldn't show up on a white horse and sweep me off my feet. He might show up in a pickup truck or a tractor or on a bicycle. But however he came he would be perfect for me. She believed it because that was what she'd found with my dad. It wasn't all sunshine and rainbows. My parents had tiffs like any married couple. But all in all they had a loving marriage and they loved me and my sister and they never failed to show us how much.

I wanted that for myself.

I wanted it badly but I was holding out for my Prince Charming and wouldn't settle for anything less.

Enter Dalton.

The first time I saw him I was grabbing a coffee. The place was packed but for whatever reason my gaze went directly to him. The rest of the people waiting in line ceased to exist. Unfortunately, he didn't look up and lock eyes with me and sweep me off my feet.

The next time I saw him I was picking up my to-go order from this hole-in-the-wall pizza joint. He was sitting by himself at a booth doing something on his phone. He didn't look up. I left feeling like I'd been punched in the stomach.

I saw him at the gym, at other restaurants. I even saw him one afternoon when I was having lunch with Wren.

I'd lived in Hollow Point my whole life and I'd never seen him.

Now, he was everywhere. And if that wasn't enough, Wren's husband Phoenix was a cop—a detective actually—and Dalton was Phoenix's partner.

Kismet.

I was meant to meet Dalton.

Now, I wasn't crazy enough to think Dalton was my soulmate but it felt like I was fated to meet him, and my boss marrying his partner solidified those thoughts. All I knew was, I was drawn to him. Admittedly it might just be I was attracted to him. No doubt he was hot and had the most unusual dark-rimmed, light-brown eyes I'd ever seen. Long eyelashes, thick eyebrows, a beard that looked like he hadn't shaved in five days but it never grew past that and I'd never seen him clean shaven. I was positive that beard would feel sublime between my legs. He kept his hair longish on top, clipped short on the sides—just enough to run my fingers through it if I ever got the chance. He was tall, lean, dressed cool, and almost always had a smile on his handsome face. So there it was—I totally wanted to have sex with Dalton.

I knew my friends, especially Wren, thought I was bold and brazen but it was mostly a front. I'd never actually approached a man and made the first move. I just put myself out there and made it obvious I was interested. However, I hadn't done that with Dalton. For whatever reason, maybe because he was attached to Wren in a roundabout way, I was holding back. I didn't want to lose my connection to Dalton should we have a romp and things turned awkward.

That would suck.

But maybe he could help me.

I pushed my way through the crowd and slowed my step when I saw Phoenix's brother, Echo Kent, sitting next to Dalton. I didn't know how I'd missed him seeing as he was the next-size-up human—the man was a giant. Wren had told me he was a teddy bear but with his piercing blue eyes and stoic expression (unless he was around his siblings or his fiancée, Jaclyn) I wasn't sure if that was true.

"I have a question." I heard Matt ask from behind the bar as he stood next to Chelsea.

"You don't have a question," Chelsea contradicted. "Go play pool with Luke. He needs some competition."

Matt ignored her and kept his eyes on Dalton.

"I have this idea."

"No, you don't," Chelsea groaned.

"How does Banging Behind Bars sound?" Matt continued.

"Like a strip club that caters to ex-cons," I blurted out.

"See?" Chelsea chirped and strutted away.

"Not that there's anything wrong with a strip club," I clarified.

Matt chuckled and shook his head. "I was actually thinking of buying a music studio."

When no one said anything, he went on. "You know, banging on instruments, laying down bars..." he trailed off, looking among the three of us.

"Dammit, now I have to admit she's right."

As soon as Matt stalked off, Echo slid off his stool.

"I'm gonna go find Jaclyn before she makes another bet and loses."

Dalton glanced over his shoulder. My gaze followed just in time to watch Jaclyn throw some cash onto the felt of a pool table.

"Good luck. Looks like she's already placed her bet." Dalton laughed.

Damn, I was a sucker for his laugh.

"Vanessa," Echo greeted.

"Hey, Echo."

"Was it something I said?" I asked and slipped onto the stool Echo vacated.

"No. Matt had to go eat crow and since I've been here Jaclyn's lost three rounds and keeps placing wagers," Dalton explained.

That made me feel marginally better. I hadn't run off his friends. But now that we were alone and I could smell his spicy cologne I wasn't so sure I wanted to ask him for help.

What if he thought I was some sort of drama queen looking for attention?

Or I was using someone following me to get into his pants?

The fake stalker ploy.

Dalton slugged back a healthy pull from his beer and I watched the muscles in his neck contract.

Good Lord, the man even had a sexy neck.

Now I was being the stalker, staring at him drinking.

Okay, I could do this. I could explain to Dalton what was going on and ask his opinion. We were friends-*ish*.

It was the perfect timing—Dalton alone, Chelsea at the other end of the bar helping a customer, all of our friends occupied.

I swiveled to face him. His knees automatically opened, my eyes dropped to his legs bracketing in mine. I liked that, liked that he made room for me, and liked the way our legs looked so close together—his outlining mine but not touching—but mostly I liked what it said. It didn't say sort-of-friends, it said something else entirely. It was intimate but not overt. I liked it too much so I slowly lifted my gaze. The moment our eyes met I was captivated and I liked that more—the way he was looking at me like he wanted to eat me and he didn't care if the whole bar knew it.

Oh boy.

All my inappropriate thoughts about how his beard would feel between my legs came rushing back and it was a miracle I didn't tip sideways and fall off the stool. A primal urge to rip off his clothes or pull him close for a kiss or at least reach up and run my palm over his beard washed over me. As if he could read my mind his lips twitched and I feared if he kept staring at me like that I might do something stupid like invite him to take a tour of the women's bathroom with me.

I heard balls breaking right before laughter rang out. Which thankfully pulled me from my trance and reminded me I was in a bar surrounded by friends and pulling Dalton into the bathroom for a quickie would've been a bad idea.

Before I could lose my nerve I cleared my throat and began. "Listen, I...um, know we don't know each other all that well but I was wondering if I could ask you a favor."

Jeez, stutter much.

I resisted the urge to smack myself in the forehead to dislodge the lingering effects of his nearness.

"You can ask me anything."

The way he said "anything" made my nipples tingle.

And suddenly I no longer wanted his help; I wanted something altogether different.

This wasn't a good idea. If I was wrong and no one was following me I didn't want Dalton to think I was a total nutcase.

I still hadn't figured out how I was going to get out of the conversation I'd started when he prompted, "What's your favor?"

Wild, crazy monkey sex until I can't breathe.

I didn't say that.

Thank God.

"Never mind, it's nothing."

I started to swivel back to face the bar but only made it as far as my knee touching his inner thigh. The thrill of that sent a current of electricity through me.

"Sorry," I mumbled, and tried to maneuver my legs clear.

Throughout this, Dalton didn't make a move to clear my way. He made matters worse and leaned in closer.

"Vanessa?"

The sound of my name sent another shiver down my spine and I was pretty sure goosebumps erupted on my arms. Suddenly I wanted to hear him breathe my name while he was moving inside of me. I wanted that with shocking desperation. So much so I could taste it.

What in the hell was wrong with me? I was a healthy, active woman who had no hangups about sex but this was something else.

"Nessa." He used my nickname and damn I liked that, too.

"Yeah?"

"You okay?"

"Nope."

Oh, hell, why did I admit that?

"What's making you not okay?"

"You're too close."

And I did it again, blurted out the truth without thinking.

"And I'm gonna get closer if you don't tell me what's wrong," he threatened.

I wanted him to get closer, a lot closer, especially when his voice was all rumbly.

Down, girl, you can't hump his leg in public. Which much to my dismay seemed like a real possibility.

"No, you close is what's wrong."

Dalton immediately reared back and freed my legs.

Disappointment flooded me.

"That's not what I meant..." I paused because at that point I'd made such a mess out of this I didn't know how to recover.

It was time for me to leave. If I didn't, I was going to make a bigger fool out of myself.

"I didn't mean that the way it sounded," I tried again. "Sorry."

I was digging my hole deeper.

"Listen, I just remembered I need to..." God, I sucked at lying. With no ready fib I lamely finished with, "I need to go. It was good seeing you."

With that I bolted.

I was out the door and halfway to my car when I felt it.

Fear slithered through me until it gripped my insides. This wasn't stress, lack of sleep, or dehydration-induced paranoia.

Someone was there.

They were watching.

I could *feel* it.

WHAT THE FUCK JUST HAPPENED?

I stared at the door Vanessa had just hightailed her fine, tight-jean-clad ass out of. I did this wondering how in the hell I'd fucked that up so thoroughly she'd fled the bar.

Oh, she'd tried to hide behind some fictitious excuse about needing to do *something* though she'd never said what that something was.

Because you made her uncomfortable, you tool.

Christ.

I needed to fix this—apologize and make sure shit didn't get awkward.

When I made it to the parking lot Vanessa's head was up, looking around, alert to her surroundings.

Good girl.

"Vanessa," I called out, and jogged my way across the lot.

Her body jerked and she glanced over her shoulder.

The parking lot was well lit. Matt had seen to that when he purchased the pool hall. He'd renovated the place inside and out. Part of the overhaul included extra exterior lighting which made it safe for his patrons to get in and out of their vehicles. So

I didn't miss the fear in Vanessa's eyes nor did I miss the way she held herself like she was readying for battle.

I'd seriously fucked this up.

I stopped at a safe distance hoping she would relax.

She didn't; the woman was tweaked.

"Listen, I didn't mean to make you uncomfortable."

"You..." she trailed off. "I wasn't uncomfortable."

I was waiting for her to say more but my attention went to the thick shrubs and overgrown grass that separated the pool hall parking lot from the gas station next door. The only area that was unkempt and not lit.

"Do you feel it, too?" she whispered.

Something in her tone had my body stringing tight and not in the normal way my body reacted to her.

"Feel what?"

"Like someone's watching."

That was exactly what I was afraid she'd say.

"How long has this been happening?"

"A while," she said immediately and I was glad I didn't have to waste time pulling it out of her.

"How long's a while?"

"About a week."

Fuck.

"I'm going to watch you walk to your car. Get in, lock the doors, and do not unlock them until I get back. Not for anyone."

"Dalton—"

"No one, Nessa."

She hesitated then briskly walked to her car. I went back into the bar, slipped into the back room, and exited the pool hall using the back door. I waited beside the dumpster and listened. Nothing but the muted thump of the music coming from inside. I slowly moved around the building, happy Matt only had minimal lighting in the back, and focused on the line of shrubs.

No sound, no shadows moving. Still I walked closer until I could see the gas station.

No one was there.

But somebody was.

I could feel them watching.

I jogged around to the front and went to Vanessa's car. By the time I was at the driver's side her window was rolled down.

"Anything?" she asked hopefully.

Vanessa Hale wasn't a timid woman which meant that hope I'd heard was fueled by genuine fear.

"No. I'm following you home."

"That's—" She stopped, shook her head, then started again. "Okay."

And there it was again. She was no pushover either; the fear was making her agreeable.

"My truck's on the side. Pull to the exit and wait for me."

Another nod.

It wasn't until we were on the road when I remembered her starting the conversation by wanting to ask me for a favor, but I'd made her so uncomfortable she'd fled before she could ask me for help.

Christ, I'm a dick.

Vanessa pulled into an older neighborhood on the outskirts of town. I tried to think of any disturbances I'd been out to in this area when I was still in uniform and came up blank. Ditto with break-ins. It was a well-kept, mid-income development with big trees lining the street. Nice yards, decent cars in the driveways, street lights scattered so the neighborhood wasn't dark but not enough to bother the homeowners. She made another turn and four houses in, she pulled into her driveway. A single story that by the look of it had new siding and stone accents around the bottom. The porch that started at the front door and made its way to the end of the house looked newish, as well as the landscaping in front of the lattice going from the dirt up the edge of the porch planks. The rest of her front yard was well established, the shrubs in front of the lattice were small, only a couple seasons old. To the left of her front door was a two-car garage. Again, the door looked modern and was gleaming white.

I waited for her to open the door and pull into the garage. When she got out of her car I pulled into her drive and parked next to her sporty silver Hyundai Elantra.

"There a reason you don't park in your garage?" I asked.

"There's no room."

A woman who lived alone, no matter the neighborhood she lived in was nice, should park in the garage.

Instead of telling her this I followed her to the porch. I was right; it had recently been updated.

"How long have you lived here?"

She glanced over her shoulder.

"Three years."

"Porch looks nice. So do the new garage doors. It's a waste you don't use it. The garage, that is."

Vanessa finished unlocking the door while muttering, "Save the lecture. My dad beat you to it and I normally park in the garage but right now it's full of paint, drop cloths, and tools."

It was good to know her dad had already paved my way. Depending on how the next thirty minutes went we'd be cleaning out her garage this evening so she could pull her car in before I left.

I couldn't say I'd spent time thinking about where or how Vanessa lived, but walking into her living room and seeing the walls painted a mustard-yellow was not what I'd imagined if I'd given it any thought. And if someone told me mustard-yellow paint would look badass I would've told them they were full of shit. But there I was, standing in Vanessa's living room with mustard-yellow walls, a couch that looked to be blue velvet—a woman would call it indigo or a muted navy or some shit like that but whatever the exact shade, it worked. The toss pillows—and there were a lot—were all different sizes and shades of the wall color. A big rug was in the center—blues and yellows—covering gleaming refinished hardwood floors. A glass coffee table with gold accents sat on top of the rug. Two raspberry free-standing chairs were positioned in front of the windows facing the street. Heavy, thick velvet curtains that were the exact shade of the walls were pulled open allowing the outside light to filter in through cream sheers. Black lacquered bookshelves were on either side of a brick fireplace that had been painted white. The mantel above it was also painted white. A large circular mirror hung above the mantel.

It shouldn't have worked but it did in a classy, elegant, but edgy cool way. It also seemed out of place in an older mid-income neighborhood.

Full of paint, drop cloths, and tools.

"Did you do all of this yourself?"

Vanessa glanced around the room then stopped and focused on me with a tilt of her head.

"It's just paint."

It wasn't just paint. The hardwood floors were real wood and gleaming. The baseboards around the room looked new, as did the framing around the windows.

"What about the floors?"

Vanessa walked farther into the house, flipping on lights as she went. I followed her into the kitchen that looked like it had all the original cabinetry and appliances from when the house was built. Neither were attractive and didn't mesh with the feel of the living room.

She tossed her purse on the old, chipped, ugly Formica counter and whirled on me.

"Those were a pain in the ass. Thankfully when I moved in here I didn't have any furniture to go in there so all I had to do was tape up some plastic here." She pointed to the double-wide opening that separated her living room from the kitchen. "The dust was unreal. I started with a hand sander but after a weekend of that I rented one of those machines you stand up and push around. That, too, was a pain. Just not a pain in my ass, it was a pain in my arms and shoulders trying to push that beast around the room and not let it get away from me."

I was seriously impressed. Sanding floors was a bitch.

"And I screwed up the first coat of finish. It had bubbles in the finish and it looked so bad I had to wait for it to completely dry, rent the sander again, and start over. I learned that cheap paintbrushes do not work on finishing."

"You did a great job."

"Thanks. I love the way it turned out and as much as I can't wait to do the rest of the house, especially my bedroom, the carpet in there is a nightmare—but I'm not looking forward to ripping it out and sanding."

At the mention of her bedroom I had the urge to ask for a full tour of her home ending in said bedroom to inspect the carpet she called a nightmare before I took my time examining other things—that weren't so much "things" as they were places, all of which had nothing to do with remodeling and everything to do with finding out how she tasted, and what kind of sounds she made while my face was buried between her legs.

I hadn't yet successfully gotten the image of her spread out on her bed out of my mind when she brought the conversation around to why I was really there.

"Thanks for following me home."

"Right. Tell me what's going on."

She bit the corner of her bottom lip which didn't help the visions I was failing to shove aside.

"I'm probably overreacting."

"Don't do that shit, Vanessa. Always trust your instincts."

Her eyes came back to mine and she relaxed.

"You promise you won't think I'm crazy?"

"I can't promise you that, but I promise to listen."

Her shoulders sagged and that worried look crept back in.

"I'm teasin' you, sweetheart."

When she stayed in her slouch I tested the waters, got closer, and when she had no reaction to my nearness I reached out and grabbed her hand. She immediately wrapped her fingers around mine and I let go of the breath I hadn't realized I was holding.

"Hey," I called and gave her hand a squeeze. "I was teasing you trying to get you to relax. I fucked up and just so we're clear on this I mean now and back at the bar. I apologized but I think it got lost in the moment so I'll say it again; I'm sorry for making you uncomfortable."

Her cheeks tinged pink and her hand flexed in mine but she didn't pull away.

"I told you, you didn't make me uncomfortable." She dipped her head like she was trying to hide her face when she softly admitted, "I was going to ask you for help but then I got nervous and then made it worse and ran away."

"Why would you be nervous to ask me for help?"

Just her eyes tipped up and fuck me...blatant interest.

"I wasn't nervous to ask you for help. I'm worried if I'm wrong I'll look like a fool."

I needed her to explain to me what was going on. But first I needed to set something straight.

"Hear this, Vanessa; there's nothing you can tell me that would make me think you're crazy or a fool." I gave her hand a shake. "I want you to tell me what's going on but I want you comfortable when you tell me. So you tell me where that's gonna be."

Her eyes flared and her cheeks flushed.

But it was the way those wide eyes heated that gave her away.

3

MY FACE FELT like it was on fire and I was pretty sure it looked that way, too.

It must be noted I had never in my life blushed and there I was standing in my kitchen with my face blistering red over an innocent comment.

All he wanted to know was where I'd be comfortable to sit and talk to him about what was going on. He didn't ask me to strip naked so he could eat me on my kitchen floor. But that was exactly where my mind had gone and if I wasn't imagining things he totally knew what I was thinking. Okay, maybe he didn't know *exactly* what I was thinking but with the way my cheeks were lit up like a glowing sign announcing I was a hussy he'd have a clue.

Jeez.

What was wrong with me and why did my voice crack when I said, "Den."

I cleared my throat and tried again.

"We can go sit in the den. It's really a four seasons room I converted. It's not as nice as the living room and the furniture in there is old so it's comfy."

Dalton's lips curved up into a grin.

My cheeks were threatening to catch fire. Seriously, I was hitting the red zone of embarrassment.

"Wherever you want."

There it was again, insinuation in his tone.

I didn't know how long I stood there staring at him—oh, and holding his hand. Not that I could forget he was holding my hand because it was tingling along with my nipples.

There was something really wrong with me. Perhaps all the stress and malnutrition hadn't made me paranoid; it had made me horny.

Ew. I hated that word. I couldn't believe I'd even thought that word.

"Sweetheart, what's on your mind?"

"Horny."

Dalton's eyes flashed, he pinched his lips together, and I knew he did this in an effort not to bust out laughing.

So, I'd been wrong.

Now, I'd hit the red zone.

Warning. Warning. Detonation fast approaching.

"Wait! I was thinking how much I hated that word."

Dalton's lips turned white he was pinching them so hard.

I didn't get the chance to dig my hole any deeper.

He lost the battle and, you guessed it, busted out laughing.

The sound was rich and deep. It felt like the sun had come out from behind the clouds and warmed my skin. I could bask in the warmth of Dalton's laugh and never, ever be cold again.

What the hell was that about?

"Holy shit," he said through his hilarity.

"I should try to explain but I'm not going to because anything I say at this point will make it worse."

Dalton gave my hand a tug. I fell forward, and braced my hand on a hard wall of muscle.

Good Lord.

"No, please continue."

Wow. Up close his eyes had flecks of gold dotting the light brown.

"Vanessa?"

"You have really long eyelashes."

The area around those unfairly long lashes softened.

"And they're really thick."

The softness went away and tiny lines formed at the corner of his eyes. I didn't need to know he was smiling.

"Thick?"

"Yeah, really thick."

Since I was now close I felt him shaking.

It took a moment for it to dawn on me what I'd said. Though in all fairness with my hand on a hard wall of muscle it was taking all of my concentration to stop myself from feeling him up so I hadn't been guarding my words.

"Maybe we should get on the couch. I mean, go sit on the couch."

Thankfully he took pity on me but not before he flashed me a killer smile that muddled my already frazzled brain.

Good Lord, I need to get a grip.

And not a grip of his dick.

Oh, my, God. My brain had run amok.

I had no control over the shit that was popping in and out all willy-nilly.

"I'd ask you what you're thinking about now but I'm afraid."

"You should be; it's a scary place in there right now."

"Scary or horny?"

"Ugh. I hate that word. I don't know why it jumped into my head."

Dalton's smile got bigger.

"You don't?"

"Um..." I let that trail off and prayed he didn't push.

Unless it was me up against a wall. He could totally push me up against a wall, shove his hands in my hair, and take my mouth.

"Advice, sweetheart? Don't ever try your hand at poker."

"I'm awesome at poker," I returned.

"So it's just me then?"

"Just you what?"

Seeing as I was much shorter than him, Dalton's head was tipped down, mine was tipped up, but still he brought his face closer to mine and whispered, "Nessa, baby." But he got no further.

My phone in my back pocket rang. I stood staring up at a now-smiling Dalton while I lamented my poor life choices as my Crazy Frog ringtone screeched *ding, ding, deed-da-ding, ding-bing-dawn.* The longer my phone rang the more the gibberish deteriorated until there were some nonsensical sound effects. Lots of *psshts* and *dongs* ending with silly motorcycle sounds before it started all over with the *ding, ding, deed-da-ding.*

"You gonna answer that?" he asked through a smile.

"No. I'm pretending this isn't happening. If I answer I have to acknowledge my phone is ringing and you can hear this ridiculousness."

Again Dalton busted out laughing. Again I watched. He was hot all the time; when he smiled—hotter. When he laughed —off the charts. So hot I wanted to kiss him while he was laughing just to see if that laughter tasted as good as it looked. It was a weird thing to think but it was the truth.

Thankfully the phone stopped ringing. Unfortunately it started again.

"Sweetheart—"

"You know if this was some rom-com I was watching this would be the part of the movie where I covered my face in commiseration with the protagonist. But it's a movie so you know the hot guy finds her cute and funny instead of ridiculous and gawky."

"Sweet—"

"But since this isn't a movie and covering my face would only embarrass me further, all I can do is wish a black hole would open up and suck us into an alternate universe where I have a badass ringtone instead."

"Vanessa—"

I ignored the humor in his tone and blathered on.

"Though in this alternate universe I'd also have the power to rewind time and not embarrass myself by running out of a bar."

"I don't know. You running out of that bar put me right here and I can't say I'm disappointed in that."

I blinked at him.

"You should answer your phone, baby, it might be important."

Baby?

It took a great deal of effort to ignore the belly flutter and the nipple tingling as I reached into my pocket to pull out my phone. I lost sight of Dalton's smile when I looked at my phone —this, too, took effort. I wanted to get lost in his smile and other parts of him besides.

My screen said Wren.

Damn.

I connected the call and heard her talking before I had my phone to my ear.

"Hey," I greeted.

"Where are you? Echo said he saw you at the bar."

"I'm at home."

"What? Why? I thought we were celebrating."

Yes, that had been the plan. We were celebrating finishing the Sunshine Center's grant proposal. The research into finding grant resources had taken longer than expected and we'd hit our deadline with a day to spare.

"I'm sorry, something came up."

Lame.

As previously noted I was a shit liar.

"Something came up?" she repeated.

"Um. Yeah. I'm sorry—"

"Are you with Dalton?" she whispered. "Echo said he was at the bar, too. But no one can find him and Phoenix tried to call him but he didn't answer."

My eyes flicked to Dalton.

"Um..."

"You are. Dalton's what came up." She was no longer whispering and I wondered if the whole bar heard. "Right on!" she yelped.

"Um..."

"'Bout time, girly."

With that she hung up. I lowered my phone and put it on silent before I placed it on the counter.

"Phoenix called you."

Dalton's smile widened.

I waited for him to do something, like say, pull his phone out and check his messages.

"What's funny?"

"Nothing, sweetheart. You're just cute when you get flustered."

I should've lied and told him I wasn't flustered but I was too busy doing an imaginary somersault.

"I thought we were getting comfortable?" I snapped.

"Yeah, we're gonna get comfortable," he drawled, full of mouthwatering innuendo.

"Dalton—"

"We're going to go sit and talk about what's going on. We'll see what happens after that."

I knew what I wanted to happen after that.

Proving that he could read my mind, Dalton winked before he let me go and swept his arm for me to lead the way.

The wink nearly did me in.

It was a miracle I hadn't jumped him then and there in my kitchen. It was also a wonder I kept my feet and led him to my den. But when he sat down next to me, angled his big body my way, and looked like he was having the same thoughts I was having now that we were on a soft surface that wasn't as big as a bed but would still provide enough room for some fooling around, it wasn't a miracle or a wonder—it was an exercise in self-control.

Without preamble Dalton started.

"Alright, Vanessa, break it down for me."

I took a breath, blew it out, and hoped he meant what he said about not thinking I was crazy.

"Okay, so, it started a little over a week ago. I was coming out of work and it was strange. I can't explain the feeling exactly but I *knew* someone was watching me. By the time I got home I'd convinced myself I was just stressed and being weird. A few days later I was at the grocery store reading the back of a bag of chocolate chips making sure I had all the ingredients to make cookies and I got that feeling again but when I looked up no one was there. I finished shopping and told myself I was in a crowded store, of course I'd feel someone watching me because, hello, it's a grocery store. The same thing happened when I went into the gym one night. And again tonight when I left for Balls Deep."

All of the flirtation had drained from Dalton's handsome face. Gone was the good-natured man and sitting next to me was Detective Dalton Neary.

"Other than that, anything else strange happening?"

"Like what?"

"Phone calls. Notes left on your car, in your mailbox. An ex hassling you. Seeing the same person at multiple places. Anything. It could be as simple as someone giving you attention."

I thought about his question even though I didn't have to. I was a single woman, I paid attention to my surroundings—most of the time. I was as guilty of checking my phone in public, or being in my head thinking about work or my house or my ever-growing list of things I had to get done on any given day. But for the most part I didn't walk around oblivious.

"No."

"All the work done around your house, did you hire out any of the work?"

"Yeah. The new garage doors, windows, the siding and accents, and the porch."

"How long ago was the work done and did anyone give you a strange vibe?"

Damn. I shifted my gaze to the new windows.

"Someone gave you a vibe," he muttered. "Do you know his name?"

Detective Neary didn't miss much. Though I suspected even when Dalton wasn't in detective mode he still didn't miss anything.

"The window guy. Tommy. I don't know his last name; he works for Precision Windows. But he was in his sixties."

"Sweetheart, there's no age cap on a creep."

Right, that made sense.

"What'd he do that gave you a bad feeling?" Dalton pushed.

And now we were back to me hoping Dalton didn't think I was nuts.

"It wasn't a bad feeling as such. He just...I don't know...was too talkative. Wouldn't catch the hint when the conversation was over and he should get back to work. He asked me a lot of questions."

"Questions?"

"Like if I was single. He said he had a son who was always hooking up with moochers and he needed to find himself an independent woman. But the way he said it was sweet like he was giving me a compliment. He asked about the work I did inside the house. He asked if I had family close. I can't remember everything. It was conversational but kind of intrusive. I never got a bad feeling about him, I just thought he was too chatty. The strange part was if he had someone here working with him he didn't speak to me. Didn't even look at me. But if he was here by himself I caught him staring at me."

"What about your doors? Did he install those?"

"My doors?"

"Your doors," he repeated. "The front door's new. Did you get new locks put in and if you did, did Tommy or Precision Windows install them?"

Oh, shit.

I felt my stomach clench and a new kind of fear crept in. Not the strange feeling I'd been having that someone was watching me but real fear that someone could have access to my house.

"Yes," I whispered. "Tommy installed the new doors. Front, garage, and that one." I pointed to the door across the room that opened to my backyard. "And they supplied the new locks."

Dalton's lips thinned and his face went hard.

"I didn't see an alarm."

He was correct. I didn't have an alarm.

I shook my head and his lips turned down.

"Are you adverse to installing one?"

Yes, in the sense I had a feeling an alarm would cost a

whack and I was saving up to redo my kitchen. An alarm would put me back months and months and I really wanted a new kitchen. Though I'd like not to be burglarized or violated more.

"An alarm is smart," he went on. "You got nice things, Nessa, they're worth protecting. But beyond that, you live here alone, and it's a matter of safety."

I'd heard that before. My dad wanted me to get an alarm before I redid my front room. I disagreed. Then he pushed for an alarm before I redid the guest bathroom but again, I didn't listen.

"I can see now this isn't going to work out between us," I grumbled.

"Come again?"

"Me and you, it's not going to work out. For my sanity we need to preemptively break up."

Dalton's brows rose and his eyes danced with humor.

God, he was hot.

"Preemptively?"

"Yup."

"You wanna explain that?"

"Well, see, you and my dad think alike. Exhibit one, me parking in the garage. Me parking in the garage would mean I'd have to find the time to clean my garage which would also mean buying shelves out there and I don't want to waste money on that or alternately moving all the stuff out there into the house and I don't want to do that either. I don't like clutter and mess. Paint cans and drop cloths and stain and tools means mess and clutter. Exhibit two, the alarm. Spending the money on that would mean delaying my kitchen and I think you can agree my kitchen needs a complete overhaul including appliances. I ignored my dad and remodeled the guest bathroom. The first time my parents came over for dinner after I finished the bathroom his head nearly exploded. But he's my dad and I cause him this sort of hassle and he'll still love me. I'm guessing men like you don't like their women giving them hassle, so you'll get fed up with it quick. Further from that, I might buckle under the pressure if I have two men coming at me about alarms and parking in my garage. I'm my own woman. I do what I do. That's not to say I can't and don't compromise—case in point I'm going to make some calls tomorrow and price out an alarm system even though I don't want to because I want a new kitchen first."

Weirdly, he didn't sound put off after my long-winded soliloquy.

"Only need to make one call tomorrow, sweetheart, and I'll make that call."

"Only one call? Dalton, estimates are important."

Gah. Now I sounded like my dad.

"No doubt. But the call I'll make is to Triple Canopy and no way they'd fuck anyone over, especially not you. I'll talk to Brady and ask if he can swing you a deal on a good system that won't break the bank."

Houston, we had a problem.

"I don't like taking advantage of friendships."

"You friends with Brady?"

Brady was married to Hadley. I was friends-ish with her. But I couldn't say I'd had more than one conversation with the man.

"No, not really, but I'm friends with Wren who is married to Phoenix whose sister is Shiloh and she's married to Luke who works for Triple Canopy. So in a roundabout way I'd be taking advantage."

"Nessa, that's not a roundabout way, that's the long way. And I am friends with Brady and with Luke and Logan, Drake, Trey, Matt, Dylan, Hadley, Nick, Carter, and Quinn."

I couldn't know for sure but I thought Dalton had rattled off all of the employees at Triple Canopy.

"And I have no such hang-up about asking for a favor," he went on. "Especially when it's something important to me."

Important to him?

"But—"

"I appreciate you're an independent woman. It's one of the many things I'm coming to find I like about you. I also like you get your safety is more important than a kitchen so you're willing to take that hit. So it's a good thing you know how to compromise because tomorrow I'm calling Brady, explaining what's going on, and asking him to swing you a deal and scratch you onto the top of his list for a quick install. And to finish, you're not preemptively breaking up with me."

Whoa. *Whoa.* Whoa.

I was finding it hard to argue my corner when I was stuck on Dalton straight-out telling me there were many things he liked about me. I was also fighting a heart attack because he wasn't accepting my preemptive breakup.

"Now you have a choice to make. Am I spending the night here or are you coming home with me and spending the night there?"

Okay.

Yeah.

Spending the night?

Now I was fighting a stroke.

"What?"

"My house or yours?" he reiterated. "Your choice. But whichever you choose you're not sleeping alone."

Yep. My heart was pounding so hard it was going to explode out of my chest.

I did a quick scan of my thoughts on this matter and found I didn't care where I slept and I didn't care that either choice would mean I wasn't sleeping alone.

"Do you work tomorrow?" I asked.

"Nope. I have the weekend off."

Staying here would mean he didn't have anything to sleep in —a definite plus. But it would also mean he'd likely roll out of here early to go home and change. That would suck. But if we stayed at his house, he might expect me to leave early and that would be life-crushing.

"I call bullshit on the whole you're good at poker gig," he stated.

That was totally insulting. I rocked at Texas Hold 'em.

"I don't know why—"

Dalton leaned in and cupped my jaw.

"Baby, you're easy to read. Your every thought is clear on your face. Mine or yours? It's an easy question. Whichever house you pick, nothing's going to happen that you don't want to happen." He paused to grin. "And seeing as earlier I read you clear, too, I'm rethinking your options. You should pack a bag and come to mine so I don't have to leave to get clothes. It might take the weekend to get through everything that was making your cheeks pink."

Holy smokes, my cheeks were burning again.

He stroked his thumb over the pink and muttered, "I see you're on board with the plan."

He was right, I was on board.

"I'll pack a bag."

With his gaze steady on mine he proceeded to rock my world.

There wasn't much distance to close but still he went slow, giving me time to stop him. Not that I wanted to but it was sweet of him to give me the option. It was thoughtful and gentle-manly. So was the first lip brush, and the chaste kiss to the side of my mouth. His tongue swiped my bottom lip. I readily followed and touched my tongue to his. It was a slow glide; again he was giving me time to pull back. Dalton kept the kiss sweet, slowly building up to the good stuff. I leaned into him, wordlessly asking for more and that was when he broke.

With a growl, the vestiges of gentlemanly vanished. The kiss went from gentle to deep in the blink of an eye. My mind blanked, the room melted away, and all that was left was me and Dalton and the magic he wrought.

Wow.

He was a good kisser.

His hand tensed on my jaw, his mouth took more and more until I whimpered.

Dalton tore his mouth from mine. I panted my displeasure. He groaned his.

Then he ordered, "Go pack a bag, sweetheart. Enough to get you through the weekend."

The area between my legs, already wet, spasmed.

I didn't move, mainly because I was so turned on from nothing but a kiss I was contemplating a quickie on my couch before I packed. (And I was totally packing for the whole weekend.) The other reason I remained still was because I was so completely and wholly captivated by the way Dalton was staring at me. I felt a burn hit my throat, something I'd never felt in my life, and held my breath.

"You keep looking at me like that, sweetheart, we might not make it back to my house."

I was fine with that.

Totally.

A sexy smirk hit Dalton's face and he shook his head.

"I see you're down with that, but, Nessa, baby, I'm thorough. And when I say that I mean, not only do I intend to take my time getting to know every inch of your body I intend to savor it. To do that right, I'm gonna need time..." Dalton paused and when he did his gaze moved to the couch. "And room." His heated eyes came back to me. "So do me a favor, go pack a bag and do it quick like, yeah?"

Suddenly I was captivated for another reason—no one had ever taken their time getting to know every inch of my body and I *really* wanted to know what that entailed.

Dalton dropped his head and sat back, giving me both the space to get up if I so chose or room should I want an out.

It was sweet. It was what I was learning was him.

But I didn't need an out.

I knew what I wanted.

Trying my best not to jump off the couch then run to my room to pack a bag, I got up, walked into my kitchen, and only picked up my pace when I was out of sight.

It was difficult, but I think I pulled it off.

4

JESUS FUCK.

I shifted my hands into the mess of pale blonde hair pooling in my lap, gathered it away from her beautiful face, and the view became better. Beautiful dark brown eyes tipped up, she groaned around my dick, and I watched with no small amount of satisfaction as she took me down her throat.

Jesus fuck.

Heaven.

Next time she took me, I'd have her positioned so I could play with her pussy while her mouth was wrapped around my cock. But right then with the taste of her climax still fresh on my tongue, the visual of her on my bed—legs spread wide while I took my time working her up until she'd taken over and fucked my face—seared into my memory in a way I knew I'd never forget. With Vanessa on her knees straddling one of my thighs, I was not complaining about the position she'd chosen to suck my dick.

Though I was close, and with each deep draw I was getting closer.

Her technique was perfection; just the right amount of

suction and tongue and she knew how to check her teeth and gag reflex. But it was more than that. Vanessa was seriously into what she was doing, keeping a rhythm that was mind-bending. Couple that with the sexy sounds she made as she worshiped my dick, I was so far gone I needed her to stop before I exploded.

I gave her hair a tug, savoring the last long pull of her mouth, fighting the urge to blow, when her suction increased as she neared the head of my cock.

"Christ," I bit out. "Your mouth."

Vanessa hummed. Clenching my teeth and hanging onto the last of my control, I ordered, "Pull off, baby, and climb on."

I let go of her hair, shifted, and reached to my nightstand to nab a condom.

Vanessa used this as an opportunity to administer her brand of torture, sliding the flat of her tongue down my shaft to my balls, and laved both my boys with attention. The feel of her wet, warm mouth was too much.

"Fuck," I grunted and focused on tearing open the condom and rolling it down. When I was covered, I fisted all that silky hair and used it to tip her head back. "Up. Nessa. Now."

Without delay she came up on her knees, reached around and unhooked her bra, slumped her shoulders forward and the last of her clothing slid down her arms.

"Next time, I get to finish," she demanded as she crawled over me.

"Sweetheart, you did finish, on my tongue," I reminded her.

Still balancing on her knees, completely naked and uncaring she was on display, she reached between us and not so gently grabbed my dick, took just the tip inside, and smiled down at me.

"Right, so next time, it's only fair I get to finish you *with* my mouth," she clarified, not moving to take more of me.

My hands went to her hips. One slid across her stomach, down, and in until my thumb found her clit.

"Next time, you want it, it's all yours." I circled my thumb and added pressure. "But the first time you make me come it's gonna to be with your pussy."

A playful light warmed Vanessa's eyes and she swiveled her hips but didn't otherwise move.

"So, what I'm hearing is you think you're the boss."

"Baby, if you don't get down to business the only thing you're gonna be hearing is yourself begging me to let you come when I show you just how bossy I can be." I tightened my grip on her hip and added, "And just a heads up with that, you'll be begging for a good long while."

It was then Vanessa drove herself down, groaning as she did, but when she had herself full of my dick she sassed, "Question for you, will I have to call you *Daddy* while I'm begging?"

I'd never been into a woman calling me daddy but hearing her say it even teasingly made me rethink my position.

"Honey, if you got it in you to speak, you can call me whatever you want." I moved my hand from her hip down to her ass and gave her a playful smack and ordered, "Time to stop fucking around."

Vanessa's hands hit my chest and she lifted herself up before she slammed back down, pulling a groan out of both of us.

"Closer, sweetheart."

She leaned forward, and with a handful of her ass, my thumb working her clit, I drew her nipple between my lips and took my fill. When I was done, I switched sides, gave her the edge of my teeth, slowly adding pressure until her pussy spasmed. I released her nipple to ask, "Can you take more?"

"God yes."

Fucking perfect.

I gave her more of my teeth at her nipple and rolled my thumb, adding a finger and pinching her clit. Vanessa's hips bucked, she lost her rhythm, and instead of bouncing she was now rocking and doing it with her cunt clamped tight around my dick, threatening to unman me.

I latched onto my control, praying I wouldn't be the one begging for her to slow down.

"Dalton."

Thank fuck.

I let go of her nipple and tipped my head back on the pillow.

"Up, baby. I want to watch."

Vanessa sat up, braced her hands on my thighs, arched her back thrusting her tits out, and gave me one hell of a sexy show while she fucked me harder and faster, chasing her pleasure. My control splintered as her climax took hold. Her pussy convulsed, wet heat flooded, coating my balls. She chanted my name, called for God, and trembled above me. The sight was enough to take me over the edge but it was the feel of her coming around my cock that had my muscles tightening, my toes curling, and my ass clenching as I exploded into the condom.

"Sweetheart," I groaned when she kept rocking, milking what felt like my never-ending orgasm.

"I'm still..." she trailed off with a moan.

Jesus fuck.

I bucked my hips and watched as she rode out her waning climax.

I knew it left her when she dropped forward and shoved her face into my throat. I wrapped my arms around her, one going high to the back of her neck, the other staying low and cupping her ass, ensuring she couldn't move.

I gave her time before I asked, "You okay?"

She nodded and I felt her still fighting to catch her breath.

I didn't know how long we laid there in the silence, her pressed against my chest nuzzling in closer, me holding her tight, not ready to disengage and have her roll off of me. And there in the quiet something strange stole over me. A feeling I couldn't place, an emotion I'd never felt. Not love. Not lust—though we were for sure going again because now that some of the edge had been carved off, I wanted to see how far I'd have to push before she begged. Not contentment. It was something else. Maybe it was the ease in which we connected, the teasing, the smiling. There hadn't been any of that first-time shyness on her part. She gave as good as she got and even one-upped me with her sassy comebacks.

I wasn't sure what it said about me—I knew who I was and what I liked and was willing to put a fair amount of effort into getting what I wanted—but I wasn't someone who cuddled, or held on tight not wanting to lose the feel of the woman I was with. I didn't finish and roll away, but when the deed was done, it was done and after a few minutes it was time to move.

Yet there I was holding Vanessa, neck and ass cheek, not allowing her the option to pull away. Unfortunately, nature being what it was I had a spent condom to deal with.

"Condom, sweetheart."

"In a second."

"Make that a quick one or there's gonna be a mess."

Not that there wasn't already a wet spot.

Vanessa lifted her head. Deep brown, sated eyes roamed my face.

Never having felt a woman study me so carefully before, I asked, "What's on your mind?"

"I was thinking."

When she didn't elaborate I queried, "About what?"

"Things that will take more than a second to explain."

"Then roll off so I can get rid of this condom and you can take the time to explain."

Vanessa started to roll but I tightened my grip on her ass.

"Kiss first."

Her lips curved up before she dropped her mouth to mine. My tongue surged in and I took over. And just like the first time on her couch, the kiss I gave her when I got her undressed, she allowed me to take what I wanted—which meant she gave.

Jesus fuck.

If I wasn't careful I could fall for this woman.

I broke the kiss thinking I bet that'd been easy, too.

"You're a really good kisser, Dalton Neary."

Fuck, she was sweet.

"Glad you think so, Vanessa Hale."

Pink hit her cheeks and this time when I saw it I brushed my thumb over the darkening color.

"You know, for a woman who not only fisted my hair while she fucked my face but also gave me one hell of a show while she rode my dick it's cute you blush when you tell me I'm a good kisser."

"I didn't fist your hair. I was making sure you didn't stop."

"Sweetheart, I think I have a bald spot, you yanked it so hard."

Amazingly her blush went away as she shrugged.

"It's not my fault you're good with your mouth. Full stop."

There it was again—her smile, the playfulness, the ease. Fuck yeah, I could totally fall for Vanessa Hale. If I was being honest, I was teetering on the edge already. Which meant I needed to lock that shit down, explain to her I didn't do commitment, and let her make her decision. We could take the weekend, fuck each other stupid. I'd help her figure out if someone was following her, get her safe, then we'd see. If she was up for it, I was game for friends with benefits. If not, I'd settle on friends.

Even though I knew what I needed to do, I didn't move. Instead I returned her smile right before I busted out laughing. I did this knowing it was the stupidest thing I could've done. Lying in bed holding Vanessa, feeling her tits pressed against my chest, my dick still wet, laughing with her in my arms, knowing it wouldn't take much to shove me over the edge.

I needed to disengage and roll away but for the life of me I couldn't do it.

5

ALRIGHT.

So, that happened.

I'd packed a bag, followed Dalton to his house, which incidentally was a condo. Not in a great area of town, not in a shit part, meaning it was in an okay-*ish* complex. This surprised me. I figured a man like Dalton who seemingly had it going on would live in one of the newer kickass apartment buildings with a clubhouse and a pool. I couldn't say I'd taken in too much of his furnishings when he let me into his condo. Just enough to know it was clean, mostly devoid of knickknacks, keepsakes, things like that. He had a couch, a smaller loveseat formed in an L shape with a cool-ass side table fashioned from a whiskey barrel positioned by the arms of the couch and loveseat. No lamp on the table. No magazines. Nothing. His dining table was the same—totally bare, no placemats or anything. I didn't get to see the kitchen. We went straight upstairs passing by an open door to a room with a bed in it. Correction, a mattress and box spring that looked to be set on one of those metal frames that comes free from the store when you purchase the mattress. No sheets, no blankets. Next I passed by a bathroom, no towels, nothing on the sink, and if I wasn't mistaken there wasn't even a shower curtain. Though in all fairness the room was pretty dark so I might've missed it.

His bedroom was a different story. Handsome furniture that looked to be expensive, and I knew it was seeing as a few months ago I'd spent a fortune on a headboard, nightstands, and two dressers and my stuff was nowhere as nice as his. The walls were boring beige but his comforter made up for the lack of color. Blues, grays, and stark white melted together in an ombre pattern. But that was all. No pictures on the walls, no lamps on his nightstands. The only mess in the room happened when Dalton tossed my bag on the floor and put his phone and wallet on the dresser.

I took in his room thinking I wasn't a slob but I lived in my house so there could be clutter. Dalton's house was so clean it didn't look like he lived in it. Either that or he had a cleaning service that came in every day. No man I knew was this clean. I stopped thinking about the state of his home when Dalton hooked me around my waist, pulled me tight against him, and once again gave me the opportunity to slow things down. Obviously I didn't. Actually I sped them up and kicked my shoes off. That had earned me a quirk of his lips. After that I made a new kind of mess in my brazen attempt to get what I wanted and pulled off my shirt and tossed it on the floor.

I'd never in my life been that bold, but then I'd never fantasized about a man taking me on my kitchen floor either. Nor had I ever had a man who looked at me like I was tempting his self-control. And I liked that. It made me feel sexy; it gave me the permission to feel what I was feeling and act on those fantasies.

Dalton wanted me just as badly as I wanted him. There was no judgment. It was easy. And never having that before, I found I could be bold and brazen and I really liked that.

So there in his bedroom, I took off my shirt but he did the

rest. My clothes came off in a hurry, save my bra. His clothes hit the floor, and I had approximately three seconds to take in his naked form—which was soul-shatteringly beautiful—before I was on his bed. But from there he made good on his promise—the man was thorough in his exploration of my body. Though, thorough might be an understatement. His memorization was painstakingly slow, so by the time he got his mouth between my legs—which, by the way, he'd bypassed my lady parts once in favor of kissing the inside of my thighs down to my knees before he licked his way up and *finally* homed in and hit a bullseye. I wasn't blowing sunshine when I told Dalton he was good with his mouth, full stop. He didn't eat me, he devoured me and didn't stop until I shouted my orgasm. Which didn't take him long. And the length of time it had taken had nothing to do with all the foreplay—though he had me so turned on it could be argued I would've climaxed if he'd simply blown on my clit. But that wasn't it, he was just that *good*.

And now I was naked, in Dalton's bed, after having the best sex of my life. It wasn't wild, there was no switching positions, it wasn't dirty nor sweet, it was just sex. Yet I'd never had a better orgasm. I'd never felt so comfortable. I'd never felt so desired or wanted or beautiful.

Never.

Those were my thoughts when I saw Dalton walk back into the room totally at ease in his nudity. Not that he shouldn't be with a body carved from stone. Not to mention other parts of him that were seriously impressive.

My mouth went dry and I licked my lips.

"Jesus," he muttered and stopped by the edge of the bed.

I tore my eyes from his dick and glanced up.

"What?"

"Sweetheart, I'm thirty-seven, not seventeen."

"Well, thank God for that or I'd be facing jail time."

I watched him smile, heard him chuckle, both of which made me sigh.

He had a great smile but when he laughed his eyes lit in this interesting way that stated plain you had his undivided attention.

Dalton crawled back into bed which had the unfortunate side effect of me losing sight of him naked, but the benefit of feeling his naked body when he hooked his arm under me and rolled me to him.

"You warm enough?" he asked.

We were lying on top of the comforter. Truth be told, I was a little chilly.

I snuggled in closer and fibbed, "I'm fine."

Proving not only could Dalton read me when he was looking at me, he could also spot a lie when he wasn't looking.

He moved this way and that, yanked the covers down from underneath us, shifted again, and pulled them over us.

The shifting and moving was impressive seeing as he hadn't let me go while he executed this maneuver.

"Now, tell me what you were thinking."

"When? Right now, I was thinking it was cool you didn't let me go when you got the covers over us. Or do you want to know what I was thinking when I was watching you walk back from the bathroom?"

"I think with the way you were eyeing my dick I can guess what you were thinking," he returned.

I bet he could guess and he'd be right.

"But I'm asking about before I got up," he continued.

Oh, right.

Damn.

"I don't remember."

"It was less than three minutes ago, how can you not remember?"

"Well, since then I've watched you walk to the bathroom, meaning I got my first look at your ass, so that boggled my mind. Then I laid in bed reminiscing about your superior oral skills which didn't boggle but frazzled my mind. And I've had time to think about the fact I'm comfortable with you, which is strange but I've decided not to think about that and instead focus on your goat game and I can—"

"My what?"

"Goat game," I repeated.

I felt the shaking start. That lasted a second before his laughter filled the room.

It was then I was afraid I'd shared too much. Maybe being comfortable with Dalton wasn't a good thing. Maybe it was bad, very bad, seeing as there were two times when I blurted shit out willy-nilly and didn't guard my words—when I was really uncomfortable and when I was totally comfortable. All the times between I could hold my tongue and watch my mouth.

"Um... forget I said that."

Suddenly Dalton rolled, taking me to my back and coming up on his elbow so he could look down at me.

Another cool maneuver, and since we were both naked that meant I could feel his dick resting on my thigh.

"Oh, no, sweetheart, spill."

Since Dalton was looming over me there was no way to hide, though I really wanted to.

"You can just look it up, but wait—"

"Nope. I want you to tell me."

I felt my cheeks flame, which as Dalton had already pointed out was ridiculous. But I could feel them getting hotter by the moment.

Good Lord, I had a big mouth.

"Goats have long tongues," I explained.

"Okay."

"And they move them really fast."

Lines formed around his eyes as his lips curved up.

"Right."

"You've never heard 'goat game' before?"

His smile widened and he shook his head.

"No, I have."

Through narrowed eyes I took in his smirk.

"So why'd you ask?"

"Because I wanted to hear you explain it. That, and seeing you blush is a serious turn-on."

"Jerk," I grumbled.

Dalton shifted over me; my legs opened to accommodate him. His lips hovered just above mine when he declared, "Let's see how much game I've got."

He said no more, not that he needed to, when his lips brushed mine and he took his time moving down my body, that said it all.

And incidentally—not that it needed to be said but it was worth the note, his goat game was better the second time around.

6

"SWEETHEART," I groaned my warning.

I'd woken up to Vanessa between my legs, mouth on my stomach, inching her way down. As soon as my eyes opened she went all-out working to take me there. And I was close.

I loosened my grip in her hair and warned again. "Last chance to pull off."

The flat of her tongue dragged up, she glided back down, and I watched her as my dick disappeared between her lips.

Brilliant. All of it. The pull of her sweet, wet mouth. Her hand gently rolling my balls. The excitement in her eyes.

Jesus fuck.

That did it.

"Fuck," I bit out and shot down her throat.

My orgasm was so powerful my back arched as she continued to blow me, taking me through my orgasm, and only slowed when I stopped filling her mouth.

Vanessa was still gliding as my muscles relaxed.

"Babe, I hate to tell you this, but I got no more to give."

Her eyes tipped up and they were dancing with victory.

"And just to say, feel free to wake me up like that anytime the spirit hits."

She smiled around my dick and I swear to God it was the sexiest fucking thing I've ever seen in my life.

"Fuck, you're gorgeous. But like this, with your mouth still wrapped around my dick after a phenomenal morning blow job, looking like you're worshiping my cock instead of sucking it, you're crazy fucking beautiful."

Vanessa shifted. Her hand circled my dick as she pulled off, then she did something I'd never had any woman do—she kissed the head of my dick before she released me, and pressed another one near the base of my shaft before she sat back on her heels.

That burn in my chest was back, only this morning it was worse.

For some strange reason those two kisses felt more intimate than anything I'd ever felt with any woman and that included my ex-wife.

"You okay?" she whispered.

I shook off the expected emotion, did an ab roll, bringing me face-to-face with the woman who would dig under my skin if I wasn't careful.

"I'm not sure why you'd ask that but maybe I didn't make myself clear enough. You give unbelievably great head and you look gorgeous doing it. So, yeah, Nessa, I'm more than okay. I'm fucking great, and if you give me ten minutes I'll show you just how great I feel."

I waited for her cheeks to tinge pink and they did, just not as deeply as they did last night.

"I need a shower first."

"It'd be a waste of time."

"Yeah? You planning on getting me dirty?"

Vanessa let out a squeal when I took her to her back and fitted myself between her legs.

I lowered my mouth to her ear and asked, "How dirty can you get, sweet Vanessa?"

She didn't verbally answer but that didn't mean her body didn't respond by trembling under me. I trailed my hand up her ribs, over the swell of her breast, her shoulder, and curled my fingers around the side of her neck and went on. "Tell me, Nessa, you want me to dirty you up?"

She nodded.

"How dirty?"

"Dirty," she whispered.

"Roll over."

I lifted up just enough for her to carry out my command.

It took some doing but she did what I asked and rolled to her stomach. My eyes roamed her back, her ass, her shoulders, the dips and ridges of her spine.

Soft and sweet and so perfect I knew I should've gotten her out of bed and into the shower and not do what I was about to do.

But need and lust swirled together in a dangerous cocktail of desire. A blend I craved with a desperation that was border-line unhealthy. I knew this had to end. I knew a woman like Vanessa deserved more than I could give her, yet I was power-less to stop my hands from going to her hips. I couldn't stop them from gliding up her sides, gathering her hair as I went, brushing it over her shoulder, then tracing the bumps of her spine down to the two indentations above her ass. I watched my hands move over her soft skin, going lower, grabbing two hand-fuls of her round, pert ass cheeks.

I gave them a squeeze and demanded, "Up on your knees."

Vanessa started to lift but I didn't wait—couldn't wait. My right hand slid lower. I twisted my wrist and glided my fingers through her wet, cupped her pussy, and helped her to her knees.

She was barely up when I slipped two fingers inside her.

"Reach over and grab a condom, sweetheart, but don't lose my fingers."

Her head turned to the nightstand, likely gauging the distance.

"I don't think I can reach."

It was doubtful she could. Still, I wanted her to try.

"Do it, Vanessa. But warning you, lose my fingers..." I gave her left cheek a squeeze. "You'll only get them back after I've reddened your ass."

Her pussy clenched around my fingers. Thank fuck she was onboard.

Christ.

Perfect.

I pushed my fingers deeper then slowly dragged them out until I found the spot that made her hips jolt.

"Here?" I unnecessarily asked.

"Yes," she moaned and rocked back.

I kept at her, fucking her with my fingers, watching her excitement turn into agitation when I edged her to orgasm then pulled back.

"*Dalton.*"

"You wanna come, you do that around my dick."

With that she set about grabbing a condom. It was an impossible task, but I had to give it to her. She tried but the nightstand was too far away.

My hand came down, a crack rent the air, and her deep moan followed. Vanessa was fumbling around trying to nab a packet when I swatted her round ass a second time.

"Better hurry, sweetheart."

She didn't hurry, she tipped her ass in the sweetest fucking invitation. I gave her a third then gave her back my fingers.

Drenched.

The sight before me, all that was her so fucking hot, I could take no more. I slid my palm over my handprint, reached between us and fisted my aching cock, smearing the bead of wetness over her ass.

"Last chance, sweetheart," I warned, stroking my dick along the crease of her ass. "I can finish you off or finish on you. Your choice but you better make it quick."

She had a packet in her hand and was shoving it in my direction.

I made quick work rolling down the latex, drove in, and stayed planted.

Ecstasy.

"You sure you want dirty?" I asked as I slid my hand up her back, putting pressure between her shoulder blades.

"Yes," she breathed.

"Cheek to bed. Keep your ass high and brace, baby. I'm gonna fuck you."

Vanessa lowered her upper body, kept her ass tipped, and fisted the sheets.

After that I fucked her hard, rough, and dirty until she was begging for me to let her come.

"SWEETHEART, YOU WANT MAYO?" I called out to Vanessa.

She tipped her head back to rest on the back of the couch but twisted her neck to look at me making sandwiches in the kitchen.

I caught her somewhat confused but soft look and smiled.

"You doing okay over there?"

"I'm sorry, I'm having trouble understanding English. What is this mayo you speak of?"

Damn, she was cute.

"I think maybe I should call in sick now," she continued. "That way when I don't show up for work on Monday, Wren doesn't get worried."

"No maybe about it," I returned before I thought better of it.

Vanessa flashed me a smile that made my dick twitch.

Thankfully my phone rang before that smile burrowed any deeper. Also thankfully it was Brady returning my text.

I nabbed my phone off the counter and answered. "Sorry to bug you on your day off."

"No worries. Your text said it was urgent. What's up?"

"You know Vanessa Hale? She works with Wren."

"Yeah, I know her."

I saw the woman in question sit upright and go alert.

"She needs an alarm, ASAP. I was hoping you could do me a favor and send someone out Monday."

"She got a problem?" And suddenly Vanessa wasn't the only one on alert. Brady's tone had changed from mild interest to very interested.

"Someone's following her. She doesn't—"

"Come again?"

"She says it's been happening about a week. At the gym, coming out of work, at the grocery store. And last night when we were leaving Balls Deep, we were talking in the parking lot and someone had eyes on us."

"What the fuck? Does she know who it is?"

Since I had eyes on Vanessa I didn't miss her shrinking back into the couch. She was worried she was wrong and if she was Brady would think she was crazy.

"She hasn't seen the person. Just has a gut feeling."

"Smart to pay attention to that," Brady returned and I wished I'd had him on speaker so Vanessa could've heard him saying the same thing I'd said. "Text me her address. I'll swing by Monday."

"She works Monday but I'll get her schedule. If she can't be there, I'll come around and let you in. She also needs new locks. Three doors."

"You gonna handle that or do you want to bring smart locks?"

"Sweetheart?" I called. "You want regular locks or keypads?"

"Regular," she mumbled.

I went back to Brady.

"I'll handle the locks."

"She's there?"

Fuck, *shit*, fuck.

I ignored his question since I didn't feel like it needed to be answered and instead told him, "She had work done on her house recently. Guy named Tommy did some of the work. He was chatty, gave her a weird vibe. She doesn't have a last name, just that he works for Precision Windows. I can't approach him and ask questions without cause. I would appreciate it if you could poke around and see what you can find on him."

"Consider it done." There was a beat of silence before he went on. "You know what you're doing?"

I liked Brady. I'd gotten to know him pretty well over the months since I'd started hanging out with him and the other guys from Triple Canopy. One of the things I liked most about him was he wasn't about bullshit—he said what was on his mind. He was also open about his past, the road he'd traveled to get over some seriously bad shit from his past. That meant over drinks one night he'd shared with me why he'd taken his wife's last name when they'd gotten married and I'd shared with him about my ex-wife and the ways she'd fucked me over before I had no choice but to leave. Further from that, I was open about my lifestyle and what I wanted for my future. That being, happily unattached.

What I didn't like was Brady questioning me. Mainly because I had no fucking clue what I was doing—I just knew I liked it and I was delaying a much-needed conversation with Vanessa. And right then with her sitting on my couch, our lunch sitting on my counter, after spending the night with her and fucking her multiple times, I was lying to myself by using the excuse she didn't have an alarm and her locks were shit so that was why she'd spent the night last night and why she was going to spend the night again tonight.

The right thing would've been to have a conversation.

I wasn't going to do that.

"Winging it," I answered honestly.

"I say this even though I know you know it—Wren and her are tight. Phoenix might have an issue with you *winging it*."

He wasn't wrong.

When my partner was single, he didn't have room to comment on how I lived my life seeing as he'd lived his the same. But then Wren came along, and just like his name, Phoenix rose from the ashes of his shit life and became a new man. There were only two other men I knew who deserved the happiness Phoenix had found as much as he did—his brothers Echo and River. Those three men were the best men I knew. They'd overcome the impossible and while they did they sheltered and protected their baby sister Shiloh.

The Kent bond was unmatched. The loyalty they had for each other and those they cared about unrivaled. So, fuck yeah, Phoenix was going to have issues.

Yet I still wasn't going to let Vanessa go.

7

I HEARD the heels clicking on the tile outside of my office and glanced at the upper right corner of my computer screen. It was twenty after four; Wren's last meeting of the day had started at three and was scheduled to end at four. My boss was efficient, she also kept a tight schedule. There was no chance her meeting had run long so I was surprised it had taken her so long to come back to my office. An office I'd only moved into a few months ago when I was promoted—at Wren's request. I was still her assistant of sorts but with more responsibility. I now did all of the grant research and wrote the first draft proposals. I also reviewed Wren's final proposals and helped her brainstorm. I liked my job before my promotion; now I loved it.

When she appeared and stopped just inside my office with her phone to her ear while speaking softly to Phoenix—and I knew it was him because I heard her say, "Okay, Phoenix, I'm in her office now."—I knew why it had taken her so long to come to me after her meeting.

Though I didn't expect her to be frowning when she showed up. After her call Friday night and her excited 'bout *time, girly* I thought she'd be smiling, coming in to dish about my weekend, not look like she was pissed at me.

"Did you forget to tell me something?" she started when she was off the phone.

I smiled at my friend even though her scowl had deepened.

"There's a lot I haven't told you since we've been slammed from the moment I walked in."

"Someone's following you?" she hissed and walked to the chair in front of my desk that was put there for the sole purpose of giving her a place to sit during the rare occasion we were in my office instead of her much larger one. "For a week?" she finished and plopped down.

Damn.

Dalton told Phoenix.

Or Brady told Phoenix.

"Who told Phoenix?"

Her eyes got big when she asked, "Does it matter?"

"Yes. I need to know who I'm pissed at. I didn't tell you because I don't *know* if someone is following me or if I'm just being weird. We were crazy busy last week, I had my mind on a thousand different things so this all could be in my head and I didn't want you, but mostly Phoenix, to know that I could be in the throes of some sort of stress-induced paranoia. He's protective and if he knew I was losing my mind he might tell you to fire me."

Wren waved her hand in front of her and lost her frown.

"Phoenix loves you, but more importantly I do. Last week was unusual but if the stress—"

"Don't finish that. You know I love my job, I do my best work under stress—that is, when I don't have five hundred other things to do, none of them business related—so I shouldn't be admitting to my boss I procrastinated getting the research done, which meant I was up until the wee hours of the morning, but it's not like my parents' fortieth wedding anniversary comes up every year so now that I've finished planning that, the other five hundred things I had to do are off my plate and I can fully concentrate on curbing my tendency to procrastinate."

I sucked in a breath to continue but Wren beat me to the punch.

"Honey, you're babbling."

Shit, she was right.

"Sorry, I'm—"

"Nessa, you only babble when you're nervous."

She was right about that, too.

"I just told my boss I was preoccupied with my parents' anniversary party so I pushed off work," I reminded her.

"Right, something I knew you were planning and knew would take up your time. The work got done so I'm not sure why you'd be nervous to tell me that. I think you're hiding the fact you're scared that someone's following you and because of that you're blowing it off. Which, honey, you have to know isn't smart."

"I know," I whispered. "But—"

"No buts, Nessa. I wasn't smart and because of that, Dalton told Phoenix. He also explained that he called in a favor and got Brady to bump you to the top of the list to install an alarm. Phoenix told me because the more eyes you have on you the better so no walking to your car alone after work and that comes direct from Phoenix. And I'm going to warn you, the guys talked, and until this is over Dalton will be accompanying you to the gym. And someone will go with you to the grocery store or when you need to run errands. My advice—don't fight this; it'll be a losing battle and a waste of time."

This was exactly what I'd been worried about. I knew Phoenix would catapult into protection mode and if I was wrong it would be embarrassing and a huge waste of everyone's time.

I didn't get a chance to explain this to Wren before my cell rang.

Wren leaned forward, caught sight of the caller ID, and smiled.

"This oughta be good," she muttered and settled in to eavesdrop on my call.

Since I took that as permission to take a personal call from Dalton while I was in the middle of a discussion with my boss, albeit a non-work-related talk, I picked up my phone and connected the call.

"Hey," I greeted.

"Hey, sweetheart. Brady called. He'll be at your house at five-thirty. Does that give you enough time to get home?" He cut straight to the point.

His crisp no nonsense tone would've worried me if he hadn't started the conversation with a sweetheart, something I'd quickly become addicted to.

"Yeah."

"Did Wren talk to you?"

I glanced up from my desk and locked eyes with my friend.

"She's in my office now."

"Good, so she told you she's walking you to your car when you leave."

No, she hadn't told me she was doing anything, just that Phoenix didn't want me leaving work alone. I wasn't sure I felt comfortable asking Wren to put herself in potential danger.

"Dalton—"

"This is nonnegotiable," he cut me off. "You don't walk to your car alone."

I sat up straight knowing I was positive I didn't like his tone.

"I'm not a fan of that word in regard to what I will and will not be doing," I snapped.

"Right, how about this?" he volleyed. "I'm not a fan of someone watching you, possibly lying in wait for the opportunity to snatch you or violate you in the parking lot, or do any number of fucked-up things they could do catching you alone and vulnerable. Wren's there and has to leave, too. There's safety in numbers and someone is less likely to jump out from behind a car and do whatever fucked-up shit they're thinking about doing to you. So she can walk you to your car or you can wait for me to get done at the station and I'll haul my ass over there and walk you out."

Throughout his ramble his patience had deteriorated. I didn't know him well enough to know if this was because he was already fed up with my situation or if he was at work and had something else going on. So it was only because he wasn't a fan of someone hurting me that I cut him some slack.

"I take it you're still at work so I'll confirm Wren will be walking me to my car with the side note in the future that I don't want my friends putting themselves in danger. As you pointed out someone could jump out from behind a car and—"

"Not only has Phoenix kitted Wren out with pepper spray but also a taser. Neither she nor you will be in danger when she walks you out. And tonight, you'll be kitted out with the same so tomorrow when both of you walk out *together* neither of you will have anything to worry about."

I wanted to mute the call so I could ask Wren how she put up with Phoenix when he got bossy like this. I also wanted to ask her why she didn't tell me she now had a taser and ask her to show it to me.

I didn't mute the call but I did note he was being over-the-top bossy.

"Are you always this bossy—"

"Only when someone I care about is arguing with me about her safety."

I ignored the fact he'd interrupted me again and gave in. But only because that wasn't the first time he told me he cared about me and I liked that. I thought it was sweet and maybe the start of something between us. Though if it was, we were definitely setting bossiness-boundaries.

"Wren's walking me to my car. Brady will be at my house at five-thirty," I recapped. "Is there anything else I need to know?"

"Yeah, I'll be at your house to meet Brady, go over your alarm, and change your locks. After that we'll order in."

He was coming over to change my locks and staying for dinner after we'd spent the whole weekend together.

My stomach did a somersault and my breath whooshed out of my lungs.

I was silently trying to catch my breath while staring at my friend who was now smiling huge.

"Okay," I readily agreed, still trying to regulate my breathing.

"Okay," he softly repeated. I didn't understand the change in his voice and I was too freaked out to ask.

"See you soon," I lamely replied.

"You will, sweetheart. Watch your mirrors coming home and call me if something feels off."

God, he was killing me.

"'Kay."

Dalton disconnected.

Wren launched in as soon as I lowered my phone.

"Now that we got that out of the way, tell me about your weekend."

I swear I felt my cheeks immediately flame.

"It was good."

"Honey, your face is so red I got that part."

I couldn't stop my hands from going to my face.

"I never blush," I griped. "I don't know what it is about him that makes my cheeks light up."

"I bet I can guess."

I bet she could, too.

"He's coming over tonight to change my locks and staying for dinner," I blurted out.

Her smile faltered but only a fraction.

"Just be careful," she warned.

"Careful?"

"You know. With your heart."

That statement along with her smile fading had me worried.

"I don't understand why would I need to be careful with Dalton? He's a total gentleman...well, until he's not. But the parts that aren't gentlemanly are really good. But he's sweet and he's made it clear that he cares about me at least in the sense he's coming over to change my locks, call in a favor to get me an alarm faster than I would've been able to get one, which you know because you came in here mad at me because Dalton told Phoenix I might have trouble and he's arranged for you to walk me to my car."

"Phoenix told me his ex-wife did a number on him."

His ex-wife?

"His what?" I hissed.

Wren pinched her lips and suddenly found the wall over my shoulder fascinating.

"Wren?" I called. "He has an ex-wife?"

"Um. Clearly you didn't talk much during your weekend together."

No, we had talked.

A lot, actually.

Between rounds of really great sex we'd talked about him spending four years in Atlanta going to Georgia State studying criminal justice and psychology. I knew he grew up in a place called Richmond Hill which was halfway from Hollow Point to Savannah. A place I'd driven through hundreds of times. He knew I grew up in Hollow Point and left to go to Jacksonville University. He knew I went there to study business analytics but changed my major to business administration. He knew I was thirty-two and I knew he was thirty-seven. We'd talked about his job, his promotion to detective which happened six years ago, and how he'd transferred to the six-twenty-eight which was where Phoenix was stationed and that was when they'd become partners.

At no point had he mentioned he'd been married.

"Well…" I started but petered out because I was a little embarrassed Wren knew something as important as Dalton being married and I was the one screwing him not her.

I was also ticked off but I wasn't sure I had the right to be.

We'd touched on personal things, but we hadn't shared in depth. We'd had a weekend of sex and I wasn't sure I was entitled to know everything about him. But still, his ex-wife doing a number on him didn't sound good and now I was thinking it was something I should know about before I got any deeper with a man who was potentially unavailable.

"What'd she do to him?" I asked.

"I think maybe this is something you should talk to him about. I don't think it's a secret he has an ex but I don't know if he talks about what she did to make him leave her."

He divorced her.

But Wren said she did something to make him leave.

Was he still hung up on her?

Did he want her back?

Oh, God, this was bad.

I was half gone for a man who was still emotionally attached to his ex-wife.

"Stop, Nessa," Wren softly demanded. "I see you're gearing up to have a freak out. If Phoenix thought Dalton would screw you over he would've told me."

Well, at least there was that.

As aforementioned, Phoenix was protective, and since I was close to Wren he'd extend that protection to me.

But still...

"I believe that, but he still said something to you that made you warn me to be careful."

Wren looked conflicted and I hated that I'd put my friend on the spot, but I'd stupidly spent the weekend thinking those two days were the start of something.

"Vanessa, I'd extend that warning to any sister who was getting involved with a man whose ex-wife screwed him over. The next woman who he gives his heart to is going to have to dig the distrust out. And you know that's true. Women who have been screwed over learn, and then go into the next relationship with their eyes open and the guards up. All Phoenix said was Dalton's made it clear he's not up for commitment."

My heart stopped.

My lungs decided they were no longer working either.

So there I was being deprived of oxygen and on the verge of dying due to cardiac arrest while Wren sat across from me with a bland expression on her beautiful face after she'd delivered a death blow.

"What?" I wheezed. "He's not up for commitment?"

"Pah-leeze," she drawled. "We all know that's a line of bull-shit men say."

That might be a line of bullshit for some men, but Dalton didn't strike me as the bullshitting type. And beyond that, I wasn't the type to play games when the result of the game could land me a broken heart.

"All it takes is for the right woman to come along and then suddenly they're all in."

She could be right about that, too, but again I wasn't willing to chance it.

"And the wrong woman gets chewed up and spit out," I educated her.

"That's why you play this smart. Be careful with your heart." Wren stood, tipped her head down, and held my gaze. "But you also pay attention. Not to what he says but how he treats you. And just to point out, he's coming over to change your locks and he's arranged for you not to be alone, not even to leave the building and walk to your car."

"He's a cop," I pointed out, as unnecessary as I thought that was. "On top of that, he's a good guy."

"He is."

"So him coming over to change my locks and arrange for me to be walked to my car says nothing. It's just him being a good guy cop."

When Wren didn't say anything I filled the silence.

"I've had my heart broken before; it doesn't feel all that great. I'm not all fired up to do it again."

My ex-boyfriend had cheated. This after he swore he loved me. His betrayal hurt. But I'd bet Dalton walking away would hurt more.

I went for nonchalant but I was pretty sure Wren saw through me when I shrugged.

"So what; we had a great weekend with lots of really great sex? We're adults, and he's not looking for a commitment. We can be friends."

Friends with Dalton.

I was right back to where I'd started.

"Vanessa—"

"I'm not settling. I know what I want. So I'm taking your advice—I'm protecting my heart and cutting my losses."

I'd only had two days with the man and the thought of not having more hurt my heart.

"I should've kept my mouth shut," she grumbled.

"And let me get hurt?"

"No, Nessa. I should've kept my mouth shut so Dalton had time to figure out you're the woman who'll bring him to his knees. You're the game changer."

I'd already brought Dalton to his knees—several times. Once to fuck me from behind and once when he knelt at the side of the bed with my legs over his shoulders and he'd eaten me until I was screaming incoherently.

I wasn't touching the game changer comment mostly because I didn't think that was the case. But, also, I wanted this sucky conversation to end.

I needed to close down my computer and get my shit together before I headed home to Dalton. Thankfully Brady would be there, then I could fake a headache and skip dinner.

"I messed up," Wren whispered.

"You didn't."

"I did, Vanessa. I messed up huge. I know you. I know when you get something stuck in your head there's no changing your mind. But I would hope you know me and you'd know I would not steer you wrong. I wouldn't set you up for heartbreak. So I really wish you'd listen to me and give him a chance—just do it protecting yourself."

I absolutely knew she would never steer me wrong.

Wren was a good friend and being that she wasn't ready to let it go.

"Sometimes the trauma someone inflicts on you makes you build walls. And sometimes if the trauma is bad enough you reinforce those walls thinking it's safer to live behind them where no one can touch you. I've lived behind those walls, Nessa. So has Phoenix. I understand Dalton. I was happy to live behind my fortress, happy to live a lonely life sheltered from anything or anyone who could hurt me and Griffin. Until Phoenix. I'd put so much work into building my wall I didn't know how to tear it down. But Phoenix did. He chipped away at those blocks and he did it unknowingly by just being him. As you said, Dalton's a good guy, he deserves to be happy but he's never going to be that living the life he's living. And I bet if you took the time you'd find it'd take barely a touch and you'd crumble those walls. And in that wreckage is where you find the real Dalton Neary and I'd also bet when you found him you'd be happy you did. But more, he'd be happy and he'd prove he was worth the effort."

With that successful reminder she turned to leave but stopped at the door to finish gutting me.

"I'd still be living behind those walls if I didn't have Phoenix, and the worst part about that is, Phoenix would be, too. Much like Dalton, much like me, he was happy to stay there spinning his wheels living a lonely life. I'm not telling you it's your responsibility to look out for him. But knowing you the way I do, you wouldn't have spent the weekend with the man if you didn't feel *something* for him. And, honey, I knew you felt that connection before you spent the weekend with him." Wren paused, gave me a tight smile, and continued. "I have an email to send then I'll be ready to walk out with you."

Gah.

Sometimes having friends who know you well sucks. They know how to hit below the belt but make that blow velvet soft and make you think.

Wren's ex-husband had done a number on her and her son. When I met her she was friendly but closed off. Anyone who got within ten feet of Wren felt the stay back vibes rolling off of her. Now she was happy. She had friends, a life outside of work that wasn't inclusive to her spending time with her son but doing nothing else.

And Phoenix...there was no way to describe his childhood beyond calling it tragic. The son of a cop killer, abandoned by his mother, and a buttload of misplaced guilt about situations that were beyond his control. The Kent family's bond was forged by misfortune and heartbreak, and due to that Phoenix didn't allow anyone close.

Until Wren.

I wanted to be Dalton's "until". I wanted to believe I was strong enough to make his walls crumble to get to the wreckage, but I was too far gone.

I was a dreamer.

While Dalton might've been my dream, I might not be his.

And if I wasn't...that wouldn't break my heart; it would crush it.

8

BY THE TIME I pulled up to Vanessa's house Brady was already there. I parked at the curb behind his company SUV, caught his frown and his posture, and didn't delay shutting down my truck and getting out.

I was halfway up Vanessa's walk when I asked, "What's up?"

"Locks are shit," he started. "Even the deadbolt. I picked it just to see how long it would take. While I was doing that, the neighbor across the street came out, saw me fucking with her lock, and just got in his car and drove away."

So much for taking care of your neighbors.

Though in this day and age there wasn't much of that anymore. People didn't want the hassle or they were too self-absorbed to care.

"I can see how that'd piss you off, but, brother, the way you look something's tweaked you."

"Obviously I don't know her neighborhood, but I've been here ten minutes and the same car's driven by three times. Florida plates. Newer white Nissan Sentra. Could be he was coming home or dropping someone off, left, then remembered he forgot something and drove back."

"Did you get the plate number?"

"Nope. First two times I didn't think anything about it. The third time, I paid attention and when I got to her driveway, car blew the stop sign and sped away."

Fuck.

"I'll talk to Vanessa, see if she knows the car."

"You do that. And the cameras I brought hoping I could talk her into just became part of whatever system she chooses."

"Appreciate—"

"I know you do. But even if you didn't call in the favor, Phoenix would've. Clearly you told him about Vanessa's problem because he called in this afternoon and talked to Luke."

I clenched my jaw until the fucker ached to stop myself from saying something regrettable. The same way I gritted my teeth when Phoenix told me he was calling his brother-in-law to make sure Brady was on top of Vanessa's alarm.

Then and now it pissed me right the fuck off my partner felt the need to make sure I was taking care of Vanessa—this after I told him I was handling it. This after he told me Vanessa was off-limits and I told him to take a hike. To say he was pissed I didn't bow to his demand would be an understatement. One could also say the rest of my day had been shit when Phoenix kept up the overprotective bullshit.

Vanessa was a grown-ass woman, what she and I chose to do was none of his business. He didn't see it that way, so he pushed. I pushed back. The bullshit only ended when we got a call about another robbery, the third in the last ten days where the only things that were stolen were guns despite there being other valuables that were easily accessible. Which meant the suspect broke into the house specifically to hit the guns. Weapons that were locked in a safe.

Since there were now stolen guns that would likely find their way to the streets, personal bullshit got set aside.

However, Phoenix hadn't thawed by the time we got back to the station, and when he overheard my call to Vanessa—not that I attempted to hide that shit—he made his displeasure known.

"I see that pisses you off," Brady rightly noted. "Good news is she's got friends who care about her. Bad news is, Phoenix didn't sound happy you and Vanessa hooked up."

"He's not," I confirmed.

Brady's gaze went to the street and I knew he heard the car making an approach same as me.

"He's just looking out for her."

"That's unnecessary."

I caught Vanessa's car pulling into her driveway. Obviously so did Brady so he quickly added, "For her safety it's a good thing having people take her back in this situation. As far as you two hooking up, brother, you had to know that'd get Phoenix up in your business. You haven't made it a secret you're not looking for anything permanent. Wren and Vanessa are tight. He's going to move in to protect her so she doesn't get her heart broken."

"I know why he's in my business but he should know me better than that. I'm not gonna break her heart."

"Does she know what this is or did she spend the weekend with you thinking it was more than a weekend fuckfest?"

I didn't get a chance to answer him before Vanessa was out of her car calling out her hello.

"Right," he murmured. "You need to get on that."

He wasn't wrong.

But the fuck of it was, I didn't want to have a conversation about where this was heading, at least not one that could take her from me.

Brady ended our huddle and walked up the steps to her porch.

"Locks are shit, Nessa," Brady said as he pushed open her front door. "Good thing Dalton's changing them out."

Vanessa cocked her head and narrowed her eyes on Brady.

"Just because you possess the mad skills to jimmy open my door doesn't mean anything."

Brady gave her a half smile and shook his head.

"It took me about seventeen seconds. It might take someone else ten minutes but the point remains."

"And the point is Dalton's replacing those locks and you're here to give me a quote on a kickass alarm so I'm not sure why you're giving me gruff."

Brady's half smile turned into a grin.

"Because it's fun and because you bailed on Wren Friday night which meant she was bored and in the mood to play pool. She challenged Hadley to a game. One turned into five. Hadley losing four of those games and since my woman hates to lose I've heard nothing but her bitch about losing the last three days. So me giving you guff is payback."

Vanessa smiled flat out and when she did I had to force myself to stay rooted instead going to her like I wanted and kissing the ever-loving hell out of her.

All day I'd thought about that damn smile—from her sexy smirk, to her playful grin, to her happy, full-fledged smile to all the varying nuances in between.

"Whatever," she grumbled. "Are we going in or are you going to bar the door and be a pain in my ass?"

Brady entered her house. I waved Vanessa to go in front of me, but she didn't move and when her gaze came to me it didn't meet my eyes.

What the hell?

"Sweetheart?"

Her shoulders jerked and she woodenly walked to the porch, up the stairs, and followed Brady.

No hello. No smile for me. Nothing.

I watched Vanessa disappear into her house thinking, *What the fuck?*

———

VANESSA WAS WALKING Brady to the front door by the time I was done installing the new locks. He called out a quick goodbye on his way past me but it was the "good luck" that had given me pause. Unluckily I hadn't had the chance to ask him what he was talking about so when Vanessa came back into her kitchen after walking Brady out I was unprepared for her outburst. Not that it would've helped me much but at least I would've been able to check my response.

"You know," she said conversationally, "I'm not one for generalizations or stereotypes but good Lord, all you men are the same."

She picked up the new keys I'd placed on the counter and turned them over in her hand.

"Bossy. Arrogant. Pushy." She finished by crossing her arms over her chest.

I was well-versed with this position. This was normally when the argument disintegrated and Layla went on a long-winded tirade about how I'd ruined her life.

Years of practice had me silently waiting for her to finish.

"I got another lecture about parking in the garage," she huffed. "I'd planned on rearranging it this weekend. But it looks like I'll be doing it tonight."

I couldn't say I wasn't happy she was going to make room for her car, though I couldn't deny it irritated me that she was willing to do this after Brady had obviously said something to her.

"I want it noted I was already planning on doing this, after *you* and not to mention my *father* talked to me about it. I also wanted it noted I'm doing it tonight under duress and only because Brady threatened to tell Quinn why I was getting an alarm. And we all know when Quinn Lancaster catches wind there's a potential problem, her DNA prohibits her from staying out of it."

I blew out a breath and relaxed.

"So, that's why you think all men are bossy, arrogant, and pushy?"

"Um, yeah," she drawled. "Did you miss the part about Brady being bossy and forcing me to do something I don't have time to do? And he got his way by being an arrogant ass and threatening to sic Quinn on me."

I had to admit, if I knew threatening to call Quinn would've kicked Vanessa into gear I would've made the same threat. There was a reason why protection was embedded into her DNA—her father Jasper Walker had passed the gene to his children. Mix that with his wife Emily's kindness and loyalty and you get offspring who do not look the other way when someone is in need.

This was when I smiled.

It was also when I knew I should've guarded my response.

"Should I take your smile as you're okay with me getting bullied?" Vanessa snapped but said nothing more as I advanced on her.

"Sweetheart, you might be bitching but we both know you're not really mad."

"Do we, now?"

"Yeah, we do. Brady's not bullying you, he's showing you he cares. Same as your dad. Same as me."

As soon as I mentioned caring about her, Vanessa shut down.

Her face was studiously blank and her gaze went to the counter.

"What's really going on?"

"What's going on is, I'm being bossed in my own house."

That was bullshit.

Vanessa was logical, it was one of the things that drew me to her. She wasn't one of those women who put wants over needs. She might've playfully bitched about spending the money on an alarm over saving for a new kitchen but she understood what was important. Same as her complaining about cleaning out her garage. She would do it and not because Brady had threatened to call Quinn but because she knew it was the safe thing to do.

"So that's it? You're pissed you're being bossed in your own house and that's why you won't look at me?"

Her eyes slowly traveled back to mine but they were so devoid of emotion she might as well have been staring blankly into an abyss.

"And that's why when you got home I didn't get so much as a 'hey, how was your day' or a smile or a kiss or any-fucking-thing?"

That earned me an eye flare.

"Brady was here," she weakly tried to explain herself.

"He was because I texted him first thing in the morning with a favor. When he called he knew you were there. Brady's not stupid; he knows I don't have women in my house, period, much less one there bright and early on a Saturday morning. So you can take from that, he knew why you were there and what that meant. Saying that to say your excuse about Brady being at your house is bullshit."

"You don't have women at your house, period?"

Fuck.

"Nope."

"That tracks," she mumbled.

"Come again?"

Vanessa pinched her lips and slowly closed her eyes. When she reopened them I was surprised to see pain.

"I'm sorry," she started. "I'm being bitchy on purpose."

I blinked at her honesty and was left speechless.

"Wren told me you were married," she softly admitted. "I guess it hurt my feelings more than I thought. I was going to tell you she told me over dinner because it's not cool I know something personal about you that you don't know I know. So you should also know she told me you don't date or commit or whatever."

Fuck. *Fuck.* Fuck.

"Vanessa—"

"No, it's okay. I get it."

She didn't have the first clue.

The poison crept up faster than usual.

The blistering pain of Layla's deception seared my insides like it always did if I gave her any thought. This was not because I was still in love with my ex-wife or holding some sort of fucked-up torch for our ten-year relationship. It was the opposite. I hated the woman and hated that I couldn't stop hating her. Though that might've been possible if the bitch didn't rear her ugly head every now and again. And I didn't make a habit out of calling women bitches. But a bitch was a bitch and Layla was the very definition of a bitch.

"No, you don't get it. Unless you married a woman who promised you the world then reneged on that promise, taking her time doing it, ripping you to shreds while she slowly came to the conclusion she hated you and you ruined her life."

Now for the hard part.

The conversation I should've had with her Friday night.

"Wren's right. I don't do relationships. Saying that, I also don't invite women to my house, yet you spent the weekend there."

"What does that mean?"

"No fucking clue, sweetheart. I just know since I divorced my ex you're the first woman who's made me wish she hadn't fucked me up, so I had something left to give."

Neither of us said anything. I didn't know what was going on in that pretty head of hers but I knew I was stunned into silence after I'd admitted to Vanessa that I wished I had something left in me, something that wasn't tarnished with the past or tainted with Layla vile ugliness.

"But we can be friends, right?" she asked in an attempt to hide her disappointment.

"Is that what you want?"

Vanessa's eyes sparked and I was happy to see some resemblance of her fun personality come out.

"Um, you just changed all my locks. Do you really think I'd let a friend like that slip through my fingers?"

I had to hand it to her—she was putting on a good front. Either that or she didn't feel half of what I felt for her because my insides were twisted and it felt like someone had stabbed me in the chest and carved out the last of my withered heart.

"Should've told you before—"

"And deprive me of the best sex-a-thon of my life? Now that would've been cruel."

Fuck.

"Sweetheart, for this friendship to work out you can't remind me I've been inside you."

Vanessa's cheeks tinged pink.

So I pushed...

Just because I was jonesing for a glimpse of that sexy blush.

"Or that I've tasted you. Or I've felt your sweet mouth around my cock and watched you swallow—"

"I get it," she wheezed with her face pink and her eyes soft and hazy.

I'd give it a shot but I already knew this friendship gig wasn't going to work out.

There was no way I could be close to her and not remember the feel of her, or the way she cuddled close at night, or how much I liked waking up next to her.

But mostly, I couldn't be friends with a woman I wanted to love but knew I wasn't going to let myself have.

9

I HAD a big mouth and on top of that I was a fool.

Be *friends?*

What the heck had I been thinking?

I knew what I'd been thinking—there was no way Dalton would've actually said yes.

But he *had* said yes. Now I was sitting on my couch in my den eating Chinese takeout next to a man I knew biblically while trying to pretend I didn't, while at the same time nursing a broken heart that I was denying I had.

But the hankering for a pint of ice cream along with a crying jag said otherwise.

I was also trying to find a safe topic to discuss now that I'd finished telling him about my new top-of-the-line alarm that would be installed at cost while trying to be grateful I didn't have to start selling my eggs at the fertility clinic to pay for it.

"What are you thinking about?" Dalton asked, cutting into my musings.

"That it's a good thing Brady gave me a discount so I didn't have to sell my eggs."

"Eggs?" Dalton's brows pinched and he looked utterly

perplexed, which sucked because it made him look almost cute instead of his normal devastatingly handsome.

"Yes. My eggs to the fertility clinic."

Dalton stared at me like I was a little crazy, which would be a fair assessment since right then I was eating dinner with him after everything we'd shared while pretending he didn't know I had a freckle on my right butt cheek—he'd kissed it twice and told me it was cute—and acting like we were old pals.

I had officially gone crazy.

This would not end well for me.

And I knew that to be irrevocably true when he busted out laughing and my world dropped out from under me.

I wanted to hear that laugh regularly and often. I wanted to sit on the couch next to him, be my normal nutty self, and make him laugh. I wanted him to think I was cute rather than strange. I wanted that more than anything.

Nope.

This friendship thing wasn't going to work.

"Yeah, sweetheart, good thing."

And really, I needed him to stop calling me sweetheart. But the thought of losing that nickname hurt my heart too much to ask.

We went back to eating in not so comfortable silence.

After a few minutes Dalton broke it.

"Earlier you apologized for something that didn't need apologizing for," he weirdly stated. "It was also cool you were honest about what Wren told you. But I didn't get a chance to apologize for being a dick and snapping at you. I don't like thinking about Layla, so you can imagine I really don't like talking about her. Still, I shouldn't've been an ass."

I had no idea what he was talking about or when he'd been an ass and my mind was stuck on *Layla*.

For some reason knowing Dalton's ex had a pretty name made my stomach clench.

Still I found myself asking, "How long were you together?"

"Ten years. Married for four, though the last year we were separated."

Ten years.

Holy shit.

I didn't have shoes that were ten years old.

Maybe I was the one with commitment issues.

"Why'd you divorce her?" As soon as the question slipped out I wanted to slap the words back into my mouth. "I'm sorry, that was incredibly rude. I can't believe I just asked you something so personal."

Dalton twisted, hitched his knee up onto the couch cushion, and waited until he had his eyes locked on mine before he answered.

"Seriously? I think we're well past *personal*, don't you?" He paused, though not long enough for me to answer. "She decided she didn't want to be a cop's wife and since I was a cop and had wanted to be that since before we started dating—something she knew since we talked about it—I ended the misery she was hell-bent on dragging out."

That didn't sound good.

"How long have you been divorced?"

"Eleven years."

Eleven years?

I did some quick mental math, which admittedly wasn't my strong suit—I mean, it was math; I could've had a pen and paper and still probably struggled—but that put Dalton in high school when he started seeing his ex.

"I'll save you the trouble," he said. "We were sixteen, stayed together through college. Got married. I went to the academy and she was all for it. I graduated, she was there playing the part of supportive wife. A year in, out of the blue she has a change of heart. The job is too much for her. She doesn't explain what exactly is too much, just that she doesn't want to be a cop's wife. For the next two years I tried to save my marriage. She was dedicated to making my life hell. Finally it got to the point where I had no choice but to give her what she wanted and leave. She wasn't happy then either and double-downed and turned something that had started pure and clean into a toxic dumpster fire of shit. By the time I filed for divorce I didn't recognize the woman I'd fallen in love with. There was nothing about her that resembled the pretty, sweet girl I thought would be the mother of my children. She took all the beauty we had and twisted it into something ugly."

Okay, that sounded worse than 'not good.'

But still, eleven years was a long time to nurse a broken heart.

Though I had no room to judge. I'd never had my life ripped away from me after someone promised me forever.

The closest I'd come was a man telling me he didn't do commitment after giving me a weekend that said the opposite. And I could confirm I wasn't all that fired up to put myself out there again. But I sure as hell wasn't going to take an eleven-year sabbatical from dating. At least I hoped I wasn't.

My phone rang—thankfully I changed my ringer back to a respectable tone—and of course Dalton had to comment.

"Got tired of the frog?"

Okay, so maybe I wouldn't take eleven years but it would take more than a few days to stop missing Dalton teasing me. And it would definitely take more than a few weeks to stop missing that smile aimed at me.

For my mental health I refrained from engaging in banter that would only make me miss him more when this friendship thing was over.

I glanced at my phone on the coffee table, saw it was my sister and as much as I wanted to ignore it, I couldn't. Malory was a worst-case scenario type of person. Not answering the phone would make her worry. Not calling her back in what she deemed an appropriate amount of time would have her taking the leap to assuming I was dead in a ditch, or sex trafficked, or at the very least in a car accident.

I reached out, grabbed my phone, and expertly engaged the call using one hand while balancing my plate of spicy beef in the other.

"Hey, Mal, what's going on?" I greeted.

I swear I heard her sigh in relief.

"Sorry to bother you. I just wanted to make sure you got my email about the flowers for Mom and Dad's party."

Shit. I totally forgot to email her back.

Another thing about my sister—she was a chronic apologizer. She started most conversations with "I'm sorry." This was a habit I'd been trying to break since we were teenagers. An endeavor that had proved fruitless even though her husband Austin—who loved and adored my sister—had picked up the mantle and did what he could to break her of it.

"I did. Thank you for handling that. Was Austin okay with you paying the extra charge for daisies?"

Daisies were Mom's favorite flower. The florist had misquoted us the centerpieces and I knew money was tight for my sister and brother-in-law. Then again, money was tight for everyone and no one wanted to pay an extra two hundred dollars for something they'd already budgeted.

"You know Austin; he doesn't get worked up about much."

That was the God's honest truth. My sister's husband was a go-with-the-flow, mellow type until something upset my sister. Then he turned into a growly beast of a man, and since he towered over most men, when Austin got pissed it was downright scary. I loved Malory had found a man who was as patient with her as he was protective.

"Other than sisterly bonding time at Mom and Dad's, is there a reason why it's good I'll be there?"

"Everything good with you?" she asked.

I was very aware Dalton was sitting next to me and I didn't want my sister to know I had company. I also didn't want him to hear me lie to my sister when I sugar-coated my life so she wouldn't worry about me.

"Perfect. But listen, I'm in the middle of something. We'll catch up on Saturday at the party."

"Yeah. Of course. So sorry to bother you. I should've—"

"Malory?"

"Huh?"

"Stop, honey, you know you're never a bother. I'm just eating dinner and you know I hate cold Chinese so..." I let that hang knowing my sister would get it.

"You're the only person in the world who hates cold Chinese."

I could hear the humor in my sister's tone, and it was times like this when some of the old Malory shone through that made my stomach tighten.

"There are like a bazillion people in the world. I'm sure I'm not the only one."

"My logical sister." She laughed and I fought back the tears.

There was a time when my sister laughed a lot. She had once been wild and fearless. A little too wild. Now, in spite of having an awesome husband and a good life, she was a shell of her former self.

"See you Saturday," I returned.

"Love you, Nessa."

Damn, but I loved hearing her happy.

"Love you, Mal."

I dropped my phone onto the cushion between me and Dalton, keeping my gaze on my plate, too afraid to look at my dinner partner. He had an uncanny ability to read me. He wouldn't miss the pain speaking to my sister brought me.

"You don't like cold Chinese food?" he asked.

"Nope."

"Sweetheart, look at me."

See?

Uncanny.

"Can you please just give me this?"

"I'd like to understand what it is I'm giving you."

With a sigh of resignation I tipped my eyes up. Dalton flinched before his expression gentled.

"Explain to me why you look like someone just stabbed you in your heart."

I think we're well past personal, don't you?

He'd told me about his ex-wife and why he'd divorced her. He deserved the same honesty from me.

This friendship gig needed to end.

"That was my sister, Malory," I told him.

"I got that."

"She's..." I searched for the right words to explain my sister.

"She's what?"

"She's different."

Dalton narrowed his eyes and I realized how horrible that sounded.

"She's different, meaning she's not who she used to be."

I held up my hand needing a moment to figure out how to explain what I needed to say.

"When we were teenagers my sister was the wild child. She was up for anything and when I say that I mean *anything*. This started when she was fourteen. At first my parents thought it was normal teenage girl stuff, but then her grades started slipping until she was failing all of her classes. Then they became concerned. I was, too, but to me she was still my big sister Malory—larger than life, everyone's friend, fun, loud, always laughing and up for a good time. But when she hit fifteen and started sneaking out, getting drunk, and my parents were being called by her friends' parents to come pick her up from their houses, I started to worry. Then when she was sixteen I caught her alone in her room drinking vodka straight from the bottle. That freaked me out. She promised it was a one-time thing. But I checked the bottle and every day it was getting emptier and emptier."

I saw Dalton shut down but I was too far into my story to process what that meant, so I kept going.

"I told my parents she was drinking in her room."

I let the guilt creep in and allowed it to wrap around me like I always did.

"What'd they do?" he asked. His tone was all wrong but again I thrust back almost nineteen years ago when I was too young to fully understand what was going on.

Not that I understood any better now, since my sister never told a single soul what had made her go off the rails.

"They tried talking to her. She blew them off, kept sneaking out, kept partying and drinking. Nothing they did worked so they sent her to a camp for troubled youth."

My heart squeezed remembering the day my dad's friend Simon showed up to take Malory to Utah. Something my father couldn't do himself so he had to have his best friend escort his daughter to the program.

Needing to get the rest out I rushed on, "When she came home she was a different person. Totally different in every way. She went from fun loving to remote. She now apologizes for everything under the sun including saying she's sorry for calling me and bothering me. She worries about everything. And I mean worries to the point she'll make herself sick with it. If I miss a call I get a text asking if I'm okay. If I don't call her back right away she'll call my mom and ask her if she's heard from me. The same goes if my mom doesn't answer, I get the call asking if Mom's alright. And that's double with Austin, her husband. He never misses a call from her because he knows it'll freak her out and he'd cut off both arms and his testicles before he'd cause her a moment of worry."

"What about your dad?"

"What about him?"

"Does she get freaked out if he doesn't answer?"

That threw me for a loop. I'd never thought of that. Actually, I didn't know if my sister called my dad with any frequency. I knew they spoke but like me I called my mom then she put my dad on the phone.

"It's weird but I think we both call my mom and she passes us off to my dad or he calls me when he has something important to talk to me about. I think he does the same with Malory."

Was that weird?

I'd never thought about why I rarely called my dad directly.

Dalton shrugged and I took that to mean he didn't think it was strange. But now that he'd planted the seed, I was thinking it was.

"So that's how she's different?"

I didn't know if that was a statement or a question but I still answered.

"It's more, and I can't explain it but it's like her spirit was snuffed out. Not that it wasn't good for my sister to stop drinking and partying. When she got home her grades went back to where they were. She was respectful. She was pleasant. I can't put into words the feeling of watching your sister who was once full of energy and light and laughed all the time just go through the motions of living. She went to college, met

Austin, they eventually got married, she loves him to pieces but still she holds herself apart. She has a job, she's good at it, but she never seems happy. And the times when she does laugh or she teases me or I see a flicker of her sense of humor it guts me. I feel like it's my fault she's the way she is. If I would've kept my mouth—"

"Your sister was sixteen drinking alone in her room, Vanessa," he cut me off. "What would've happened if you didn't do the right thing and tell your parents?"

That was the part I struggled with.

What if she would've grown out of the teenage rebellion on her own?

What if I'd kept my mouth shut and she hadn't been sent away and I'd still have my sister?

Or what if I didn't tell and it got worse until she was in serious trouble?

The what-ifs piled up like the guilt.

"Do you blame your dad for sending her away? Is that why you don't call him as much as you call your mom?"

My den suddenly felt suffocating, like sweltering hot mixed with the worst Georgia humidity. I felt a bead of sweat form on the back of my neck while I tried to suck in enough oxygen to live.

"Sweetheart?"

Dalton leaned closer but his face was nothing more than a blur.

"Vanessa?"

"I don't know," I whispered. "I don't think so."

But now that he asked I couldn't help but to wonder. Did I blame my dad for sending Malory away? My mom was against it. They fought about it. My dad's friend, Simon, had found the place, told my dad it was for the best. The camp would help Malory; she'd come home back to her regular self.

She never did.

Simon and my dad were wrong.

Very, very wrong.

"Maybe," I croaked.

"Hey?" he called from close.

I blinked away the haze and found Dalton was much closer than I thought. Nearly nose to nose. So close I could see those long, thick lashes I'd admired all weekend. His lips so close I could kiss them, but they weren't mine to kiss. They never really were and they never would be.

"I think we need to stop being friends," I blurted out.

"I think we need to absolutely stay friends," he contradicted.

"I don't think—"

"No offense, sweetheart, but right now I don't care what you think."

Well, that wasn't very nice and it was exactly what I needed to pull myself out of my misty-eyed funk.

"You know when someone says *no offense* it doesn't take the offense out of the statement."

"Okay, how about this..." Dalton abruptly stopped, his eyes went over my shoulder. But before I could figure out what he was looking at he was up off the couch, his container of General Tso shrimp hit the coffee table, and he was on the move. "Lock the door after me and stay in the house."

"What?"

"Lock the door and stay inside," he repeated as he prowled to the door.

I had just gotten to my feet when he slipped out the door and quietly clicked it shut. It wasn't until I was turning the lock that I realized my backyard was illuminated and it shouldn't have been unless something tripped the motion sensor light.

Okay, now I was officially freaked out.

Freaked out and grateful and stupid.

I needed to move away from the window—someone could be out there lurking in my yard.

Watching.

That got my legs unrooted and I ran into my bedroom to grab my baseball bat. I made it to my closet when there was a knock on the front door.

Did stalkers knock?

I found my old softball bat, and like some sort of idiot I tiptoed down the hall, keeping my back to the wall, ran through my kitchen into my living room, and crouched down. Not that there was anything to hide behind but standing made me feel exposed.

Another knock came followed by, "Sweetheart, open the door."

I rushed to the door and swung it open.

Dalton's gaze dropped to the bat, his lips twitched and under his breath he muttered, "Good girl."

I ignored the tingling between my legs those words inspired and narrowed my eyes.

"We need a safe word," I declared.

With a hand to my chest he gently pushed me back and followed me into the house.

"You planning on getting rough with me, baby?"

"No, you dope. A code-safe word. Like an all clear, or something so I know it's safe to open the door and you're not knocking under duress."

Dalton locked the door and turned to fully face me.

My heart rate ticked up a few dozen notches.

Not at our proximity, though he was close and getting closer. Not at the way those intense brown eyes were roaming over my face. Nope, my heart felt like it was going to explode out of my chest because I really, really loved the way it felt as those eyes glided over my features getting darker and darker the longer he stared at me.

"Hear this, Vanessa," he rasped. "We don't need a safe word or a code word. Do you know why that is?"

I was too mesmerized by the steely edge of his voice to form words so I shook my head.

"I would never bring danger to your doorstep. Ever. No matter what."

I believed him.

Though the danger Dalton brought wasn't to my front door.

The kind he brought was far, far scarier.

The man was hazardous to my wellbeing.

Dalton Neary was the white knight my stupid heart had been waiting for and it was going to hurt like hell when I watched him ride off into the sunset alone.

He'd have his commitment issues.

I'd have a broken heart.

This just plain sucked.

10

FRIENDS.

Fucking *friends*.

I must've lost my damn mind.

Actually there was no 'must have' about it. I'd straight up lost what was left of my good sense. I could lie to myself and use the excuse Vanessa had an unwanted admirer who was not only following her but doing drive-bys of her house and that was why I'd stayed for dinner. Or I could use the bullshit excuse that she was friends with my friends and we needed to keep things copasetic for all involved but not even in my delirium could I convince myself that was why I was still there. All it would've taken was me stepping aside and Phoenix would've had someone from Triple Canopy playing bodyguard.

That would've been the smart thing to do.

But it wasn't what I was going to do. And as much as I wanted to continue to stand in Vanessa's living room with her looking at me like I was some sort of romance hero straight off the big screen, someone had been in her backyard.

"Vanessa, sweetheart?"

Those big brown eyes stayed locked with mine.

"Yeah?"

I mentally calculated the hours it had been since I'd watched those same eyes get hazy with lust and pleasure. It hadn't even been twenty-four hours and already I was jonesing.

Christ, I had a problem.

"Do you know anyone in the neighborhood who drives a white Nissan Sentra?"

Vanessa snapped out of whatever trance she'd been in and blinked. I felt the loss of her attention immediately and again, I had a fucking problem. I shouldn't want the woman to look at me like I was anything but a bad idea. The sooner she came to her senses and decided that I was a shit friend and we went back to acquaintances the safer I'd be—I mean, her. The safer she'd be.

"I don't know..." She stopped, tipped her head to the side like she did when she was thinking, then asked, "Why? Is one out there?"

"Not anymore," I told her honestly.

Her brows pulled together and she took a step back.

"But there was?"

Instead of answering I asked, "How well do you know your neighbors?"

"No way, Dalton. You saw someone?"

I wasn't sure if that was relief at the confirmation that someone was watching her, since she'd mentioned several times she didn't want anyone to think she was crazy if she was wrong, or if fear had finally kicked in.

"Earlier when Brady was waiting for us to show, he saw a white Sentra drive by three times. And just now when I got to the front of your house I saw the taillights of a white Sentra."

Though I hadn't heard a car start. So either he left the car idling on the street, there was someone else in the car waiting, or it was someone who lived in the neighborhood who just happened to be driving by. The last would be one hell of a coincidence and I didn't believe in those.

The second option scared the fuck out of me.

"Was the gate open?"

"If you mean that rickety excuse for a fence, no, there was no open gate."

I expected her to remark on my dig, not widen her eyes and ask, "Did you hop the gate?"

"Sweetheart, what you're calling a gate is really nothing more than a waist-high hurdle."

Vanessa's gaze slipped to the bank of windows and as cute as she looked staring off into space we had important things to discuss.

"Your neighbors?" I prompted.

"Shh."

"Why are you shushing me?"

"I'm not done fantasizing... I mean, picturing you hopping the gate."

Yeah, this friend thing was not going to work.

"Vanessa." What was meant to sound stern came out as a groan.

"Right, my neighbors." She mercifully came around to the topic we needed to discuss. "Mrs. Thompson lives on the right, or the left if you're in the backyard facing my house. She's in her eighties fighting her son's wishes to move into an assisted living facility while at the same time fighting with her daughter wanting her to move in with her and her family. She's sweet, capable, but her kids are right, she's getting too old to live by herself. My other neighbors are kind of jerks so I don't know them well and what I do know I don't really like so I don't speak to them."

The gate Vanessa was talking about was on Mrs. Thompson's side. It was unlikely she heard or saw anything.

I needed to call Phoenix and text Brady but when Vanessa's gaze slipped to the door and she started worrying her bottom lip, that need shifted.

"You're safe in here with me."

"But when you leave—"

"I'm not leaving."

Suddenly we were right back to where we'd been when we were in her kitchen before we'd ordered dinner—Vanessa's expression blank, looking anywhere but at me.

"I don't think that's a good idea."

It wasn't a good idea, it was a seriously horrible idea, yet I was still going to spend the night.

"I'm taking the couch," I told her. "Though tomorrow you're back at my house. We haven't cleaned out your garage and Brady won't be back to install your alarm for a few days."

"Dalton—"

"I have an alarm. I also have a garage you can park in and a spare bedroom. My house makes more sense. Unless you want to clean your garage tonight and you have an extra room for me to stay in."

She transferred her bat from her right hand to her left then back to her right. The movement had me wondering if she was planning on using the damn thing on me.

"I'm scared," she admitted. "The car casing my house is freaky but the motion light..."

She let that hang.

Not that I needed her to finish to understand that someone in her backyard was what had her scared.

"Is your Chinese too cold to eat?"

"Probably," she mumbled.

"How do you feel about microwaved Chinese?"

Her nose scrunch said it all.

"Gross but I'm hungry so I'll suffer through rubbery noodles."

I could totally fall in love with her.

The clarity with which that thought hit had me terrified. Not that it was the first time I'd thought that but it was becoming increasingly more difficult to deny it.

Love led to ruined lives and shattered dreams.

It was the beginning of the end.

The root of devastation and destruction.

Nevertheless it felt inevitable.

"Go nuke your noodles." The rest of my instructions died on my lips when Vanessa's curved up into a ridiculously cute smirk.

Fucking hell.

"Nuke your noodles," she repeated with a smile. "Number six-hundred-twenty on the list of things I never thought I'd hear Dalton Neary say."

"That's some list you got. What's number one on that list?"

Her smile faded, sadness crept in, and she shook her head.

"I love you."

With that successful blow to my heart she turned and walked into the kitchen, not having the first clue she'd gutted me.

Could've been hearing those words come out of her mouth made me wish she was saying them *to* me, rather than *at* me, or it could've been knowing I never would. Either way I found it hard to catch my breath as I dug my phone out of my back pocket.

I waited until I heard her moving around in the kitchen before I hit Phoenix's contact.

Two rings later my partner picked up.

"Yo, everything good?"

Pure Phoenix Kent. We'd left work pissed at each other but

I was calling after nine at night—something I no longer did now that he was married with a family—and the first thing he asked was if everything was okay.

Something loosened in my chest. Something I wanted to continue to shove aside and not think about. Something I would have to deal with sooner or later and later was coming fast.

"Tomorrow we're gonna have to carve out some time to chat with Vanessa's neighbors."

"Brady called and told me about the Sentra."

Of course he had.

Instead of feeling bitter I was choosing to view it as a time-saving measure and went on.

"Tonight the driver was in her backyard."

"Are you fucking serious?" he grunted.

"I saw the motion sensor light go on. Apparently he did, too, and got spooked. By the time I got outside and around to the front he was in his car driving away."

"Are you staying there or is she going to your place?"

No animosity, just curiosity.

"Here tonight. My house until the alarm's installed."

"Then what?"

Good fucking question.

"Then I'm gonna have to come up with a really good excuse as to why I'm sleeping on her couch or she's in my guest room. Right now she's given in; when she's got the alarm she won't be so amicable."

"The couch?"

"We've decided to be friends."

The words tasted like acid.

"Friends?" he choked.

"She deserves—"

"For you to pull your head out of your ass. Vanessa is not Layla."

"Don't piss me off," I warned.

"Like you're not already pissed at me," he rightly noted. "And since you already are, I'll take this as my opportunity to remind you when I was going through my shit with Wren you told me I was acting like a bear with a thorn up my ass. Which I have to tell you is better than acting like a fucking coward."

My temper flared and my insides boiled.

"Phoenix—"

"Repeat after me, asshole, Vanessa is not Layla. She's not a spoiled, weak-minded bitch who's going to turn into a raging alcoholic and blame you."

I was seriously regretting telling him about my ex-wife.

"I'm hanging up before I tell you to go fuck yourself."

"You do that, brother. And after you hang up, think about what I said."

I didn't get a chance to hang up on the asshole.

The fucker hung up on me.

Instead of texting Brady I shoved my phone into my pocket and went in search of Vanessa. When I found her she was standing in the open archway that led to her den, staring out the window and not seeing anything because it was pitch dark in her backyard.

"Do you want me to close the blinds?"

She jolted and spun to face me.

The fear I saw earlier was now in hyperdrive.

"I wish I could go back to thinking I was having dehydration hallucinations."

"Come again?"

"It was better when I could just blow it off because I had no proof. And no one wants to look like a malnourished fool in front of her friends. But now there's proof. Someone was out there. Someone's following me. Someone wants—"

Vanessa stopped, her eyes turned glossy, then I was on the

move. I got to her as the first tear fell. I had her wrapped up tight before I felt her body hitch and the first sob broke loose.

I waited until sobs turned into muffled cries then I waited a little longer until I heard her sniffling.

"We're going to find whoever is following you and you'll be safe while we do it."

Vanessa nodded.

"Was that you agreeing or were you just wiping your snot on my shirt?"

"I believe you."

"Good." I bent and kissed the top of her head. "Now for the bad news."

"I can't handle any bad news right now," she told me, her voice nasally.

"Okay, then how about this? Something new to add to your list of things you'd never hear me say."

"How high up on the list is it?"

Christ, I wanted to love this woman.

"I'm thinking top-twenty."

"Hit me with it."

"If you still want your rubbery chow mein you're gonna have to eat it off my chest."

There was a beat of silence before her body went stiff.

Her head slowly tipped back. I dipped my chin, and suddenly our lips were close. Too close.

Mere inches.

Close enough the ever-present electricity I felt when I was near her was firing to life.

Close enough I was wondering if I could convince her to add benefits to this sham of a friendship we were playing at.

It only got worse from there when Vanessa pressed her tits and hips closer to keep the container of Chinese that was crushed in her hand from falling to the floor. There was no hope of stopping my dick from stirring to life, especially when her lips parted and she sucked in a breath.

"This isn't smart," she whispered.

"It's not," I agreed.

I watched the war raging in her eyes. Part of me hoped she lost the battle and decided that being smart wasn't all it was cracked up to be. The other part hoped she won and told me to fuck off.

Slowly her lids drifted closed, cutting me off from her thoughts.

"I wish I was the kind of woman who could separate sex and feelings. I wish I could take you to bed and enjoy a meaningless fuck then let you leave in the morning and go about my day happy with the orgasms you gave me. But I'm not."

And I wished I was the kind of man who could take care of a woman. But I'd already proved that wasn't the case and I'd never chance ruining Vanessa the way I did Layla. For once it wasn't the thought of my ex that had my gut churning.

"Nothing about our weekend was meaningless," I corrected. "Nothing about you could ever be meaningless so don't ever wish you were a different kind of woman. You're perfect just the way you are."

"Dalton—"

The hope I heard in those two syllables further proved I couldn't be trusted around Vanessa.

"Your noodles," I prompted in an effort to put some distance between us.

Whatever light was left in those gorgeous eyes dimmed. I should've been grateful. Instead I felt like the world's biggest asshole.

"I think they're ruined."

Better your noodles than your life.

"You can have the rest of my shrimp."

That cute nose of her scrunched and I wanted to beg her to fix me. To take a chance on me knowing the outcome would be devastation.

"The only thing worse than rubbery noodles is rubbery shrimp."

I lifted a brow and asked, "The *only* thing?"

Christ, I just couldn't stop myself.

"Well, not the only thing but there's a woman code to protect so it wouldn't do for me to blab about penis size in relation to how hot the owner of said penis is."

Yeah, this had to end.

All of it.

The closeness.

The teasing.

The falling in love.

Yet, I didn't step back and allow the noodles to fall to the floor. I pressed closer, trapping her hand, her meal to my chest.

"Penis size in relation to how hot the owner is?" I questioned.

"Eh, it's always a disappointment when a hot guy has a small penis. Not that you'd know about that," she mumbled the last part miserably.

I couldn't deny my ego and my dick liked knowing she hadn't been disappointed.

"Is that because I have—"

"You don't have a vagina so this conversation is officially over before I'm kicked out of the girl gang."

The woman was a never-ending source of amusement.

One day she'd find some asshole who was worthy of her and the lucky son of a bitch would spend the rest of his life beside a beautiful, independent, funny woman who would make him laugh.

I hated the dick already and she hadn't even found him.

I hated knowing one day, I'd be nothing but a distant memory, or worse—a regret.

I hated that Phoenix was right. I was a fucking coward.

Better a coward than a selfish piece of shit who shattered Vanessa's perfect life.

11

"YOU LOOK..." Caroline, our new admin, said but paused to give me the once-over.

"Annoyed," Wren supplied from her desk without looking up from the application I'd handed her.

"No, that's not it," Caroline returned.

"Frustrated?" Wren went on.

Sexually frustrated would've hit the nail on the head but I wasn't admitting that.

"Closer..."

"Confused?"

"That's it." Caroline snapped her fingers and bobbed her head. The tips of her jet-black hair brushed her shoulders and her pretty face broke into a smile.

I liked Caroline. She was a little younger than me, had two kids she was raising alone since her husband had up and run off with a woman who was nearly twice his age and had a son only a year younger than him. He now lived in Tennessee with his sugar mama. Caroline and her kids got a monthly support check that Caroline suspected was guilt money from the mistress and not fatherly concern or obligation from her husband. She was hard-working, a good mom to her two young children, and despite her husband's fuckery she never bad-mouthed him. I thought that said a lot about the type of woman she was. She'd also recently hired a divorce attorney and I'd heard her in the break room tell the lawyer she only wanted out of the marriage and her fair share when she could've taken the cheating, child abandoner to the cleaners.

She was beautiful, smart, and sweet. If she wanted to find someone new she'd have no trouble.

"I'm not confused," I lied.

I was totally confused and as mentioned, sexually frustrated. Unfortunately that was only the tip of the iceberg of the things I was. I was also freaked out and scared someone was definitely following me, and ever since Dalton had asked if I was angry at my dad for sending Malory away I couldn't stop thinking about it. Was I mad that my sister spent her seventeenth birthday locked up in a camp for troubled youth that seemed to do more damage than good? Eighteen years was a long time to harbor ill feelings and not realize it but I loved and adored my sister so if I was mad—and I wasn't sure I was—I could hold a grudge for eternity.

But could I do that subconsciously?

Damn Dalton for bringing it up.

Damn him for spending the night on my couch, making it so I got no sleep wondering if he was uncomfortable.

Damn him for making me second-guess myself and what I knew I wanted.

But mostly damn him for still being hung up on his ex-wife.

Yes, I knew that was unkind to think but my stupid broken heart didn't feel like being logical or kind. It felt like being petty and mean.

"Don't listen to her," Wren told Caroline. "She's confused and in denial. Apparently that has an adverse reaction to her normal sunny disposition that makes her snappy. I'm ignoring her today. You should, too."

I glared at my boss.

"Welp, I was just coming in to see if you needed anything before I left for the day."

"Thank you but no." Wren smiled at Caroline, something she hadn't done with me all day seeing as I had been snappy with her. "Have a great night."

"Thanks. You, too." Then Caroline transferred her smile to me. "I know you don't know me that well but I'm a good listener. If you need to talk, my door's always open and I always keep a bottle of wine and a fresh pint of mint chip on hand. You're welcome to it any time."

Damn Dalton.

I was in a shit mood and taking it out on my co-workers.

"Thanks, Caroline. Sorry if I've been a pain today. I didn't sleep well last night."

"*If,*" Wren mumbled.

"Fine," I snapped before I thought better of it. "I'm sorry *I've* been a pain today."

"You haven't been but if you're not sleeping well you should get one of the mattress toppers. They work wonders."

See?

Caroline was a total sweetheart. Her husband was an idiot-fool for leaving her and a huge douche for abandoning his children.

"Thanks."

"See you tomorrow."

I watched Caroline leave Wren's office with a skip in her step and for the first time in my life I felt real, honest-to-God jealousy. I had never been one of those women who coveted what other women had—not success, not men, not material things. If I wanted something I worked to earn it—my father had taught me that. My mother had taught me through example how to lift people up, both the men and women in my life. I didn't need to dim someone else's light to make mine shine brighter. When you're busy cheering people on you don't have time for something as trivial as jealousy. Thus I'd never felt the emotion. But seeing Caroline skip-walk out of Wren's office knowing everything she had going on at home made me feel inadequate, which led me to being jealous of her perseverance and determination.

There I was sulking like a toddler because the man I had a crush on—okay, more like was mostly in love with—didn't like me back the same way. And worse, I'd made it Wren's problem with my moping.

"I think I'm mad at my father for something he did eighteen years ago," I blurted out.

"Whoa there," she whistled. "Warn a girl when we're switching lanes. I was readying my mattress topper comeback and you drop a nuclear warhead on me."

Wren moved her mouse, tapped it a few times, then gently closed her laptop and gave me her undivided attention.

"Okay, sock it to me," she offered.

"It's a long story," I warned.

"The important ones always are."

Another reminder of why I adored Wren.

I gave her the abbreviated version of my sister's teenage angst but more context and detail than I gave Dalton. When I was done she looked pale.

"First, I'm sorry your family went through all of that. All of you experienced varying degrees of trauma."

I sensed there was a *but* there and I was right.

"But as a parent I can sympathize with your mom and dad. I don't know what I would do if Griff started acting out, especially the sneaking out and drinking part. That's dangerous and scary. You know I met Phoenix through the Hope Center. He was Griff's mentor-slash-big brother."

Shit. Dammit.

"I'm sorry. I shouldn't be—"

"Don't do that, Vanessa. I placed Griff in the program because I didn't want there to come a time when Griff acted out because he no longer had good male companionship. But even if there had been a problem you'd still have nothing to apologize for. I still worry about Griff. Kids, especially teenagers, go through so many changes. High school is a battlefield but for girls I think it's worse. It's where we learn toxic behavior in the name of fitting in. It's a time in a young girl's life when she learns lessons she's too young to learn. Immaturity and lack of impulse control is a dangerous combination. As a mom, that's one of my biggest fears—drinking, driving, sex, jumping off the roof of a house into a pool, trying to outrun a train. Teenagers are scary, fearless creatures. I can't say if what your parents did for your sister was the right call or not. Maybe her going to that camp saved her life. Maybe it changed her in ways that were harmful. The only person who can answer that is your sister."

Wren was right. For most people high school was something you lived through and when you were done you slammed the door behind you, happy you made it out alive. I supposed there were people who had a great time though I was not one of those people. I was an early bloomer. That meant I was chesty before my peers, started my period before them, and had the acne to prove my hormones were raging. I didn't peak in high school like some, I was the ugly, shy duckling who didn't understand—even though my mom had drilled it into me—what true beauty was until I understood the kindness I'd given to others also extended to myself.

"She won't talk about her time in Utah."

"Won't or doesn't like to?"

"Won't. Not then, not now. It's like that seven months she was gone didn't happen."

Worry suffused Wren's features, a look I was positive I myself had during the many times I'd attempted to talk to Malory about the therapy she'd received in Utah. The same look I was sure I had when instead of asking her about the camp I tried to talk to her about what had been going on in her life that had led her to go from wild and fun to off the rails.

"What do your parents say?"

"Nothing. Not a thing. It's our family's dirty secret that gets swept under the rug. No one talks about that time. They don't even bring up anything I did during that time. It's like we live in a time warp where those years do not exist—period."

"So the real question is, are you mad at your father? Do you blame him?"

Before I could answer Wren, which would be to tell her I had no clue, my phone pinged with a text. She leaned forward to look at my cell and announced, "Dalton."

I snagged my phone off her desk, hoping he was telling me my alarm had been installed early and he was canceling our sleepover.

I opened the text and sighed.

"Problem?" Wren asked.

"I was hoping Brady installed my alarm today and I'd be left in peace."

"You could stay with me and Phoenix if you don't want to stay at Dalton's," she offered.

Did I want to stay at Dalton's when I couldn't touch or kiss or be on the receiving end of multiple orgasms—no. Did I want to stay with him knowing that I never had a chance with him— double no. Did I want to bring trouble to Wren and Phoenix's house with Griffin living in that house after the kid had survived a fire and watching his stepdad almost die—that was a hell-to-the-no no.

"I'm just being a whiner."

I tapped out a quick response and tossed my phone back on the desk.

"Well?" she nosily prompted just as her phone started binging.

I sat back knowing she was likely getting the same message from Phoenix that I'd received from Dalton.

"Ugh. Why is it he always runs late when it's his turn to cook?"

She might've been complaining but I knew it wasn't real.

"Because he's a man."

"Yeah, that's probably why. So, our men are going to be late. What do you say I swing by my house, grab Griff, and we all go out to dinner?"

I was stuck back on the "our men" part of that question.

"We could try that new burger place, I've heard it's good."

Burgers sounded awesome.

My stomach growled, accepting Wren's invitation.

"You know I'd hate you if I didn't love you so much," she grumbled. "You eat like a toddler and have that body."

She waved a hand in my direction.

I didn't bother dignifying her craziness with a response. The woman had a rocking body and unlike me she didn't go to the gym three times a week.

"Will Griff groan and moan if we talk about the application while we wait for our food?" I asked as I stood.

"Have you met my son?"

Yes, I'd had the pleasure of meeting her very handsome, very smart son many times. But since her question wasn't really a question I remained quiet.

"He won't even know we're in the booth with him until I

pry his phone out of his hands. Then suddenly he'll look around and realize he's not in his room and there's a plate of food in front of him and we will become invisible again as he scarfs down his meal."

That sounded like normal teenage behavior.

And thank God when I was his age, cell phones weren't what they are today or I'd be living in a cave somewhere dying of embarrassment that my teenaged stupidity was well documented and forever preserved for all to see.

"Let me grab my purse and we'll walk out together."

"Damn right we will."

Right.

Stalker.

How could I forget?

Dalton, that was how.

Everything could be blamed on him.

12

"MR. RYAN, if you know something and you're holding back..."
Phoenix let that lay.

The gun store owner's gaze slid to the other side of the U-shaped display cases, landed on his son, and took his time answering.

"We've heard about the robberies," Clint Ryan admitted.

"What've you heard?" I pushed.

Clint fixed his focus on me. He shook his head, exhaled through his nose, and I settled in for the familiar refrain I knew was coming but didn't have time for.

"I remember a time when people around here didn't have to lock their doors."

I heard that a time or ten from the old man.

"People respected other people's property."

That, too, was something Clint had pointed out before.

"Times have changed," I unnecessarily reminded him, wanting to get to the point of our visit while resisting the urge to look at my watch. "What's the word on the break-ins?"

"Word is nothing was taken but firearms from locked safes."

That was correct, and concerning that small detail had made its way to the street.

"What else?" I asked.

"Nothing." Clint shook his head and glanced back at his son. "But me and Josh were talking last night."

"Have you had any problems here at the store?" Phoenix inquired.

"You know better than that, Kent," the elderly man scoffed. "Our inventory is locked up."

"Bet the homeowners who are now missing their firearms thought the same," Phoenix countered.

"We don't rely on safes, at least not the conventional kind and you know that."

This was true. Clint and Josh Ryan went above and beyond what the law required. The vault was reinforced cinder block around a steel cage. A thief would need explosives and a blowtorch to get into their storage room.

Clint was still holding something back which was unusual for the man. He had strong opinions on gun ownership mixed with stronger opinions about breaking the law. Over the years he'd tipped us off to illegal backdoor sales and was quick to call us with any rumor involving unlawful activity. His tips normally panned out—that was why we were there.

"You got anything for us, Josh?" Phoenix called out.

"Just a theory," he answered on his way to his father's side.

"What's your theory?"

Josh looked at his father before asking his own question, "Remember a while back there was that case in Oregon? Law enforcement had a warrant to seize weapons from that jackass making threats but he wouldn't give up the code to his safe?" Josh paused long enough for Phoenix to nod. "The feds called the manufacturer of the safe and got the master code."

Fucking shit.

I had a feeling I knew where this was going.

"You think someone's got the master code?"

Josh looked at me and shrugged.

"Don't know. But there's a reason we don't use safes at the store. There is no master code to get into the vault."

"Before you ask, I haven't heard any talk about a master safecracker in the area and that's what it'd take to break into a modern safe," Clint rejoined. "And you know I'll call if I hear anything about guns being pawned."

Thankfully Phoenix took that as our cue to leave. "Appreciate your time."

"Tell that sister of yours if I don't see her soon I'm going to think she's cheating on me."

"I'll let her know she's due for a visit."

There had been a time when Clint was angling for Shiloh Kent to become Mrs. Josh Ryan. That was until Sunny met Luke and it became clear Clint wouldn't be welcoming her into the family, but he still liked to flirt with her when she came in.

Normally I found this banter amusing. Today, not so much. Not after a fourth robbery; the last two happening within three days of each other, which indicated the perpetrator was getting more confident and escalating. Not after we'd canvased Vanessa's neighborhood that morning asking her neighbors if anyone knew the owner of a white Sentra. Frustratingly no one had seen the car or knew of anyone in the neighborhood who drove one. Not after I'd lost the right to sleep next to Vanessa so I'd slept on her couch last night, with her just down the hall in her bed. Not after a morning where I had to fight back the urge to kiss Vanessa goodbye.

I was in a shit mood, made shittier with another break-in which meant I was running late getting to Vanessa. Last week I would've welcomed the overtime. Last week I had no reason to rush home. Last week I'd given Phoenix shit when he complained about leaving the station twenty minutes after his shift had ended.

Now I got it and that understanding pissed me off. Ten years ago I had a wife at home and never once had I ever wanted to rush home to see her. Phoenix had the life I thought I'd be living. That didn't piss me off—Layla fucking me over and stealing my future did. The woman was off doing whatever jacked-up shit she did and a decade later I was still dealing with the fallout—the consequences of my failures taking away any chance of happiness.

"What are your thoughts on Josh's theory?" Phoenix asked, pulling me back to the present.

"I think it's worth looking into."

"So do I."

"I'll pull the reports when we get back and check—"

"Tomorrow," he cut me off and rounded the car to the driver's side.

I clenched my jaw, preparing for another near-death experience. The man drove like we were running the Fallujah gauntlet and not driving the city streets of Georgia. I triple checked my seat belt was good before I broached the subject we'd both been ignoring all day.

"About last night," I started.

"Is that how you start your morning-after conversations before you slink out of the house?" Phoenix chuckled. "Because I have to tell you, that sounds like a bad breakup line."

I flipped him off and braced my hand against the dash as he slammed on the brakes.

"Who the fuck taught you to drive?"

"Unlike you, not my grandma."

I ignored the jab about my superior driving skills, including knowing how to brake without giving my passenger whiplash and went on, "I was a dick."

"If that's your idea of an apology I'm gonna need more than that seeing as you're a dick most of the time."

A five-year-old's idea of a comeback was on the tip of my tongue. I refrained from telling him it took one to know one but just barely.

Unfortunately, tamping down my impulse took too long and Phoenix continued.

"Bet you thought about what I said," he mumbled.

The fucker was right. I'd thought about little else as I laid awake on Vanessa's couch and he was right—there was no comparing Vanessa and Layla. But he was more wrong than right.

"My ex wasn't a raging alcoholic when I met her. That's who I turned her into."

"Are you fucking kidding me?"

"Wish I was."

I'd been partners with Phoenix long enough I could anticipate his movements when we were in the middle of a takedown. I could follow his train of thought when interrogating a suspect. I could easily read his body language and facial expressions. Which meant when the vibe in the car went frosty I knew to brace.

"Tell me, Dalton, how the hell did you turn another human being into an alcoholic?"

Christ, I should've kept my trap shut.

"According to her, it was between college and when I went into the academy."

"According to her," he spat. "So let me get this straight; you held her down and poured wine down her throat."

When I had no answer to that he pushed forward.

"No? I see. So you graduated college, planned your wedding, and explained to her that you wanted nothing more in this world than for her to start drinking and do that to such excess she was to be slaughtered when you came home from work every night, and her being the loving fiancée vowed to do just that."

"This isn't a fucking joke," I ground out, losing the hold on my temper.

"You're wrong, brother. You thinking you have the power to turn someone into an alcoholic is a joke. Did you ever stop to think that maybe her blaming that shit on you was an excuse?"

Thankfully Clint Ryan's gun store was only a few blocks from the station. I needed to get the fuck out of this car and away from Phoenix before I said something that I couldn't take back.

"Your silence speaks volumes," he muttered as he pulled into the parking lot. "You know my father was a drunk, so are you telling me that his drinking problem was my fault? My brothers'? Sunny's?"

"That's not even close to the same thing."

"It's exactly the same thing, Dalton, and since I know you're not stupid you're purposefully being stubborn. You've latched onto her excuses so you'll never open yourself up again. I get that. I get why you'd hold on to her selfishness to protect yourself. So I'll say it again in hopes that maybe you'll fucking hear me this time. Vanessa. Is. Not. Layla."

"No shit." I spat out the words and reached for the door. "As you pointed out when you told me to stay away from Vanessa, she's too good for me. Sober, my ex doesn't come close to the perfection that is Vanessa."

"You're a dumbass."

"Thanks, you've already pointed that out several times."

I opened the door but didn't exit fast enough before Phoenix verbally sucker-punched me.

"I didn't tell you to stay away from the woman. I told you not to fuck her unless you planned on sticking around when you were done. Then I told you to pull your head out of your ass before you lose your shot at her. And lastly I called you a coward because for whatever reason the woman is gone for you and you keep running."

"Yeah, brother, I keep running. But clue in; I keep running back to her, and if I don't figure out a way to stay the fuck away from her I'll ruin her the same way I ruined Layla. You think I'm being a coward holding on to excuses but I'm telling you, I'm fucking weak and can't stay away. I'm not being stubborn, you asshole, I'm trying to protect Vanessa from throwing her life away."

"Dalton—"

"This conversation's over."

I swung the door open, got out, slammed it closed, and made it three steps away before Phoenix called out, "You need to tell her."

I didn't bother with replying.

I was nearly to the back door of the station when my phone vibrated with a text. I pulled my phone out of my pocket, halted long enough to read Vanessa's message and reply. I changed directions and walked to my truck.

Vanessa was done with dinner with Wren and I was done with Wren's husband's bullshit so the timing was perfect. Phoenix could finish the paperwork by himself.

I'd just pulled onto the parkway when my phone rang. I ignored it.

The phone rang again. I glanced at the caller, sucked in a breath, and tried to hide my irritation when I answered.

"Hey—"

"There's a white Sentra behind me," Vanessa rushed out.

Those knots in my stomach tightened and I forced myself to push everything out of my mind but Vanessa and what I needed her to do to keep herself safe until I could get to her.

"Where are you?"

"I'm on Oglethorpe leaving that new burger place next to the Applebee's across from the Chevy dealership."

I had no idea what burger place she was talking about but I knew the Applebee's.

"I'm on Main," I told her. "I want you to make a right on Memorial. I'll meet up with you at the roundabout."

"Okay."

Her voice was shaky and her "okay" sounded more like a whoosh of air than an actual word.

"Everything's going to be fine, Vanessa. All you need to do is get to the roundabout and I'll take it from there."

"Okay."

"I'm going to call—"

"Don't hang up with me," she pleaded.

The fear in her voice cut me to the bone.

"I'm not hanging up, but I need to call Phoenix on three-way."

I passed a car going forty-five in a thirty and wished I was still on patrol and had a vehicle with lights and sirens.

"Don't put me on hold, Dalton."

Fuck.

I pressed down on the accelerator, uncaring I was now twenty over the posted limit.

"Okay, baby, tell me what's going on."

"What's going on?"

"How far back is the Sentra?"

"Right behind me."

Jesus fuck.

"What's the driver look like?"

"Um, I don't know. It's too dark."

"Male or female?"

"A guy. Young if I had to guess. I'm turning onto Memorial."

"I'm two blocks away from the roundabout. You're doing great, Vanessa. I'm almost there."

"He went straight," she announced. "I mean, he didn't turn with me."

Thank fuck.

"That's good but I want you to keep your eyes on your rearview until I'm behind you. I'll follow you back to my place."

I heard her blow out a shaky breath and I knew what was coming.

"What if—"

"Don't do that. Better safe than sorry."

"There has to be a thousand white Sentras in Hollow Point."

"There are," I agreed. "And one of them is driven by a man who is stalking you. So until this is over you call me every time you see one."

I heard another long exhale.

"I'm at the roundabout."

Just as she said that her silver Elantra came into view.

"I see you."

"Before we go to your house can we stop by mine? I forgot something."

"Is that something vitally important?"

"On a scale of one to ten I'd say my nightly face moisturizer is not only vital but essential."

The smile her comment elicited was against my will. I'd had a shit day, had broken about a dozen traffic laws to get to her, was still freaked the fuck out someone had been following her, and yet she could still make me smile.

"I don't suppose we could stop and get this moisturizer at Walgreens?"

"*Gasp!* Does my face say drugstore moisturizer to you?"

The woman actually said "gasp" which was ridiculous and cute as fuck at the same time.

Before I could tell her that her face said a lot of things—all of them beautiful—she wiped away my shit-day with three whispered words.

"You found me."

A simple statement of fact since indeed I had found her.

Yet I felt those words pour over me like acid peeling away layers of hardened scar tissue, leaving me exposed and raw and wanting nothing more than to be a whole, emotionally undamaged man worthy of her.

If only I'd found her first.

13

I PULLED INTO MY DRIVEWAY, killed the ignition, grabbed my purse off the passenger seat, and jumped out of my car.

My heart rate had slowed to a gallop instead of the thundering beat it had been ten minutes ago but there was something lingering in my chest I couldn't get rid of. I didn't care if I'd been wrong and the car following me hadn't really been following me but instead just innocently driving behind me. I didn't care if I looked foolish. I didn't care about anything but getting to Dalton. I also didn't care what it said about me that I needed him to get rid of the last vestiges of fear or adrenalin or whatever it was that was pumping through me. I needed to touch him, to feel his strong arms wrapped around me, to thank him, to hear him tell me I was safe.

I knew I was being irrational and probably a little dramatic but I didn't care about that either as I ran across my yard and threw myself at him. Upon impact he wrapped one arm around my waist, one around my shoulders, and just like I knew he would he pulled me against his chest, both arms locking me in place.

"Let's get inside," he murmured. "I want you off the street."

There it was again, Dalton looking out for me—making me safe.

I didn't want to move out of his arms but still I murmured back, "Okay."

I moved but didn't get far when Dalton tucked me close and walked with me to the front door. I unlocked the door and the deadbolt, both of which he'd installed. He let me go, shuffled in behind me, and slammed the door closed. But that was as far as I got when he hooked me around my waist and yanked me back. With his chest plastered to my back he shoved his face into the side of my neck and breathed in.

I closed my eyes.

He breathed out.

In that moment, our position was not something that friends shared, not even after one friend had run into the other's arms. There was something far more intimate about the way he was holding me. I should've put a stop to it but stupidly I lifted my hand, found his forearm, and held on.

"Fuck." His raspy curse vibrated on my neck, causing an unfriendly-like tremor between my legs.

"Dalton—"

"You okay?"

I was safe in my house snug against Dalton's hard body—no, I was not okay. This after he rushed to help me. This after I'd kissed, licked, and tasted every inch of him. This after he'd returned the favor. In other words, I needed to step away from him before my body reacted in a way I'd regret.

"Are you?" I asked instead of answering.

"Fuck no."

Alrighty then.

I didn't know how to respond to that and I didn't get the chance before there was a knock on my front door.

Without warning, Dalton let me go and spun around to face the door while at the same time he herded me behind him and motioned for me to stay there. Then his right hand went to his hip and in a smooth, upward motion he drew the gun I hadn't noticed he was wearing.

"Kitchen, baby," Dalton snapped. "Phone out, ready to call 9 1 1 if you hear something you don't like."

I was still processing my abrupt departure from Dalton's hold when he snapped again, "Kitchen. Now. Out of sight."

I decided the kitchen was my best course of action seeing as Dalton's demands left no room for negotiation. Say, like me answering the door or him doing it without his gun out, which would likely scare the pants off of one of my neighbors.

A second later I was in the kitchen digging through my purse when I heard Dalton's angry voice boom, "Who the fuck are you?"

"I'm looking for Vanessa Hale," a voice I'd never heard returned.

"Didn't ask who you were looking for, I asked who the *fuck* you are and while you're at it you can explain to me why the *fuck* you're following my woman and creeping around her house."

Dalton didn't shy away from cursing, but I'd never heard him enunciate his f-words in that furious tone before.

And *his* woman?

What the heck?

"I need to talk to her."

"Listen, kid, I don't give a fuck what you need to do. Who are you and why are you here?"

Kid?

I peeked around the corner of the wide archway, trying to get a glimpse of who Dalton was calling a kid. The person didn't sound like a kid and I knew Dalton well enough to know he would never curse like that to an actual child. I couldn't see who was at the door with Dalton's big body barring entry but I could see a mop of tussled, dirty-blond hair.

"My name's Sullivan Wooten."

I didn't know anyone by that name.

I took a step to get a better look but halted when Dalton proved he had some sort of supernatural hearing and irately commanded, "Don't come out here."

I wasn't sure which part annoyed me more—the part where he was barking commands at me at all or barking the commands irately.

Obviously Dalton didn't feel this "kid" was a real threat or he wouldn't be standing in the doorway speaking to him. And for all he knew, the "kid" could've been one of my neighbors.

"If Vanessa's home, I'd like to speak to her please," Sullivan said.

"And I'd like to know why you've been stalking her."

"Stalking her?" I heard it then, the crack in the guy's voice. He wasn't a kid but he wasn't yet a man. "I'm not stalking her."

"So what do you call following her? Driving by her house. And creeping around her backyard?"

"The backyard was a mistake," he amicably admitted and I inched back into the kitchen. "But the rest wasn't stalking. I was watching her."

I heard an angry growl coming from Dalton and I wondered if now was when I should call 911. Not because I thought Dalton or I were in danger but by the sound of Dalton this Sullivan guy might be.

"Please don't shoot anyone on my porch," I called out. "It's new and I'm not sure how easily blood comes out of cedar."

"Is that her?" Sullivan asked hopefully. "I really need to talk to her."

I thought there was excitement—or was it nervousness?—in his tone and I wasn't sure what it meant that some random guy I didn't know who'd admitted to watching me sounded excited I was in the house.

"That's not gonna happen," Dalton denied.

"Why are you watching me?" I asked from the safety of my kitchen.

"Jesus fuck," Dalton snarled.

It wasn't funny but still I had to pinch my lips to stop myself from smiling.

"I think you're my aunt and I just wanted to talk to you."

Aunt?

That was impossible.

"You have the wrong person!" I yelled into the living room, thinking it was ridiculous I was having this conversation by shouting across my house.

"I'm...um...I'm pretty sure I'm right."

"Sorry—"

"Five minutes," he pleaded.

"Not gonna happen, kid. This is your warning—turn around, leave, and stop watching Vanessa Hale. Absolutely never show up at her door or at her work. No joke, Sullivan, this is the only warning you get. Next time I see you I'll arrest you."

This Sullivan kid must've been brave because he completely ignored Dalton and yelled back to me, "I took a DNA test. I have it with me. All I want is five minutes. If I'm wrong I'll leave and you'll never see me again."

A DNA test?

What in the world?

"Five minutes," I returned.

"Vanessa," Dalton growled but it was too late; I was moving through the living room toward the door.

It was then I got my first look at Sullivan Wooten.

I was right. His hair was a mess of sandy blond—a shade darker than mine. Tall, lanky, maybe eighteen or nineteen, meaning he hadn't finished filling out. Hazel eyes with more brown than green but just enough to cut through the brown and make them beautiful. His jaw was squarish, cheekbones high, straight nose. Overall, he was a cute young man who would grow up to be a very handsome man.

And he looked familiar.

Very.

Like I'd been looking at a female variation of him for thirty-two years.

He looked like he could be my brother.

My stomach clutched in an uncomfortable way.

A thousand scenarios ran through my mind, ranging from my father having an affair, to him having a second family out there, to my mother giving her firstborn up for adoption and this young man standing in front of me was the result of some scandalous family secret that was about to be exposed.

Dalton stepped in front of Sullivan, cutting off my view of the boy-man who was definitely my family.

"Come in, shut the door, sit down, and don't fucking move or I swear to God I'll shoot you."

After he was done threatening Sullivan, he turned. I didn't miss his flinch before he prowled to me, hooked me around the shoulders, and led me to the hallway. Dalton didn't stop until we were in my bedroom.

"Talk to me," he demanded.

"I don't know what to say."

"Let's start with your sister," he prompted.

Malory?

"She's thirty-five. That guy in there has to be like nineteen.

Besides, my sister doesn't have children and she wouldn't hide something like that from me."

"Your dad?" he cautiously asked.

"So you think he looks like me?"

Dalton pulled me closer, kissed the top of my head, then very gently told me, "Hair's a shade darker, eye color is different, but yeah, baby, he looks like he could be your brother."

See?

"That's what I thought, too."

Dalton didn't reply.

My stomach was in knots and panic started to claw its way up my throat.

"Hey," Dalton murmured softly.

What if my dad had an affair?

Oh, God, what if he's still having an affair?

"Hey, baby, stop."

What if Sullivan showing up breaks up my family?

Oh, God, I'm a total asshole. Who blames a child on breaking up a family?

"Nessa, baby, you're freaking out over nothing."

"Nothing? My family—"

"You don't even know for sure who he is."

If I had the energy I would've tipped my head back and glared but I didn't so I continued to stare at the ugly carpet in my room thinking I really wished I'd ripped it out when I did the living room.

"Before we go back out there and talk to him I need to ask you where he'd get your DNA sample to test."

Huh?

"What?"

"He said he has a DNA test."

My mind whirled back five years to a time I was feeling

overly ambitious and was going to make my mother a family history book. Nothing ever came of it because I got too busy but I'd taken the DNA test and signed up on the company's website.

"I did one of those at-home DNA tests to track genealogy."

"Alright," he returned softly. "We're gonna go back out and hear him out. But before we do, you need to remember he could be full of shit. This could be—"

"Dalton, you saw him."

"I did and he looks like you. But, Vanessa, there are all sorts of criminals and scammers out there. We could get back out there and find he's already taken off with your purse and china."

That would suck. Canceling credit cards was a pain in the ass but some part of me hoped Sullivan had jacked my purse and run away.

"Does it make me a horrible person to wish—"

"No, it doesn't."

"You didn't let me finish."

Dalton's arm loosened. He shifted me away from him just far enough so that he could use his hand to tilt my head back and catch my eyes.

When he had my attention those golden-brown orbs held infinite kindness. I wanted to hate him—should've hated him for showing me everything I could never have.

It was at that moment, with a stranger sitting in my living room and knowing in my soul my life was about to be forever changed, I realized Dalton Neary was unsurvivable. One day I would fall in love, get married, have a family, and Dalton would be the man I looked back on and wondered *what-if*. He would forever be the one I wanted but wasn't allowed to have.

I should totally hate him.

Instead, I fell further into the abyss of that stare and clung to the vestiges of his strength knowing he was going to take it all away.

"Brace, Vanessa, this is gonna hurt."

"Which part?"

Dalton caught my meaning and his eyes slowly closed.

"All of it."

14

"I NEED TO CALL MY SISTER," Vanessa announced as we walked hand in hand down the hall. "She only lives ten minutes away. She should be here for this, too."

From what Vanessa had told me about her sister Malory, I didn't agree.

"Are you sure that's a good idea?"

"No," she sighed. "It's a horrible idea but I need her here so she's going to have to buck up and be my big sister."

Reading between the lines—Vanessa needed someone she trusted and knew she could lean on for emotional support to sit next to her while she heard the kid out. Taking that a step further, that person wasn't me.

I absorbed that gut punch, took in the kid sitting ass-to-the-edge of the couch cushion, bouncing his knee like he nervous as all fuck, looking like he was regretting knocking on the door.

"Nessa, sweetheart, I think right now it should just be you who talks to him," I told her softly.

"Me? Wait." She squeezed my hand and dug her heels in, stopping us at the mouth of the hall. "*Just me?* Are you leaving?"

"Fuck no, I'm not leaving you alone with him. Kid or not, he's been following you. Until we know for sure who he is and why he's here you're not to be alone with him. Period."

I expected her to push back, tell me to go fuck myself. Instead, her shoulders sagged in relief.

"Thank you."

"If you're having second thoughts, I can get rid of him." I offered her an out she looked like she needed. "Or you can wait in your bedroom while I get his story."

I liked the second option, but I knew Vanessa, and the stunt she pulled from the kitchen only proved what I already knew—she would not sit idly by and let me handle the situation for her. She might've been amicable when she thought she was in danger, smart enough to let me take the lead, but now that she'd laid eyes on the person who'd been creeping her out—that person being a teenager who looked to be nonthreatening—Vanessa wouldn't sit on the sidelines.

Part of me couldn't find fault in that, admired her fortitude. But a bigger part that included the cop in me found this troublesome. Looking a certain way, especially nonthreatening, didn't mean shit. Sullivan being young didn't mean shit. I'd been a cop long enough to know looks could be deceiving.

"As long as you stay, I want to hear him out."

Fuck.

"I get the first go," I told her.

"First go?"

"I get to talk to him first," I explained.

Vanessa's eyes got wide but there was humor there.

"Will this be an interrogation, Detective Neary?"

Good Christ, she was cute.

"Yes."

"Will you be cleaning your service weapon on my coffee table while you perform this interview?"

Yeah, she was cute as fuck when she forgot I'd fucked her—literally and figuratively. There would come a time when she woke up and ended this tentative friendship we had and when she did she'd remove herself from my life. The thought made me irrationally afraid. Not angry, not annoyed, just scared. One day I'd lose her and I'd have no one to blame but myself. I couldn't even lie and hide behind Layla being the cause of my issues. Not when it came to Vanessa. The truth was I was exactly what Phoenix said—a fucking coward.

"No, sweetheart, the smell of Hoppe's lingers," I teased.

"Hoppe's?"

"I'll explain later but to answer your question, no, I'll refrain from cleaning my weapon with the warning if he upsets you he's out on his ass. This after I call a unit out and he gets an official notice from a uniformed officer if he doesn't back off he'll be slapped with a restraining order."

"I don't have it in me to argue with you about your caveman act so I'm reserving the right to give you shit about it later, especially if you try to kick him out without me learning the whole story."

"You know I can hear you, right?" the kid called from the couch. "Hoppe's is a brand of gun cleaner and the guy's right; the smell lingers. My mom hates the smell and makes my dad clean his shotguns out in the garage. And I don't need an official warning or a restraining order. I just have some questions, then I'll leave."

I had questions for the kid about his father's shotguns but Vanessa got to Sullivan first.

"Who are your parents?" she asked as she walked farther into the living room.

I pulled her to a stop and redirected her to the farthest chair from the couch. It was still too close for my liking but at least it kept the coffee table between them.

Vanessa tipped her head back, rolled her eyes, but other than that outward show of annoyance didn't argue about the seating arrangements.

"Will and Pam Wooten. I'm adopted. I don't know if my parents had intended on keeping it from me or if they'd always planned on being open about it but it was hard to hide when my mom has red hair, my dad has black hair, and I was taller than both by the time I was thirteen."

There was no animosity in his tone. He rapped out the information like he'd recited that same speech a time or two.

"How old are you?" Vanessa went on.

"Eighteen. My birthday's next month."

I looked down at Vanessa and could see the wheels turning.

"Why don't you explain why you're here?" I cut in.

Sullivan went from looking at Vanessa to me. Two things happened at once. Both made my stomach clench and my chest tighten.

The kid smiled and Vanessa sucked in a breath that sounded painful and her shoulders snapped back.

I understood her reaction. There was no denying the striking resemblance between Vanessa and Sullivan, but when he smiled that significantly ratcheted up the likeness. He had the same small indentation at the corner of his right eye that Vanessa had when she smiled.

Whoever this boy was he had to be related to Vanessa in some way. And seeing as her parents had been married longer than this boy was alive, whoever he belonged to was going to have some explaining to do.

And that explanation would likely lead to Vanessa's family being torn apart.

"Are you going to sit?" Sullivan started. "Or are you going to stand there like Vanessa's bodyguard and glare at me? Because you're making me nervous, and, dude, it's taken me almost two weeks to get the nerve to knock on her door."

"Yes, he's going to sit," Vanessa wrongly answered for me. "Is that why you've been following me, because you were trying to get up the nerve to talk to me?"

"Yeah," he breathed. "It's not every day you roll up to a stranger's house and say, hey I think you're my aunt, can I come in for some cookies and bonding time."

"Well, I don't have cookies but I do have chocolate-covered pretzels. They're my favorite."

Christ.

Sullivan smiled again and shook his head.

"I promised I'd only take five minutes of your time and I have a feeling he's..." Sullivan jerked his head in my direction. "Keeping track."

"Sit, Dalton." Vanessa smartly tapped the arm of her chair. "Oh, and, Sullivan, this is...my friend, Dalton Neary."

Friend.

I sat on the arm of Vanessa's chair and rested my arm over her shoulder. Sullivan took in our position and grinned.

"My parents don't know I'm here and they don't know I took the DNA test and found you." Sullivan dropped his eyes to the floor and went on. "They're good parents. I love them so this isn't anything against them. I was just curious so I did it... the DNA test, that is. I didn't think I'd find anything or I guess anyone but then you popped up and I got more curious. Like, if I had an aunt maybe I had brothers or sisters."

I noticed he hadn't mentioned his birth parents.

"So do you live around here?" Vanessa questioned.

"No. I live in California."

Vanessa sat up straight and when she spoke there was nothing but concern in her voice, "Did you run away? Do you need to call your parents so they won't—"

"They think I'm in Florida on vacation," he grumbled. "We have a condo in Jacksonville. That's where they think I am. My friends think I'm visiting a girl I met online so they're covering for me."

"Sullivan—"

"Everyone calls me Sully," he interrupted Vanessa. "And I know it's shitty I'm lying to my parents. I feel bad, but I had to know."

"Know what?" she softly inquired.

"Who I am."

Vanessa leaned into me and I knew this kid had her. The woman in the curve of my arm had a soft spot she didn't bother trying to hide. Whatever was going on was going to cause her pain but she was going to give this stranger what he needed to feel whole.

"I don't have answers for you," Vanessa quietly admitted. "I only have one sister and she's too young to be your...birth mother. And..." She stalled out and glanced up at me before she went on. "And, well, I just don't know. Maybe we're cousins or something," she offered.

"We share twenty-five percent DNA. You're my aunt."

That statement hung in the air.

And the longer it did the stiffer Vanessa became.

"I don't want to cause any trouble," Sully whispered. "I'm not asking you to do anything. I just wanted to meet you. That's all. I know it's selfish and I'm really sorry."

"Wanting to know where you came from isn't selfish, honey," she murmured back. "My parents—I guess your grand-parents—have been married forty years. I have a sister, so you have another aunt. Our grandparents, that is your great-grand-parents are both gone. They lived in Atlanta and moved out here when my dad was a kid. My mom grew up in Savannah. Malory and I grew up in Hollow Point. I never..." Vanessa shook her head. "I took that DNA test because I wanted to track our genealogy but I never got around to it. I actually never went back into that account to look at the results. I meant to, but life got busy. So I don't have a lot to give you but if you want, maybe tomorrow I can pull out some pictures and you can at least... I don't know, see who your family is."

Shit.

Vanessa was going all in.

Sully's eyes came to mine and I'd swear the kid was asking for permission to come back. I wanted to tell him he'd gotten all that he was going to get from Vanessa. That he'd knocked on her door and tore open something that had been buried and now had altered her life in a way that couldn't be undone—that was, if his story checked out and he was indeed Vanessa's nephew. And before this went any further I wanted to make sure this kid wasn't some sort of grifter out to do Vanessa harm.

"You said you had your DNA test with you?" I rejoined.

"I printed the results from the Family Finder website, yeah," he confirmed and leaned to the side to pull a folded-up piece of paper from his back pocket. He put it on the coffee table.

"Tomorrow I'm going to run your information," I told Sully. "If your story checks out Vanessa will call you and if you want you can come back and look through pictures."

Something that looked a lot like gratitude washed over the kid and he slumped back in the couch looking every bit of the teenager he was.

"Please don't contact my parents," he begged. "I'm still not sure if I want to tell them what I've done. They're good parents, they love me, and I don't want to hurt them."

"As long as you're telling the truth and you're over eighteen, you're an adult and I'd have no reason to call them."

Sully stood, pulled his wallet from his back pocket, opened it, and pulled out his ID.

"Here." He reached across the table to hand it to me. "I have nothing to hide."

The *kid* might not, but someone did.

I took the ID, glanced down at the California driver's license, checked the date of birth, and noted the address was in Westwood. Beverly Hills adjacent, that explained why the Wootens had a condo in Florida and an eighteen-year-old recent high school graduate was spending the summer vacationing instead of working.

Without hesitation, I yanked my phone out of my pocket and snapped a picture of the license before handing it back. I tagged the folded paper off the table.

"Can I keep this?" I asked.

"Yeah. I brought it for Vanessa."

I wouldn't need the test results—or more to the point Brady wouldn't when I punted the information to him—but I still wanted to look at them. I could look into Sullivan myself, but I'd have to explain why I was looking into him and I had a feeling Vanessa wouldn't want me telling a story that wasn't mine to tell. With Triple Canopy there would be no chance for the situation to leak. Brady wouldn't breathe a word to anyone outside of the company and no one involved with TC would go outside of the organization. Her personal matters would be safe.

Vanessa got to her feet and gave Sullivan a long, studying look before she gave him a sad smile.

"I don't know what to say," she whispered.

"I'm sorry I—"

"Please don't apologize," she interrupted the kid. "Whatever this is, whatever is happening, it's not your fault. I don't have the answers you're looking for but I promise I'll help you find them."

Goddammit.

Sully dropped his gaze to the table and took a breath. His eyes went back to Vanessa and he exhaled.

"I didn't know. I mean, I couldn't know if you knew about me or not. I just...I don't want to cause you any trouble. I don't... maybe I shouldn't have come."

The fuck of it was, I actually believed the kid. He looked miserable and apologetic along with perplexed.

But it was too late now.

Pandora's Box had been opened.

Vanessa looked just as miserable. She also looked like she wanted to pull the kid in for a hug, something she thankfully refrained from doing and leaned into me instead.

"Let's start with the test and make sure it's right. But since I feel like I'm looking at the boy...er...young man version of my sister with a little of me mixed in there, I'm inclined to believe you're my nephew, which means my parents or at least one of them has been keeping secrets. It doesn't feel real good to know I've been lied to but that's not your fault and it's not mine. At this point I feel like we all deserve the truth, don't you?"

"Not if it means my existence ruins your life."

"Sully, knowing you exist can only add to my life. It means I have a brother or another sister out there I didn't know about. It means my family is getting bigger. Whatever you decide to do with what you find is up to you. You have parents who love you; I understand if you don't want to share with them what you learn, but, honey, I want to know you and my other sibling. I won't force you to be a part of my life but I want you to know that option is open to you. Your parents as well; they're family, too."

Christ.

All-in didn't begin to describe what Vanessa was.

The woman knew her heart was going to get trampled, yet

she was welcoming this boy and his family into her life and doing it with love and grace.

When Sully didn't respond she went on. "We'll exchange numbers and coordinate tomorrow."

I had to fight the urge to yank Vanessa's phone out of her hand as she unlocked it and handed it to Sully.

He took it and programmed his number in and was handing it back when he said, "I'm sorry I scared you. I wasn't following you...or, I was but I didn't mean to scare you."

"I get it, you were nervous. And now that we know I don't have a stalker I can cancel the fancy alarm system I was going to have installed and put that money back into my kitchen remodel fund."

Like hell she would.

The alarm would still be installed.

"I'm so—"

"Stop! I was teasing you. It's all good."

It wasn't all good.

It was the beginning of the end.

Five minutes later when I closed the door on Sully I learned something new about Vanessa... she was a damn fine actress.

Gone was the good-natured, accepting, kind woman who had openly welcomed a stranger in at his word.

"Sweetheart..." The rest of what I was going to say got lodged in my throat and a chill slithered over me at the look of raw emotion in her eyes.

She'd held it together in front of Sullivan.

Now her mood blanketed the room and that mood cut me so deep I flinched at the anguish in front of me. So much of it I was surprised she was still standing.

"I'm not sure who I'm supposed to be mad at," she whispered. "And that's making me irrationally angry because I don't know who is hiding what and why they'd hide it."

"Vanessa—"

"I'm trying to remember there might be a perfectly good explanation but this feels...wrong."

I watched the tremors start in her hands. The shaking moved up her arms until she crossed them over her chest.

She drew in another shaky breath and I was done watching and waiting from a distance. I took a step in her direction and that was all it took—just like she did on her front lawn she launched herself at me. Only this time my hands went to her ass and hefted her up. Vanessa's legs immediately circled my waist and she shoved her face into my neck.

That was when the first tear fell but it wouldn't be the last. She cried into my neck as I walked to her bedroom. She cried when I laid her down. And she was still crying when I came back to her after locking up the house and crawled into bed next to her and tucked her to my side.

"I don't know what to say," she muttered.

"Nothing to say, sweetheart."

She nodded against my chest, snuggled in closer, and whisper-soft asked, "Will you stay?"

I didn't answer mainly because I was fighting back the emotions that had been clawing at my chest since the first time I had her in my bed. That feeling of contentment, the ease, the way my body warmed when she was in my arms.

The feeling of overwhelming *rightness*.

"Yeah, sweetheart."

"Here, with me?"

I closed my eyes and made the decision I should've made two days ago.

"Yeah, Vanessa."

Her arm resting across my chest gave me a squeeze.

And there in Vanessa's bed with her soft body wrapped around me, I stopped fighting the inevitable.

15

PHOENIX WAS ALREADY at his desk when I made my way through the bullpen juggling two cups of coffee.

I was nearly to my desk when Phoenix called out, "One a' those for me?"

After I set mine down on my desk I reached across the desks that were butted up against each other and handed Phoenix his.

He took a sip, swallowed, and smiled.

"You must feel guilty," he rightly noted.

If I stopped to grab coffee on my way into work I always got one for Phoenix, too. Though I never ordered him his favorite. Mainly because it was a pain in the ass to rattle off his complicated order.

"No man should drink coffee that includes three pumps of brown sugar syrup, two pumps of cinnamon caramel syrup, two shots of espresso, and a dusting of cinnamon on top of frothed oat milk. Just saying, partner—real men drink their coffee black."

"Says the man who puts seven sugar packets in his coffee."

"Yet it remains black."

"Right. Apology accepted."

Good to know my peace offering hit the spot.

"You were right," I told him as I typed in my password to my computer. "Thought about what you said, why I was acting like an asshole determined to hold onto something that wasn't my fault, and why I was hellbent to push away a good woman who makes me happy in a way I've never been."

"Good you thought on that, Dalton, but a man doesn't do an about-face in less than twenty-four hours after holding onto some serious shit for over a decade."

"He does when he's faced with losing the best thing that's ever happened to him."

Phoenix took another sip of his froufrou girly drink and cautiously asked, "Did something happen last night?"

I took a slug of my coffee and thought about how to answer without giving away Vanessa's personal business.

"Yes, something happened but here's the problem. As my partner, as a cop you should know exactly what's going down. However, I'm gonna do you a favor and not explain the details."

Phoenix leaned back in his chair and scowled.

"How's that doing me a favor, and more importantly how's that helping Vanessa? She needs—"

"I know what she needs, Phoenix. And me not telling you is part of what she needs. The other part of that is not asking you to keep something from your wife and that's also me giving Vanessa what she needs and saving you from having to keep a secret Wren will not be happy you kept. What I will tell you so we can get to work is, Vanessa's safe. Someone was following her but last night that ended. The person who was following her knocked on her door and explained. If Vanessa wants to tell Wren, that's her business."

"They knocked on the door?"

"Yep."

Phoenix leaned forward and placed his elbows on his desk, all the while holding my gaze.

"And just like that, she's safe?"

Physically, yes.

Mentally? Fuck no.

But I couldn't explain that to Phoenix without breaking Vanessa's trust.

"Just like that she's safe," I confirmed. "I was there, I listened, I watched, and this is gonna piss you off but after we're done with this conversation I'm calling Brady and asking him to run some information for me. I'll also call Vanessa and urge her to talk to Wren. She's going to need her support and I'm going to need to run this shit by you so I don't miss something that could blindside Vanessa. But what I won't do is get between you and your wife by asking you to keep this under wraps."

"That doesn't sound like she's safe, Dalton," he pointed out.

"Okay, I'll amend. She doesn't have a stalker and the person who was watching her means her no bodily harm. Emotionally, she's shredded and it's only going to get worse from here."

"Fucking hell," he muttered. "She's got until the end of the day to tell Wren so you can let me in on what's going down. If not, I'm taking your back."

There it was—he'd keep a secret from his wife to have my back.

"I'll talk to Vanessa. But first I have to call Brady and get him on some searches."

"You do that, then we'll run down the case with Brennon."

I pushed back from my desk and dipped my chin toward his desk.

"Drink up. That frilly, seven-thousand calorie wannabe coffee costs eight bucks."

"Small price to pay to put me in a good mood."

He wasn't wrong.

"I feel like I've said this to you too many times in the last few days...I was a dick."

"You were," he confirmed. "But I get you. I know the road to self-forgiveness. It's long, winding, and bumpy as fuck especially when you're forgiving yourself for being stupid and holding onto shit that was never yours to hold onto. Layla did you dirty. You didn't want to feel that again. I understand your need to go cautious. I'm glad you pulled your head out of your ass—for you and for her. But mostly I'm happy you're letting go of Layla. It's way past time."

The blow that Phoenix delivered was unintentional but that didn't mean I didn't feel the concussion of it wind me.

Letting go of Layla.

Was that what I'd been doing the last eleven years—holding onto my ex-wife? Was staying pissed at her, allowing her to place the blame of her alcoholism at my feet and buying it all in an effort to stay connected to her?

Christ.

If that was what I'd been doing it was well past time to let her go.

IT HADN'T TAKEN me long to fill Brady in on last night's big reveal. I texted him the picture of Sullivan's license and the picture I'd taken of the DNA printout. He told me he'd have something for me in a few hours. After I hung up with Brady I'd called Vanessa, got her voicemail, and asked her to call me back when she was free.

Now I was sitting next to Phoenix in Captain Brennon's office and I'd just finished telling him about our chat with the Ryans.

"You got the retailer?" Brennon said, looking at me.

"Phoenix did. All four safes were purchased at Outdoor Goods. All four safes were SafeCo brand."

"Next step?" Brennon asked.

One of the many things I liked about the man, he asked questions. He allowed his detectives to work a case how they saw fit. He rarely interjected his opinion unless asked. He also had an open-door policy which every person under him took advantage of and kept him informed on their every move. This wasn't because he demanded to know; it was what he inspired by being loyal to those he was in charge of and a good leader.

"We're going to look into SafeCo before we head to Outdoor Goods and start asking questions," Phoenix relayed.

"Good plan. If someone at Outdoor Goods has an in at the manufacturer and is getting the master codes you going in there asking questions is going to tip them off."

When Brennon was finished he sat back in his old, worn leather chair and steepled his fingers in front of his chest—his signature 'thinking pose.' Rumor had it, he bought that chair and brought it in the day he'd made detective and started sitting behind a desk. No one knew why after fifteen years he still had the same chair but the thing would likely be bronzed upon his retirement in a few years. That was if he didn't take it home with him when he left the department.

"You might want to talk to Frank," Brennon suggested. "His wife Cara works at Outdoor Goods. She does the books."

I glanced at Phoenix in time to see him nod.

"We'll talk to Frank."

Frank Bristol was a thirty-three-year-old rookie who decided he was wasting his life behind the service counter of a local car dealership instead of living his childhood dream of being a cop. He was a little older than the other new hires but he used that to his advantage and became a leader among his peers. Good guy—smart, intuitive, and a go-getter. He'd move up the ranks quickly and if he wanted a shot at detective he'd have no problem doing that.

"He's on shift today," Brennon continued. "Call Lina; she'll know when he's due back from patrol."

Lina worked the front desk, a civilian who was a grandmother of twelve and looked it due to five of those grandchildren living with her along with her daughter and her son-in-law. She was a sweet old lady who needed a long vacation alone on an island somewhere.

"Thanks, Cap," Phoenix finished and stood.

We were on our way back through the bullpen when Phoenix pulled out his phone, checked the screen, and announced, "Clint Ryan," before he swiped his screen and answered, "Kent."

By the time we'd hit the back of the large open space where our desks were tucked in the far-right corner, Phoenix was ending the call.

"Appreciate the call, Clint, we'll look into it." There was a pause then, "You know I can't comment on an active investigation." Another pause, this one longer before. "Right. We'll make some calls. Later."

Phoenix tossed his phone on his desk, pulled out his chair, and the damn thing groaned when Phoenix lowered his sizable heft to the seat.

"Clint got word this morning two antiqued, gold-finished, leaf-engraved revolvers with polished cherry grips have found their way to South Carolina."

Victim number one had two antiqued gold finished, leaf engraved revolvers with polished cherry grips stolen from his safe. They had more sentimental value than actual monetary value and they also weren't in working order. The man's father had removed the firing pin. The thief would have no way of knowing the revolvers he or she had stolen were nothing more than display pieces.

"Did he say why he's calling you about it? That detail isn't or shouldn't've been known by the public."

"Yeah, guy up in North Carolina uses Clint and Josh to do transfers to Georgia. He also knows Clint collects revolvers and thought he might be interested in what he called paper weights."

Holy fuck.

"Did he get a name?"

"Yep. Though he suspects it's fake." Phoenix couldn't hold back his smile when he said, "William Bonney."

"Why'd he think that's a fake?" I asked.

"Billy the Kid?"

"What about him?"

"His name was Henry McCarty, his alias was William H. Bonney," Phoenix explained.

I stared at my partner across the desks and wondered how the fuck he knew that.

Phoenix chuckled and through his amusement he informed me, "Don't be impressed. I had no idea what the hell Clint was going on about until he explained."

That tracked.

"So did Billy the Kid leave a number?"

"Nope. But he's supposed to come back in this afternoon. Clint informed his friend he's interested in purchasing the revolvers."

Interstate transfer of stolen property was a federal crime. If these were the revolvers that were stolen the feds would be taking over. Some cops had issues with the feds; I was not one of those cops, neither was Phoenix. Working the gun unit, we'd had our fair share of interaction with the ATF and the FBI. That collaboration led to illegal firearms being taken off the streets and prosecuted in federal court which meant tougher penalties.

I wanted the stolen guns returned to their legal, rightful owners more than I wanted the arrest and I knew Phoenix felt the same.

"That's good news, but why did Clint think they're tied to our case?"

"He knows Tommy Bennet."

Tommy Bennet owned the revolvers.

"So Clint knew more than he shared yesterday?"

"Clint said Tommy came in today and shared his safe was broken into and wanted Clint and Josh's recommendation on an upgrade. He said he was going to call us but then he got the call from his friend in North Carolina and called right after he hung up."

That made more sense than Clint holding out on us.

"Small world," I muttered.

"Got that right."

I glanced down at my ringing phone and was surprised to see Brady's name on the screen.

"Gotta take this." I nabbed my phone, stood, and started to move away from my desk.

"Brady," I greeted.

"Preliminaries are in, the kid's clean."

"What about the adoption?"

"That's going to take time. California is a closed record state so any adoption is sealed. It's going to take some digging to find out if he was adopted. I have his birth certificate, parents listed are William and Pamela Wooten. State of birth is listed as Utah. Seeing as the search I did on the Wootens bore them both residing in California and owning joint property there for thirty years, not to mention their work history is only in California, I'd say the boy being born in Utah is a good indication he's indeed adopted. I ran property searches in Utah. The Wootens don't own property and I haven't found any rental agreements for the time frame of Pamela's pregnancy or any time."

"Utah?"

"Yeah, why? What's in Utah?"

Fuck.

"Vanessa's sister was sent to a camp for troubled youth in Utah. I think Vanessa said Malory spent her seventeenth birthday there."

Brady muttered a curse, then I heard him clicking away on his keyboard.

"Did she mention the name of the camp?"

"No. All she said was a family friend had taken Malory because her father was too distraught to take her himself."

"I need the name of the camp."

Shit.

"I'll get that for you tonight."

"Now would be better."

"I get that but I'm at work and this is a question I need to ask face-to-face. Vanessa's gonna want to know why I'm asking and I want to be with her when I explain there's a possibility her sister was pregnant and gave her child up for adoption."

I didn't know which scenario would be worse for Vanessa—one of her parents having a child and giving that child up or having the answers to why her sister went away and came home a different person. I wasn't a woman nor was I a father so I couldn't begin to imagine what it would feel like to give a child up for adoption, even if it meant it was the kindest, most loving sacrifice a parent could make.

My guess was it could change a person.

"I'll run Vanessa's parents while I'm looking for camps in Utah just to be thorough."

"The Wootens are clean, too?"

"William is a famous architect. He's sixty-one, no arrest record, minimal debt, excellent credit score. Pamela works as the accounts manager for the architectural firm the couple owns. She's sixty. Never been arrested and like her husband she has excellent credit. They jointly own their home in California, a condo in Florida, a BMW, a Yukon, a Toyota, all registered in California, and a Nissan registered in Florida. Again, this is all preliminary but on the surface they check out. That's not to say when I dig deeper I won't find shady shit; you know how it is. Sometimes people look like normal, decent people until you find they're bad people. But if you're worried about the kid running a con on Vanessa to get money out of her, I'd seriously doubt that. The parents are loaded and Sullivan until he graduated high school—with honors by the way—held down a job at a Starbucks and his bank account says his parents also give him an allowance. Unless baristas now make five grand a month and if that's the case, I'm changing careers and making coffee. Less money but less stress and I can live with a few grand less a month if it means I don't go home at night wondering what the fuck is so broken in people they do the fucked-up shit they do."

There was a lot to unpack there, including Brady making a few thousand dollars a month over five K. I was thinking I was the one who needed to switch jobs. Then there was the fact the kid had five thousand dollars a month going into his checking account. It was California and I understood the cost of living in the Sunshine State was a fuckton higher than Georgia but what kid needed that kind of cash?

I didn't ask that. Instead I asked, "So you think we're good to let the kid come over and look at pictures tonight?"

"It was me, I'd let him in the door. Also it was me, I wouldn't leave my woman with him until I get more. And the more I need is the understanding about Utah and what went on there."

My jaw clenched at his insinuation.

"Are you thinking black market adoption?"

"I'm not thinking anything beyond a newly turned seventeen-year-old girl went to a camp for troubled youth nineteen years ago and a kid shows up nineteen years later who's nineteenth birthday is coming up in a month."

Fuck me.

"I'll talk to Vanessa tonight after Sullivan leaves."

"Call me when you have the name and don't worry about the time."

Brady wanted to dig in.

I got that. I didn't like loose ends.

Speaking of, I had a case to work.

"Right. Appreciate you looking into this."

"Anytime. Later."

I pocketed my phone and went back to work.

16

WITH EVERYTHING that had gone wrong at work one would think it was Friday the 13th and five black cats had continuously walked in front of me on a constant loop. I had two missed calls from Dalton I hadn't been able to return but I had found time to text him back to tell him I wasn't ignoring him, I was just slammed with work. He texted me back telling me that Sullivan was good to come over to look at pictures.

So between the phone system being down and then the network being inaccessible I sent a quick text to Sullivan inviting him over. He promptly replied he'd be there at six. I relayed this information to Dalton. He messaged back he'd be there before Sully showed.

Then because I couldn't get the documents I needed off the server I decided to text Malory and ask her to come by on her way home from work. She said she would but only after she asked if I was okay and if I needed her to stop and pick me up anything like medication for the illness I was positive she'd imagined I was dying from. That was only a semi-joke seeing as my sister's mind would go there before she'd think I just wanted to see her *and* she did ask if I needed medication so it wasn't a stretch. I put her mind at ease and told her I just wanted to see her and talk about Mom and Dad. She assumed it had something to do with their anniversary party. I didn't disabuse her of this notion, meaning I lied *but* I couldn't explain what was going on over the phone and especially not over text without her freaking out.

Suffice to say with all the crap going on at work I didn't have time to fill Wren in on what had happened the night before. 'Crap' was an understatement of course. Last night had been life changing on many fronts. The first being I had a nephew I hadn't known about—his very existence was going to rock my family and not in a good way.

Then there was Dalton.

Something had changed, I just couldn't place what it was exactly. He'd been different and that started before Sullivan had knocked on my door, but definitely more so after. And even more when he carried me to bed and let me mourn the loss of my peaceful life in the form of tears leaking from my eyes while he held me close. At some point I'd felt him roll away from me. I heard him walking through my house, then he came back, got into bed, and curled his big, warm body around mine, pinning me.

He was different this morning, too. He'd quietly watched me get ready for work. This after he'd made coffee and brought me in a mug, setting it on the bathroom counter before he went into my bedroom and sat on my bed. He gently teased me about the horrible carpet in my bedroom. He continued that teasing, telling me how ugly my bathroom was and how violently my baby-pink with pretty white flowers shower curtain clashed with the horrendous off-white vanity and worn yellow tiles. All of this was done in jest. It was gentle, it was lighthearted, it was meant to give me something to banter about instead of dwell on what was to come. He coupled the banter with touches. His hand on my lower back guiding me to the kitchen when I was done getting ready. His knuckles sliding down my cheek. My hand in his while he escorted me to my car. And finally, a kiss to my forehead before he opened my car door and helped me in.

Suffice it to say I was a mess.

A muddled, frenzied, frantic mess.

I probably shouldn't have invited my sister over—that was what I was thinking when I pulled into my driveway at 5:39. But now I was stuck. If I canceled she'd worry and I'd get ten calls before the night was over to ascertain the state of my health or to make sure I didn't hate her.

Too late now.

I studiously avoided looking at my beautiful new garage door knowing I still hadn't cleaned out my garage. Dalton would start in about that again soon, and my father would ask if I'd cleaned it out on Saturday at the party.

A party I no longer wanted to attend.

Someone was lying, had been lying for going on nineteen years, and obviously had planned on lying for the rest of their lives. So I wasn't all fired up about celebrating forty years of marriage when someone had a secret.

Secrets and lies.

My family was good at sweeping stuff under the rug. They were experts at avoidance, but lying... I'd never imagined any of us would flat-out lie to each other. Well, that wasn't entirely true; Malory had lied about a lot when she was a teenager. But since then, since she'd gotten back from Utah I hadn't caught her in a single fib. She'd gone from wild to the perfect daughter.

Sometimes I wished my crazy, fun, happy sister would break free from the timid, boring, happy*ish* woman she'd become. Minus the sneaking out and excessive drinking.

I unlocked my door and was pushing it open when I heard

Dalton's truck. I turned and watched Sullivan's Sentra pull in behind him and park.

It was weird how two conflicting emotions could crash into each other.

Anticipation and dread.

Excitement and fear.

And as I watched Dalton and Sullivan walk toward me, I wasn't sure which emotion belonged to which man. The newest mixed-signal Dalton was sending put the fear of God into me. I felt like I was being set up for a fall I wasn't prepared to take. Yet seeing him made me anxious in a good way.

Then there was Sullivan, my nephew who also scared the hell out of me but for different reasons, but the resulting heart-break of his appearance would hurt no matter what reason. However, I wanted to get to know him. I wanted to learn about him and the possibility that I had a big brother or another sister was overwhelmingly terrifying but I wanted to know them, too.

What a mess.

"Hey," Sullivan happily greeted me when he was halfway up my walk.

"Hey, Sully."

I transferred my smile to Dalton, took in his worried expression, sucked in a fortifying breath, and tried but failed not to allow his trepidation mix with the nervousness I already felt.

Dalton stopped at my side, kissed my temple, and whispered, "All good, sweetness."

His words didn't match his expression though they did make me feel marginally better.

Prematurely I would find.

"We'll talk after Sullivan leaves."

At his declaration my body tensed. I knew he felt it when he slid his arm around me and tucked me to his side.

"Inside, Nessa."

Right.

Inside.

Together we walked into my house with Sullivan walking in behind us.

"Mind shutting the door, bud?" Dalton asked though he didn't turn to look at Sullivan.

And bud?

It wasn't exactly a declaration of friendship but it certainly wasn't combative or hostile. Not that Dalton had been either of those things last night but they hadn't made it to 'bud' status.

Interesting.

And confusing.

"Sure."

I heard Sullivan's mutter, the door click closed, and for some reason I didn't know what to do. Like I was a guest in my own home.

Did I offer Sullivan a drink?

Did we go back to the back room where it was less formal and more inviting?

Did we sit at the kitchen table?

I was saved from making this decision when Dalton took charge.

"Want something to drink?"

Dalton hadn't let go of me so when he stopped, I stopped. And when he turned, I turned.

Connected.

I liked that. I was feeling weird and uncomfortable. Strangely or maybe not so strangely having Dalton at my side made me feel minutely better. But just a fraction.

"I'm good. I just rolled through Taco Bell on my way here."

I opened my mouth to tell Sullivan Taco Bell was Malory's favorite fast-food restaurant and she and I bickered nonstop about which was better, soft or hard-shell tacos—I was in the hard-shell camp, she was soft tacos all the way—when there was a knock on the front door.

Shit.

Malory was way earlier than I expected.

I hadn't had a chance to tell Sullivan his other aunt would be joining us.

"You expecting someone?" Dalton asked.

"Well, I invited Malory over. I thought it would—"

I stopped talking when Dalton's body not only jerked but turned rigid.

"I'm sorry, Sullivan. I was going to talk to you about it but she's early."

Sullivan's gaze was bouncing between me and Dalton.

"I don't mind," he muttered.

"Fuck," Dalton clipped.

"I'm really—"

My apology was cut short when the door opened and Malory poked her head in.

"Oh, sorry, I didn't realize you had company." Malory stammered, her wide eyes taking in Dalton.

I watched in morbid fascination as her gaze glided to Sullivan. At first she looked startled to realize there was someone else in the room then her face went white and she looked like she might pass out or throw up or both.

"Malory," I called.

My sister didn't move. Not a muscle. Her eyes were locked on our nephew like she'd seen a ghost.

"Malory!" I tried again.

Nothing.

She continued to stare at Sullivan.

"I can explain," I started. "This is—"

"How?"

"Fuck," Dalton whispered.

I didn't understand her question nor did I understand Dalton's reaction. What had come clear was that I'd made a mistake.

A grave mistake.

"*How* what?" I asked.

Malory's gaze snapped to mine.

Pain.

All I could see was pain. It was written all over my sister—it was pouring out of her, filling my living room, seeping into the walls never to be rid of.

So much pain I burrowed into Dalton.

"What's happening right now?" Malory whispered.

She was barely inside the door. It was still open and I was afraid she was going to run from my house screaming into the night.

"Mal, come in and shut the door. I'll explain."

"I can't... I have to...how..." she stammered, not making any sense.

"Sweetheart, you need to go to her," Dalton murmured. "Get her in the house and back to the sunroom."

It was a den but I didn't think now was the time to correct or explain the difference.

I disengaged, moved toward Malory, and as feared she started to back out the door. I quickly lunged and caught her hand in mine.

"We're gonna go in the back room and talk a minute," I told her then turned to Sullivan to tell him we'd be right back. But my words died.

They died a slow, pain-filled death when I saw the way Sullivan was staring at Malory.

I glanced back at my sister.

Then back to Sullivan.

Only then did it hit me.

Same color hair.

Same coloring.

Same eyes.

Same...

Impossible. The similarities were due to lineage.

My grip tightened around my sister's hand. She squeezed back.

"Sullivan, let me talk to Malory. We'll be right back."

"Okay. Sure."

Malory whimpered. Sullivan didn't miss this. His attention on my sister became acute. My gaze went to Dalton. He, too, was staring at Malory. Jaw clenched, alert, ready to jump in if I needed. What he didn't look like was confused at my sister's reaction to Sullivan.

I guided my sister through the living room to the kitchen. I heard the front door close as we entered the den. I didn't offer my sister a seat, I cut straight to it.

"I don't know where to start," I muttered. "I guess the beginning so you understand. A few years ago I had this idea to research our family and make Mom a family tree. A real one with all the census reports and immigration documents. I took one of those DNA tests." I watched as my sister slowly closed her eyes and I pushed on. "I got busy and never did anything with it. But that's how Sullivan found me. He's our nephew."

Malory's eyes popped open. The color in her face hadn't returned but if it was possible she went paler, making the dark under her eyes seem darker. Her eyes were dead and lifeless—more so than normal. There were a great many times I missed my old sister but never more than right now. I wanted to shake her out of her stupor and tell her I needed her to be the big sister. I needed her support. I needed her to be at my side if I decided to confront Mom and Dad.

"Obviously we have another sister or brother out there. I

don't know what to do with this. Sullivan loves his parents. They don't know he's here and he's not sure if he wants them to know. But I'm not sure if I can know Mom and Dad or at least one of them has been lying and not call them out on it."

"He loves his parents?"

I didn't know if Malory's whispered words were a question or if she was just repeating what I'd said. Still I answered.

"Yes. He told me they love him very much, too. It sounds like he comes from a happy family. He just wanted to know where he came from."

"No, he doesn't," she spat. Then with more backbone than I've seen in over a decade and a half she went on. "You need to tell him to go back to his family. The one who loves him. There's nothing good for him to find here."

I was taken aback by the vehemence in my sister's tone.

My family was far from perfect, but we had a good one. My parents loved us and didn't hide how proud they were of us. Even Malory when she came back from Utah. They showered her with love, attention, and praise.

So really her assertion there was nothing *good* for Sullivan to find with our family was offensive.

"He's an adult, Malory. He's also the one who made the approach to find his kin. I think in our current situation, he gets to call the shots and make the rules. If he wants to meet his grandparents then I'll help him." When I stopped speaking my sister looked like I'd slapped her and I sighed. "I know this is a lot and I'm sorry I blindsided you. I should've told you about Sullivan,"—another flinch— "a different way. He showed up last night with his DNA test in hand announcing I was his aunt. Since then all I've thought about is Mom and Dad and which one of them has another child out there they never told us about. I need you to help me understand what's happening."

"Listen to me," she snarled. "Tell him to go home to his parents."

Malory, my quiet, boring, apologetic, overly sensitive sister actually snarled at me. An honest to God growl, baring teeth.

What the hell?

"No. He's our nephew. He wants to know—"

"You don't understand what you're doing!" she shouted.

"Sweetheart." I heard from behind me. "Grab the photo albums and go sit with Sullivan. I need to speak to your sister."

Dalton was using his Detective Neary voice. I didn't know if he'd been eavesdropping the whole time or if he heard my sister shouting at me and he was moving in to protect me. In the grand scheme of things it didn't matter if he'd been listening in; I would've told him about my sister's behavior anyway. But I didn't need protecting from my sister, but my nephew obviously did. Which shocked the hell out of me.

"Dalton—"

"Now, Vanessa."

That was the second time he'd ordered me to do something in my own damn home. And it would be the second time I obeyed. However, unlike the first time due to unforeseen drama tonight when everyone left I was going to explain—in great detail—how much I didn't appreciate being ordered around.

"You have a boyfriend," Malory accused.

"No."

"Yes."

Dalton and I gave conflicting answers at the same time.

Mine was the 'no'.

His was the 'yes'.

I shifted so I could scowl at Dalton.

"Now's not the time," I hissed.

Dalton was annoyingly unaffected by my scowl.

"Go talk to Sully, sweetheart."

I glanced back at my sister who was much better at giving the evil eye than I was, I just hadn't seen it in so long I'd forgotten how *much* better she was.

Wordlessly, I moved out of the den and through the kitchen, but was halted when Dalton's arm shot out and I found myself plastered to his chest.

"Sully's freaking out, Nessa," he murmured quietly. "You need to smooth that over."

Smooth it over?

I had no idea how to do that.

"How?"

"Be you."

That was sweet but I didn't know how being me would smooth anything over after the disaster I'd made of the night.

With a kiss on the top of my head he let me go.

I had to admit the rest of my short journey into the living room was done on wooden legs and with more than a little apprehension, and when I saw Sullivan sitting on the couch, both knees bouncing, my apprehension knotted in my belly.

"Hey," I called and Sullivan's eyes tipped up but his knees kept bouncing. "I'm sorry that didn't work out the way I'd hoped."

"Dalton explained," he offered.

Did he?

What exactly did he explain?

"What'd he say?"

Sullivan's eyes shifted to the double opening to the kitchen.

"That she's shy and reserved and doesn't handle surprises well."

Well, that was a good-natured excuse as to why my sister was behaving so out of character I wasn't sure if I was pissed or beside myself with glee a little of the old Malory had come out.

I moved around the coffee table to the built-in shelves where

I kept my albums and I did this saying, "I got ahead of myself and messed up. I wanted you to meet her and her you. I rushed it and screwed everything up."

"Is she okay?"

That was sweet of him to care.

I pulled two thick albums from the shelf and answered, "She's...fine."

Sullivan grinned and once again I was taken aback by his smile.

"Are you asking me or telling me?"

On a sigh I sat next to him.

"I don't know what she is," I quietly answered. "But whatever she is, it's my fault."

"Actually, it's my fault."

Shit.

Without thinking I grabbed Sullivan's forearm.

"None of this is your fault."

"I came here—"

"None of this is your fault," I repeated. "You came here looking for answers and I messed that up by asking your other aunt to join us. That's on me. I blindsided you and her. That's my fault."

"She looks like me, too," he mumbled. "Only more like me than you do."

He wasn't wrong about that.

I opened the first album and flipped the pages until I found the picture I was looking for and pointed to the snapshot of me, Malory, Mom, and Dad.

"I was about ten in this picture. Malory would've been about thirteen. You and Malory have more of my dad's coloring. I take more after my mom."

Sullivan stared at the picture and I knew why. He looked like he'd fit right in. Sullivan was tall like my father, and thinking about it after seeing the resemblance he shared with Malory and my father, if I had to guess, I'd say Sullivan was the product of an affair my father had. He looked like me, Malory, and Dad—not my mother.

"May I look at more?"

Damn, the kid was killing me.

I removed my hand from his arm to give him room to look through the pictures without me weirdly crowding him.

"Of course."

"You did what?" Malory screeched from the den.

Next to me Sullivan went stiff.

I closed my eyes.

Yes, I'd made a grave mistake.

However, I didn't know that mistake would open old wounds and unleash an unimaginable hell on all of us.

17

I'D SEEN a lot of desperate people during my tenure as a cop, more so when I made detective. When I was assigned to the gun unit I experienced a whole new level of desperation, the kind a person renders when they knew the penance for the crimes they'd committed was so great they'd do *anything* to avoid being caught.

That was Malory.

The desperation seeped out of her pores.

It went far beyond the son she'd given up for adoption sitting in her sister's living room.

And Sullivan Wooten was Malory's son. Any doubts I had after my conversation with Brady vanished when I witnessed her shock melt into shame.

Now that shame had switched to terror and desperation.

She leaned toward me and shrieked, "You did what?"

I'd just finished explaining to her that I had a friend looking into Sullivan's birth parents and his adoption.

Her response was over the top.

Yeah, no doubt whatsoever she was Sullivan's mother, and for whatever reason that went *way* beyond her being thrust into a situation that would normally be painful—she was freaked the fuck out.

"Malory," I said slowly. "I'm a cop. I'm seeing your sister. Do you really think I'd let someone into her life when they entered it the way Sullivan did?"

"You... It's not...tell them to stop."

"What's happening?" Vanessa hissed from the kitchen.

Malory whirled to her sister and pointed at me.

"He needs to stop."

"Stop what?"

Sullivan walked in behind Vanessa and Malory rocked back like someone had punched her in the stomach. As if to punctuate the blow, her arms were wrapped around her middle.

My attention went back to Malory. There was no denying she was a very pretty woman. I was sure when her face wasn't pale and splotchy, when fear wasn't dripping off of her, and wild panic hadn't set in her eyes she'd be beautiful. Not stunning like Vanessa but they had similar bone structure and facial features. Malory was a little taller and would be more so if her shoulders weren't hunched.

Vanessa had said her sister was different—that might've been true but she was also broken.

Broken in a way that made me fear she'd shatter any moment.

I seriously wished Vanessa would've told me she invited her sister.

Now I was stuck.

Did I pull Vanessa into her bedroom and tell her neither of her parents had lied to her and hidden a secret love child, that there was no other sibling out there for her to find because Malory was Sullivan's mother? That would leave Sullivan alone with Malory and I wasn't sure which one of them would break first.

Did I take Sullivan for a walk and explain that Malory was his birth mother and she was having a difficult time processing the situation? That meant telling the boy before I told Vanessa and I didn't see that going down all that well.

"I should leave," Sullivan said as he backed out of the room.

Vanessa caught her nephew's hand and pulled him to her side.

"Absolutely not," she declared then turned to her sister. "Mal, I'm sorry I messed up and didn't explain to you what was going on before you got here. I know I took you off guard and this is a lot but you need..." Vanessa paused and narrowed her eyes. "Did you know? Did Mom or Dad tell you?"

Shit. Vanessa was misreading Malory.

"Nessa—"

"Answer me, Malory," Vanessa spoke over me. "I know this is a surprise, finding out we have more family we didn't know about but you're not being...you."

The firmer Vanessa's tone got the more Malory shrank into herself.

"Vanessa, sweetheart, please let me talk with Malory in private."

"No, Dalton. I want my sister to answer me."

I should've known it would be Sullivan who asked the million-dollar question. He'd been watchful, studiously so. From the moment Malory had walked into the house the boy went on alert.

"Are you my mother?"

The question was asked softly like that little bird in that book my own mother had read to me a hundred times.

Malory reared back.

"No, Sullivan, I told you..." Vanessa scowled and shook her head.

Fuck.

I was too far away from Vanessa but I feared if I moved the bomb would explode.

Then it did.

All over Vanessa's kitchen.

"Are you?" Vanessa whimpered. "You... oh my God. Is that why... wait." She dropped Sullivan's hand and I watched helplessly while she pressed the fingers of both hands to her forehead. "Is that why you went away?"

"I don't... I'm not—"

"Now's not the time to start lying, Malory," I warned.

"*You knew?*" Vanessa flung her accusation at me.

"I suspected when Brady called me this afternoon after he looked at Sullivan's birth certificate."

Malory's sob rent the air.

Sullivan stepped back.

Vanessa gave me wide eyes and a frown.

"Sullivan's records are sealed." I stopped thinking better of talking about the kid as if he wasn't in the room and changed direction. "Last night I told you I was going to look into you." Sullivan nodded so I went on. "This morning I had a friend do that. Your adoption records are sealed but your birth certificate isn't. Your parents live in California and have since before you were born. They also own property in Florida. But you were born in Utah."

Both women sucked in audible breaths. Vanessa's was accompanied with her reaching out to hold onto the door frame. Malory's was tinged with more pain.

"This was not how I wanted to share this information. Unfortunately with Malory showing up this is what we have to work with," I finished.

"So it's my fault my sister—"

"Baby," I interrupted Vanessa. "I didn't say that. We have

enough going on. You can be pissed at me later but right now this is about Sullivan."

Sullivan and Malory.

The kid might've been technically an adult but he was still the most vulnerable one. Malory was an adult, so she needed to pull it together. Not my kindest moment but not untrue.

Suddenly Malory swiped her tears from her face, the movements jerky and erratic.

"I'll tell you everything as long as you stop."

We all looked at Malory and waited for her to say more. Like who she was speaking to and what did she want to stop.

"But I can't do it right now. I need to... think."

"Malory?" Vanessa gently called.

"Yes. Okay, yes," she whispered and lifted her eyes to Sullivan. "Yes. I'm sorry. I'll explain everything. Tomorrow. I'm sorry it wasn't my choice. I never. I didn't want to do it..." she paused again and the tears started again. This time they weren't panicked, they were sad and heartfelt and damn if I didn't want to pull the woman close and give her someone to hold onto. But that wasn't my place.

Vanessa took a step away from the wall. Malory's hands shot out in front of her like she was warding off an attacker.

"Don't, Vanessa," she said, still whispering. "I'm sorry."

Vanessa wasn't exaggerating. Malory was overly apologetic.

"I think we should go into my room and talk," Vanessa suggested.

"No. I need to get home. I need to think."

Then her eyes darted around the room until she found the courage to look at Sullivan.

"You grew up to be..." Malory sucked in a breath. "Beautiful. I knew you would be."

With that she dashed out of the house. By that, I mean she skirted around Vanessa and Sullivan and ran.

The front door slammed.

The kitchen was still heavy with emotion.

Vanessa broke the silence and it was a repeat of what she'd said last night.

"I don't know what to say."

"I think maybe nothing," Sullivan offered. "That was..." he trailed off.

"Traumatic?" Vanessa supplied. "A cluster fuck. A dumpster fire. A monumental fuck-up on my part. A fucking disaster."

"Welp, it's good to know my aunt doesn't shy away from the f-bomb. Neither of my parents cuss so I always wondered where I got that from."

"Are you teasing me?" Vanessa snapped.

"Um, *yeah?*"

"Listen up, Sully, something you should know about me. I don't like to be teased when I'm gearing up for a rant."

"Something you should know about me, *Aunt* Vanessa—"

The kid didn't finish. Vanessa's forehead collided with his shoulder, her arms wrapped around him, and from across the kitchen I saw her squeeze the breath out of the poor guy. Sullivan stood stock-still then he relaxed and hugged his aunt back.

Fuck.

A dumpster fire didn't touch that scene.

"I didn't know about you." I heard Vanessa's muffled cry. "But if I had, I promise I would've loved you and spoiled you rotten."

I watched the kid who was really a young man battle his emotions. It took him a while but he beat back the tears before they fell.

18

"THAT WAS BAD."

Dalton's arm tightened at my whispered understatement.

"It didn't start great but I think it ended okay."

I wasn't sure I believed him.

After the nuclear explosion happened in my kitchen, Dalton got us all back into the living room. He ordered pizza while I called Malory to make sure she hadn't crashed her car on the way home and Sullivan went back to the albums.

It had taken three calls before Malory picked up only to tell me she was sorry she didn't pick up but she was driving. I gritted my teeth hearing her apology but didn't correct her. I also didn't ask her any questions. I just told her I loved her no matter what. She returned the same sentiment and we rang off.

The pizza came, we moved—taking the albums with us to the back den so we could eat and be comfortable. Dalton and I on the couch. Sully on the floor with his plate on the coffee table, album open.

When we finished eating, Dalton took the remnants of the desecrated pizza and the plates to the kitchen while I told Sully stories behind some of the pictures. He studied each photograph like he would be tested on the subjects and the world's future depended on him answering correctly.

Throughout storytime my heart hurt.

There was still a part of me that was in disbelief that my sister had a son. Another, bigger part ached for my sister.

It wasn't my choice.

I didn't want to do it.

I couldn't imagine my parents forcing her to hide her pregnancy and give her child up for adoption. They were not those people.

Then again I couldn't imagine my sister hiding her pregnancy from me.

So what the hell did I know?

Another secret to pile on top of all the rest.

It wasn't my choice.

Those four words replayed in my mind the entire time Sullivan and I went through those books. Then I had to explain —the very abbreviated version seeing as I was telling him about his birth mother—why the photos jumped from Malory's early teen years to her college graduation. And during that time there were very few pictures of me. It was like as soon as Malory had been sent away our lives had stopped and they didn't start back up when she'd gotten home either.

It wasn't my choice.

That explained the change.

That explained why my big, fun, loud, smart, funny sister turned.

Sullivan hugged me goodbye, promised to text me tomorrow, and shook Dalton's hand then took off. We watched him drive away. Then with me tucked to his side, Dalton walked around the house turning off lights, and double checking the doors were locked before he led me to my room. Once there he let me go only so he could open and close drawers until he found what he needed. A not-so-cute pair of ratty old sweats, an equally not-cute pink t-shirt I only wore when I cleaned the house. He tossed those on the bed and undressed me down to my bra and panties. I said not one word. Mainly because I was curious, but also because no one had ever undressed me only to redress me in ugly PJs. We then moved to the bathroom—yes, that was *we*—and he guided me in, then stopped in front of the basin and asked me if I needed to wash my face while he put toothpaste on my toothbrush. I nodded. I brushed my teeth while he watched. When I was done, he took my toothbrush, loaded up more paste, and stepped to the side so I could wash my face. He did this with *my* toothbrush in his mouth.

I said nothing.

I mean, what was there to say? I'd kissed him. He'd has his mouth on me. I'd had my mouth on him. And seriously, he'd dressed me and put toothpaste on the brush for me.

He was taking care of me.

That much I understood. I just didn't know why.

Did friends go to such extremes to take care of their friends? Sure, *girl*friends did. I would undress, redress, and brush Wren's teeth for her if she needed me to. I'd also floss them and bathe her if necessary. But did boy-girl friends get down to their underwear in front of each other?

When I was done with my nightly bathroom routine Dalton again guided me to my bed. He pulled back the covers, helped me in, went to turn off the light, then climbed in after me.

"I should've told Sully to text me when he got home," I mumbled into the dark. "Do you think I should call him now and tell him to let me know when he's home?"

Dalton pulled me closer but he didn't answer. Or maybe I didn't give him enough time before I fired off my next question. "Do you think it makes me a bad aunt that I didn't ask him where he's staying? Jacksonville's a two-hour drive. Maybe I should've told him to stay here tonight. That's too long for him to drive back and forth. Especially after a night like tonight. It's only been thirty minutes. I should call him and tell him to come back. He can—"

"Sweetheart."

I waited for Dalton to give me his opinion.

"Well?" I prompted when he didn't give it.

"I think Sully's been driving back and forth for almost two weeks. Or he's rented a hotel in town, which is unlikely if he doesn't want his parents knowing he's coming up to Georgia. I agree he's too young to be driving two hours late at night. I also know he's been doing it and doing it safely since he's fine. Also, the kid learned how to drive in Southern California; it's likely he's a better defensive driver than me. Let's give him time to process all that happened tonight. A long drive might do him good. Clear his mind. Tomorrow when you talk to him and invite him over, you can ask him if he wants to stay the night. But, baby, you need to be prepared in case he says no. This is new for all of you. You're his aunt but you're a stranger."

Dalton was right. I was mostly a stranger.

"You know what's weird?" I asked.

"What's weird?"

This! I thought. Lying in my bed for the second night when there was no danger (there was only drama) but Dalton didn't need to be here to protect me.

I didn't say that.

"A few days ago, I thought he was stalking me. Now if I'm not careful he'll think I'm some crazy woman who's stalking *him*."

Dalton twisted, shifted, and rolled to his side taking me with him so we were facing each other.

His hand found mine in the dark. His fingers threaded

through mine and he brought our hands to rest in the small space between us.

"I know tonight was a lot," he began.

"You could say that again," I mumbled.

He didn't, instead he said, "Something else you need to prepare for, baby."

I didn't like the sound of that.

"Sullivan's made it clear he loves his parents. He's also communicated he doesn't know if he wants to tell them he's found you. So we can take that as a read he wouldn't want to tell them about Malory or your parents."

Damn.

"Which means you need to hold yourself back."

"I don't know how to do that. He's my nephew."

"No, baby. He's Sullivan. He's a young man who shares your blood but he has a family. A good, loving family who opened their lives and hearts to him. Who raised him. Who love him."

God, that hurt.

"I want to love him."

"And you do that by giving him what he needs even if what he needs is for you to let him go. That might not happen. He might want to keep in contact with you. I just want you prepared. Have a mind to your heart but also to his."

I didn't know how to do that either. My stupid heart had led me astray. Case in point, lying in bed with Dalton, holding his hand, having a hard time remembering he wasn't mine and never would be.

"You're right," I grumbled.

"He graduated with honors."

I jolted at Dalton's swift change of subject.

"Yeah?"

"Brady didn't get far today. But what he did find looks good.

He worked at a Starbucks while he was in high school. His parents are extremely well off, highly respected. His father, Will, is an architect. His mother works at the firm with her husband. They're in their sixties. No other kids. It's a guess but seeing as they didn't adopt him until they were in their forties I'd say they wanted kids but couldn't have them."

"He doesn't seem spoiled. Other than vacationing in Florida instead of working before he goes off to college. Though if I had a son who graduated with honors while holding down a job and I owned a condo in Florida and could afford it I'd probably give that to him, too. Though my dad would lose his mind if I invested in a second property and it wasn't income generating."

"Income generating?"

"My dad's a financial planner."

"Explains a lot."

"What's it explain?"

"You saving money for projects instead of taking out loans."

"Loans?" I fake-gasped. "And endure a seven-hour lecture about interest rates complete with graphs and charts. No thank you."

I heard Dalton chuckle. More importantly I felt it, reminding me how close he was.

"Tonight was a lot," he repeated his underestimation of how shitty the night was. "But I need to know if you're up to talking about something else."

"That depends," I answered honestly. "If you're going to tell me that I have another relative out there and they, too, will be at my door soon to turn my life upside down then no, I don't have it in me to talk about more. Or if Brady found something that's going to freak me out, maybe we save it for tomorrow."

"Us."

Oh, no.

I wasn't prepared to talk about anything that had to do with us.

Yet, I still queried, "Us?"

"You and me and what's happening between us," he terrifyingly clarified.

"We're friends," I weakly reminded him.

"We are that. But what I want to talk to you about is going back to what we used to be."

For reasons I didn't want to admit to myself that hurt—a whole lot.

To hide that hurt my response was snippy if not curt when I reminded him, "I already told you, I can't give you that."

"You already did."

Oh. My. God.

Was he saying he thought I was a...floozy?

I tried to unlink our hands. His fingers tightened.

"You need to let me go and leave."

"Tried that, Vanessa. It didn't work."

What the hell did that mean?

Nope. It didn't matter.

"Try harder," I spat.

"Only so hard a man can try to push a woman away before he wonders why he's trying so hard to run away from someone who means something to him. Only so much a man can fight his feelings before he realizes he's a coward."

Dalton yanked my hand, untwined our fingers, and placed my palm on his chest and went on with his confusing confession. "I fucked up. The other night when you came home after talking to Wren, I let you believe what she told you. You'd already had it all figured out in your mind and I didn't correct you."

"Let me believe what? She told me you weren't interested in

a relationship and you confirmed you weren't. What was there to correct?"

"Instead of telling you what I was feeling for you, I did what I'd trained myself to do. I retreated because I knew if I didn't I'd fall in love with you. I tried to fight the pull of you, the promise, the beauty, but I didn't get far did I, Vanessa? I didn't do the smart thing and let you go and stay away. I found every excuse to come back and be close."

Belatedly I understood why he'd placed my palm on his chest. His heart was pounding double time. His voice was hoarse. His body tight. It might've been dark in my room but he was showing me something.

Something special.

I still didn't trust it.

I couldn't.

And he needed to know why. Which would mean I'd have to tell him the truth and give him back the gift he was giving me knowing it was for naught.

"Before I met you I saw you around. I lived my whole life in Hollow Point, only leaving to go to college then I came right back. I'd never seen you before then suddenly you seemed to be everywhere. Then I found out you were Phoenix's partner and in my mind that solidified my fanciful belief."

"What was that, baby?"

I didn't answer him. I wasn't done explaining.

"All my life my mom told me to hold out for my Prince Charming. She filled my head with all things soulmates and true love. She told me never to settle, that the man who was meant for me was out there." Dalton pressed my hand tighter against his chest. "I'm not sure if I truly believe her or if I just fell in love with the idea that there was someone out there who was meant to sweep me off my feet. That he was waiting for me. But I never stopped believing. And then there you were. At my gym, at the pizza place I go to, at the coffee shop, eating lunch at the same place I was. I convinced myself it was all part of the universe's plan to put you in my path. Then you gave me a weekend. Two days and I took my fill. I was greedy and binged. I thought I'd been right, it was fate. But I was wrong."

"You weren't wrong," he growled.

I ignored the full-body shiver.

"I was, Dalton. In my dream, in my fantasy, my Prince Charming doesn't want a friends-with-benefits sex relationship. He wants all of me and in return he'll give me all of him. I already told you, I know myself well enough to know I cannot separate sex and feelings. Some people can, I can't. And frankly I'm beyond that. I'm thirty-two, I want a family. I don't want to waste the next five years having meaningless sex only to start looking for something serious in my forties. I'm here—I mean, I'm there now. I'm ready. And going back to what we had won't work for me. I'll get lost in you. I'll get—"

"You're not listening to me, Vanessa."

"I am, Dalton," I countered. "You said you wanted to go back to what we had."

"No, baby, I said I was done being a coward."

I took in a stuttering breath, then another, and found I was at a loss for words.

Dalton wasn't.

"I'm going to point out again that there was nothing meaningless about the weekend we spent together and that most especially includes the sex. Every kiss, every touch, every time I was inside of you meant something to me. Correction, it meant *everything*. I'm also going to repeat something I told you the other night. No woman since I shared one with my ex-wife has been to my house. Not a single woman. And not because in my divorce I gave my ex every last stick of furniture. Actually, I gave her everything. Anything that was in the house we shared, went to her. I took my clothes and personal items and left her with the rest. Got a place and didn't bother decorating it. I had no reason. But that's not why I didn't bring women to my place. That gives the wrong impression. It says something to a woman when she wakes up next to a man and for eleven years I went to great lengths to make sure I never got close to a woman."

Well, that explained why his house looked like no one lived there. Because he didn't. He existed in that space but he wasn't living. And that made me sad for him but I didn't understand why he was telling me any of this.

"Dalton—"

"The point is, that first night I could've stayed here on your couch or in your bed, yet I maneuvered you into coming to mine with a bullshit excuse because I wanted you in my bed. I wanted you in my house. I wanted that because from the very beginning I knew you were different. And the beginning was from the moment I was introduced to you, not when I followed you home from the bar. The beginning was when I first saw you. That's when the battle started. That's when I had to remind myself that I fucked up my marriage and you were too good for me. I lost that fight and spent the weekend with you in my house—in my bed—knowing deep down you were meant to be there. Yet, I still didn't correct you when you told me you knew what you knew. I fucked that up and I've spent the last two days in my head wondering why the hell I'm such a dumb fuck that I'd let the woman who I know *I've* been *waiting* for, walk away."

Wren's words echoed in my mind, *all it takes is for the right woman to come along and then suddenly they're all in.*

My heart loved every word he'd said.

Yet, I still needed to understand about his ex.

"What about Layla?"

Dalton went solid under my palm. The downside to him placing my hand over his heart was I felt it go from pounding to hammering. I also felt the words thunder in his chest before I heard them.

"What about her?" he asked.

"I don't know. You tell me."

"She doesn't factor in our lives and certainly not when we're in your bed."

That was kind of sweet of him not wanting to bring his ex into my bed. Or it could be an excuse because he was still hung up on her.

"Right."

Suddenly we were no longer lying on our sides face-to-face with my hand on his heart. I was flat out on my back and Dalton was moving above me.

The lamp on my nightstand clicked on, flooding the room with a dim glow.

Dalton settled onto his elbow on the bed beside my shoulder and scowled down at me.

"That woman does not factor into anything that has to do with us," he mostly repeated.

"I disagree seeing as she's the reason you don't want to be involved in a relationship."

His scowl melted into raw torture. A chill seeped into my bones as the air between us grew heavy.

"No, baby, she's the excuse I used to protect myself."

"Why?" I bravely asked.

"Why?"

"Yes, Dalton, why did you use her as an excuse to protect yourself?"

He was silent but that didn't mean something wasn't running through his mind. It was fascinating to watch. His right eye twitched, his brows pulled together then relaxed, a muscle jumped in his cheek. Whatever he was thinking were not happy thoughts. Finally, he forcibly made his body relax. I knew this because he blew out a long breath and leaned deeper onto his elbow, giving me more of his weight.

"Remember when you told me Malory was different?"

"Yeah."

"I understand that kind of pain. Loving someone so much then watching them change into someone else. When I met Layla we were young. We grew up together and I mean that in every way a person can grow. We went to high school together. We experienced college life together. We matured and grew. Throughout this she was the same mellow, levelheaded, fun, sweet girl turned woman. Then when I was at the academy she started going out with friends, mostly to bars. She rarely drank because she didn't like getting hangovers. That started happening more and more. The drinking got heavier and heavier until she started coming home trashed. The next day she'd moan about her hangover and how she was never drinking again."

Oh, no. I'd heard the 'I'm never drinking again' line before.

"I don't know when, and I've thought about it a lot but she started drinking at home. A glass of wine with dinner. That turned into a glass when she got home from work and another with dinner. Eventually she graduated to a bottle a night. Every night."

Yep. This was going where I thought it was going.

"So I say something to her because she's my wife and I love her. A bottle of wine every night and going out with her girls on the weekend getting hammered. Only now she's not getting hangovers."

His tone was abrasive, grating, deteriorating into something that was hard to hear.

"Dalton," I whispered.

"Are you getting it?"

"Yes."

"Do you want me to continue?"

I wanted him to put Layla out of his mind, roll us back to our sides, let me hold his hand, and try to get him to relax.

"No, but I think you need to."

He dipped his chin and continued, "Needless to say she didn't like me asking questions. She mistook my concern for me trying to control her. The more I tried to talk to her about it, the worse it got. The drinking progressed to two bottles. Sometimes a bottle and a few vodka tonics. She didn't hide how much she was drinking, she threw it in my face. Told me it was my fault. Blamed it on me being a cop. One bullshit excuse after another. She couldn't sleep when I was on shift because she was too worried about me and the wine helped. She was lonely at night so she drank. I wasn't paying her enough attention so she drank. She had about a hundred excuses. But her favorite was to tell me I'd ruined her life."

"I'm sorry," I spat. "*You* ruined her life?"

Dalton flinched and I immediately regretted my outburst.

But in for a penny...in for a pound...

"Were you stepping out on her?"

"Fuck no."

"Did you hit her?"

Dalton didn't bother answering my preposterous question and I didn't need him to. There was no way he'd lift a hand to a woman.

"Did you treat her like she was less than? Did you expect to come home and have your house spotless, clothes washed and ironed, dinner on the table, treating her like she was your maid not your wife?"

"No."

I didn't think so. Though Dalton's condo was scarily clean, I figured it was because it was only him living there and he probably wasn't there enough to make a mess.

"So you just showed concern for your wife and she accused you of ruining her life?"

"No, Vanessa. We fought about it and toward the end it got ugly. I participated in those fights, hell, most of them I started. Coming home to my wife smashed, stumbling around and slurring—"

"Hurt you," I interrupted.

"Pissed me off," he corrected.

"Pissed you off because you were *hurt*."

He didn't need to admit I was right, I saw it wash over his features. I knew what it was like to see someone you loved in that state over and over again. I couldn't imagine that person being the person you married.

Then it hit me—something he'd told me the other night.

"Promised you the world then reneged on that promise," I muttered.

"We had our life planned out. At sixteen I thought I found everything I wanted. I thought she found everything she wanted. I worked hard to give her the life we'd planned. And in the beginning she did, too—until she didn't. I went from going to sleep at night thinking I had it all; the woman I loved sleeping next to me, a nice house that one day we'd fill with kids, a job I loved, to dreading coming home. And I'll be honest with you and it's going to make me sound like an asshole but part of that dread was knowing I'd have to get into bed and sleep next to a sloppy drunk who reeked of wine and vodka. The other part of that is I was pissed she forced me to watch the sweet, ambitious, fun-loving woman I married turn into a functioning alcoholic who refused to admit she had a problem."

I hated all of that for Dalton.

"You didn't ruin her life."

"Maybe not but—"

"No buts, Dalton. I'm sorry she has a drinking problem, but

it's *her* problem. And before you tell me all the ways you could've done things differently, I'll remind you *she* has to want to get help. *She* has to admit *she* has a problem. That's not me being unkind or negating your pain. It's just the plain truth."

Dalton's eyes slowly closed. I stared at his long lashes, the creases between his brows, and wondered if he'd spent the eleven years since his divorce believing he'd ruined her life.

I bet he did.

He seemed to be the kind of man who would carry that guilt.

Just like me.

I'd spent more than half my life feeling guilty for ruining Malory's life. For telling my parents about her drinking causing them to send her away.

"My sister was drinking while she was pregnant," I whispered, the truth hitting me. "If she was pregnant before she went to Utah...and she'd have to be because she was only there seven months."

Dalton's eyes opened, he lowered his lips to my forehead, and murmured, "Don't take that on, Vanessa."

"I won't if you admit you didn't ruin Layla's life."

His head came up and he looked down at me with a scowl.

"Emotional manipulation."

He didn't sound pissed, just resigned I was willing to pull out the big guns every woman held in her vast arsenal.

"When I told you I felt guilty for telling my parents about Malory's drinking you asked me what would've happened if I hadn't," I reminded him. "Now with the addition of Sullivan in that equation I'm struggling not to blame myself for putting my sister into a situation where she might've felt giving him up for adoption was his only option. So, here's my deal; you help me come to the understanding that Sullivan has had a wonderful life and was raised by good people who he loves deeply, and you let me help you come to the understanding that not only is Layla's drinking problem not your doing but you didn't ruin her life."

"Our deal?"

"Yup. Our deal. Shake on it." I wiggled my arm free from under the comforter and awkwardly offered him my hand.

Dalton glanced at my hand and smiled.

"You know what they say," he drawled. "A deal's a deal."

"And you can't break a deal especially when it's been sealed with a handshake," I finished.

"Should we make a pinkie promise, too?" he teased with a smile.

"Sure."

"I'll shake to your deal if you pinkie promise to mine."

Before I could ask what we were promising Dalton's smile faded and he wrecked me.

"I'm no Prince Charming. But I want the chance to prove you're the one I've been waiting for. I want us to go back to what we were. Just you and me getting to know each other without anything between us."

That scared the hell out of me but I wanted it.

"I'm not hearing a promise in there," I pointed out when he didn't go on.

"Promise me you'll give me that chance."

No promise from me about what I'd give him in return.

I nodded.

Dalton shifted all of his weight to his elbow, took my hand in a strong grip, and gave it two pumps. After that he let go, twisted his hand, and hooked his pinkie with mine.

Before he let go, I bent my pinkie so he couldn't pull away.

"I promise to be worth the wait," I whispered.

Dalton's eyes flared, those beautiful brown orbs bore into mine.

"You've already made good on that, sweetheart."

I loved how he thought that.

I guess Wren was right.

Sometimes all it took was the right person to come along and the walls came crashing down. I just hoped I didn't get buried under the rubble because I had a feeling we'd barely scratched the surface.

That night I fell asleep in safety and warmth in Dalton's arms not knowing the very next day my heart would shatter into a million pieces.

19

I HEARD POUNDING on the front door.

My eyes shot open.

Vanessa rolled away and before I could stop her she was climbing out of bed.

"Don't you dare," I growled, coming to my feet and nabbing my jeans off the ugly-assed carpet.

Last night after I got Vanessa settled and she'd finally fallen asleep, I'd gotten up and undressed. Now I felt like my eyes had only been closed ten minutes but the clock told me it was five forty-five so it was more like five hours.

Vanessa flipped the light on.

The pounding stopped.

She glared.

I continued pulling my jeans on.

The pounding started again.

I nabbed my gun off her nightstand. Her eyes got big.

"Are you going to shoot someone?"

"Possible."

"Seriously, Dalton, that's not necessary. I live—"

"Sweetheart, you could live in a gated community with

security patrolling, have two Dobermans, and I'd still be answering the door with my gun."

"It's—"

"Just coming on six and someone's pounding on your door pissed," I finished for her and stalked out of the room.

Vanessa was trailing after me. Since I knew I had no chance of her doing what I asked, I didn't bother telling her to stay in her room.

I got to the door, caught Vanessa by the hand as she tried to skirt by me to go to the windows, and shook my head.

"Who is it?" I called.

"Austin!"

"That's Malory's husband," Vanessa said, pushing her way to the door.

"If I asked you to stay behind me would you?"

Her 'you're an idiot' look was the answer I'd expected.

The pounding started again.

"Christ!" I bit out and opened the door.

As soon as I did, a very pissed-off dark-haired man shoved into the door and came to a rocking halt in front of me when I didn't move.

"Who are you?" he angrily asked and his gaze dropped to the gun in my hand at my side.

"Detective Dalton Neary." I matched his biting tone. "Now, you want to explain why you're pounding on the door at the ass crack of dawn?"

"I need to talk to my sister."

Vanessa wasn't his sister, she was his wife's sister. I didn't bother pointing that out.

"I guessed that, seeing as it's her door you're pounding on."

"What's going on?" Vanessa entered the conversation.

Austin's eyes moved to Vanessa and narrowed.

"I didn't expect that from you."

"What?"

"That shit was lowdown," Austin went on like Vanessa hadn't spoken. "She's completely fucking undone."

"Oh, God," Vanessa whispered.

"That shit is on you!" Austin bellowed.

I pulled Vanessa to my side, stepped in front of her, then took a step back, forcing her to move back with me.

"I can see you're pissed—"

"I don't know who the fuck you are and I don't give a fuck. You're not in this."

"Wrong. I was here last night. I know what happened. Even if I wasn't there's no way I'd stand aside and let you tear into my woman. Period. But especially when she didn't do a damn thing to earn your anger. You either calm down or I'll show you the door."

Austin glowered.

"The fuck she didn't. Vanessa knows how her sister is and she still calls her and asks her over then treats her to that shit."

I wondered what exactly Malory told her husband.

"And what shit would that be?"

Vanessa's hands went to my sides and the pads of her fingers dug in.

Then she spoke to my back but her question was for Austin.

"Why don't you come into the kitchen? I'll start coffee and we can start over and you can tell us what happened after Malory left here last night."

At Vanessa's quiet suggestion the man looked like he was working hard trying to find calm. He also looked like he was struggling. From the interaction I'd had with Malory, and from what little Vanessa had told me about her, I understood Austin. His wife may've once been outgoing and vivacious but she was now timid and anxious. I could see him moving in to protect her and being pissed she'd come home to him upset.

My understanding stopped there.

It wasn't my job to protect Malory; it was to shield Vanessa.

Austin blew out a breath. Then another before he turned back to the front door and closed it.

I took that as our cue that we were moving into the kitchen. I patted Vanessa's hand and she let go but didn't move until I twisted and grabbed her hand.

"Go get a shirt. I'll start coffee. And lose the gun, Detective," she bossed.

I hadn't yet decided how I felt leaving an angry Austin alone with Vanessa when she went on, "He loves my sister beyond reason. But he loves me, too, and he'd never hurt me. He'll calm down and when he does he'll feel like shit he yelled at me."

"She's right," Austin said from behind us.

Instead of issuing a threat to the pissed-off husband of my girl's sister—which would likely only escalate the situation, seeing as if I was in his position and I thought someone had fucked with Vanessa I'd tell them to shove their threat straight up their ass—I refrained. Instead I kissed the top of Vanessa's head and left them in the kitchen.

I also didn't bother because I'd be quick.

I left Vanessa to make coffee, trusting she could handle her brother-in-law while I went back to her room to get dressed in yesterday's shirt. Then I brushed my teeth with her toothbrush. I did this thinking I had to go by my house before work and pack a bag so tomorrow I wouldn't have to make an unnecessary stop before work. I also wasn't going to ask or mention it to Vanessa, giving her the opportunity to overthink me staying with her or to tell me no. But tomorrow night she was staying at my house.

I'd just hit the kitchen when I heard Vanessa ask, "Did you know?"

Austin took the mug Vanessa was offering and gave a slight nod.

Fuck.

"Seriously?" she hissed.

Without taking a sip, Austin set his coffee on the island. He watched me make my way to the coffee pot and Vanessa. He watched as I slid my arm around her waist and pulled her to my side.

He didn't miss my point.

I wasn't leaving them to have a private family discussion.

But still I told him, "I think you get what this is. I also told you I was here last night and I talked to your wife. So whatever you have to say is gonna be said in front of me."

For his part, Austin clenched his jaw but didn't argue.

"She told me she promised she'd be back tonight to explain," Austin started. "But she's not going to do that."

Vanessa startled then slowly she went stiff.

"Why not?"

"You have no idea what this has done to your sister."

"You're right, I don't. Want to know why, Austin?" Vanessa asked but didn't give him a chance to answer. "Because she's never talked to me about it."

"And maybe that's because for her sanity she needed to keep this buried."

"I have a nephew."

"And she has a son who she loves but was forced to give up for adoption," he trumped.

That was the second time the word *forced* was used in regard to Sullivan's adoption.

"Did my parents—"

"No," Austin interrupted. "Your parents didn't know she was pregnant when they sent her to Utah and they don't know anything that happened there and they don't know about Sullivan now and they'll never know about him."

That last part was said with authority. The part about Utah was said with disdain. But surprisingly, his tone softened when he said Sullivan's name.

"They have a right to know," Vanessa countered.

"They don't," Austin said firmly. "And when I explain you'll agree with me."

I wasn't fond of talking in circles. I was a get-to-the-point-and-do-it-quickly type of person. In order to facilitate that I broke into the conversation.

"Sweetheart, get yourself some coffee so we can sit and Austin can explain."

Vanessa tipped her head back and to the side to catch my eye.

"Bossy much?" she sassed but moved to get herself a cup of coffee.

Austin watched this as well, his eyes bouncing back and forth between me and Vanessa.

"When did this start?" he finally asked.

I waited for Vanessa to field the question and she didn't disappoint.

"Why don't we table the discussion of my love life until after you explain why you're here instead of my sister."

"You know why," he volleyed.

"Yeah, I do. And you know because we've had this conversation a lot over the years. I hate that my sister won't talk to me about what happened in Utah. I hate that everyone tiptoes around it like it never happened. I hate that she's changed and that change means I no longer have a sister. I'm glad she's at least opened up to you. However, I'm hurt that you knew why my sister had changed and you never gave me the first clue you knew."

"Nessa, honey, I get why you'd be hurt but one day you'll understand that, too. If you think about it, you already do. You said it yourself; I love your sister beyond reason. That means I love her more than anything or anyone including you. I love her enough to protect her secrets even when I know doing so will hurt someone else."

Alright. So, I was beginning to like this guy despite the rocky beginning.

Though I wasn't going to tell Vanessa I agreed with her brother-in-law. In my opinion it wasn't his place to tell her his wife's secret, it was his place to guard it.

"What does forced mean?" I broke in.

"It means Sullivan's biological father is a well-connected, powerful man. He was nineteen years ago and he's more so now."

The implication churned my gut.

"Was she violated?" I gently asked.

Austin scrubbed his hands over his face, his movements jerky and agitated.

Fuck.

Vanessa abandoned her coffee and slid under my arm.

"In the eyes of the law, no. According to her, no, it was consensual. According to me, a man near on her father's age taking advantage of a sixteen-year-old girl—fuck yes. However, Malory still insists the relationship didn't start until after she turned sixteen and continued until she left for Utah and during that time, she was never coerced, pressured, or was gaslighted into believing this man was in love with her or that he'd leave his wife for her. She maintains it was purely sexual in nature and at no time did she feel uncomfortable or used."

I had to hand it to Austin. Throughout his explanation he'd remained a fuckuva lot calmer than I would've been.

"But he held power over her. Age of consent has stipulations," I argued. "The power dynamic holds merit. Say, a teacher entering into a relationship with an underage student."

"I didn't say he held power over her. I said he was and is a powerful man."

Well, fuck.

"Do I know this man?" Vanessa inquired.

"Yes."

Vanessa wrapped her arms around me tighter and nuzzled her cheek on my chest. She did this silently, almost like she was attempting to gather strength for what was coming next.

A second later, I learned I was correct.

"Simon," she whispered.

"Your dad's friend who took her to Utah?"

"My dad's friend who suggested Malory be sent to Utah," she corrected. "Then, yes, took her there. My dad's friend who always paid more attention to my sister than me. Back then I didn't think anything of it. He was like an uncle. But as an adult, thinking back, it was creepy."

Austin remained quiet.

"Am I right? Is Simon Sullivan's birth father?"

"Yes."

"Simon talked my dad into sending her away because she was pregnant," Vanessa deduced.

"Yes."

With that confirmation Vanessa detonated.

She tore out of my arms, slammed her palms on the worn Formica of the island, and exploded into a rant that was painful to hear.

"That asshole!" she shouted. "That disgusting, asshole pig. He's my father's best friend. He's sat at our table. He was there for Malory's sixteenth birthday, with his wife and two sons. His wife! He's my father's age and he..." Vanessa abruptly stopped and shook her head. "He's why I lost my sister." Again she paused. "I can see it. I can see him forcing her to give up the baby."

"Why?" I asked then amended. "Outside of his age, his marital status, and the fact he's a family friend."

"Back then Simon was an attorney. A very successful one. Now he's a judge."

Fuck.

"He's the county's Chief Judge of the Superior Court," Austin added.

And the plot thickens.

"Are you talking about Judge Rodman?" I asked.

"Yes," Austin grunted.

I'd testified before him numerous times. Rodman was known for his no-tolerance policy on drug cases and maximum punishments of felonies, therefore he was well liked by the sheriff's department, local police, and state patrol. He didn't play the good ol' boy game but that didn't mean he didn't call in favors should one of his cronies get stopped for speeding. Though I'd never heard of him asking for a serious infraction like a DWI to be overlooked. It was also known his sons were assholes and his wife delirious with her perceived power at being the wife of the top judge in the county.

Vanessa curled her hand around my forearm.

"Do you know him?"

"I've testified before him and I've been at FOP functions where he and his wife have been in attendance. I also had a run-in with him early in my career when I was still on patrol and I pulled his son over for reckless driving. Jake, I think his name is—"

"James," Vanessa corrected. "James and Connor."

"Right. James. He was all bluster and posture. Actually called his father during the traffic stop and had the judge on speakerphone when I approached. Rodman told me to write the ticket. James continued to bitch, but to his father about my abuse of power. Rodman shut that down, too."

"That's Tracy's doing," Vanessa told me. "I can't tell you how many times my mother complained about that woman and her sons after they..." Her nose scrunched and she dropped her head to finish on a whisper, "this is so disturbingly disgusting."

That was an understatement.

"Malory doesn't know I'm here," Austin announced. "She wants to come clean but I hope you get now why I'm not going to allow that to happen."

"Austin—"

"He made threats," Austin cut off Vanessa's retort. "He's now in a position to make good on those."

"What kind of threats?" I asked.

"The kind that could ruin Jeff and Holly."

"My parents," Vanessa helpfully clarified. "How could he possibly hurt Mom and Dad if they didn't know?"

"Just because they don't know doesn't mean Simon can't twist it to make it seem like they did. But that's not what he's threatening. Your father is a financial advisor. He manages a lot of wealthy people's money. People who, with one call from Simon, would drop him. Still, that's not the threat that silenced your sister. It's Sullivan she's worried about."

Vanessa straightened and something beautiful stole over her —the lioness roared to life for a young man whom she barely knew.

"What about Sully?"

"Simon threatened to take Sullivan from Malory and raise him should she say anything. Now that he's over eighteen I think Malory feels this is no longer a worry but she forgets Sullivan's adoption might be called into question. Malory lied on the adoption paperwork and on the birth certificate."

"Lied about what?"

"She listed the father as unknown. Simon instructed her to do this but she has no proof. He can and will make things difficult for Malory and Sullivan if his paternity is exposed."

I wasn't understanding what the judge could make difficult.

"I'm seeing it as the opposite," I rejoined. "Rodman would want to distance himself."

"Right and to do that, he'll say Malory went away, had the baby, then gave his child up for adoption without his knowledge."

"She was sixteen fucking years old," I spat. "He was old enough to be her father. He's the one who has something to lose, not Malory and not Sullivan."

"Yes, Dalton. And think what he'll do to protect his place in the community," Austin lobbed. "His position on the bench. Sullivan's existence won't make it to the court of public opinion because he'll shut that shit down before it gets that far. Sullivan will be target number one, Malory will be number two, then he'll go after anyone else he feels is a threat. The man has the money and power to do it."

"Not if we come at this from a position of knowledge."

"I get you think that," Austin sneered. "But it's my wife who will be target number one. My wife, who has spent the last eighteen years mourning a child she was forced to give up. The woman I adore who is so riddled with so much guilt she will not have a family with me because she has convinced herself she doesn't deserve it. And finally, the woman I will protect at all costs from the barest possibility someone will hurt her. And Simon poses more of a threat than you understand."

Austin looked at Vanessa. "I know you think your sister's fragile and she's not who she was before she gave up Sullivan, but she's stronger than you know. Every single day she wonders about her son. Every day she lives with the repercussions of her actions. She refuses to see she was taken advantage of. She believes she is responsible for her actions and she owns them. She wants the truth to come out. She wants Sullivan to know she didn't want to give him up. She wants to tell you about her time in Utah. She wants your parents to meet Sullivan. But I'm asking you, Nessa, to help me protect your sister."

The silence that ensued was wrought with anger and pain as Vanessa and Austin faced off. The fuck of it was I could see Austin's point. I didn't agree with his assessment of Simon Rodman but I fully understood his play. He was going to do whatever he could to make sure his wife was safe from the man who'd violated her. Vanessa, on the other hand, wasn't going to let this go and I knew it. I was beginning to understand—she saw black and white when it came to right and wrong. While most of the time I agreed with that, my job had shown me the various shades of gray between the two. She was going to demand Simon's ass be held to the fire. Austin was going to fight to see that didn't happen and it was me who needed to end this here to give Vanessa time to process all that she'd learned.

"Nessa, baby," I called.

She tore her gaze from her brother-in-law.

"I already know what you're going to say," was her lead-in. "You're siding with him."

"My side is next to you, always. But I think you need to take some time with what you've learned. If after that, you want to firebomb the judge's life, I'll help you light the match. But this isn't about what you want or what Austin wants or even about Malory. This is about Sullivan and how this can and will impact his life. If you out Simon and he makes good on any of his threats Sullivan will be stuck. And by that I mean his parents will likely be dragged through the mud right alongside Malory, Austin, your parents, Sully, you, and me. But again, I'm at your side whatever you choose."

Austin started in again. "I'm not going to let—"

I interrupted Austin by telling him, "It's not your place to *let* Vanessa do anything. You make what moves you feel you need to make when it comes to Malory. But Vanessa's choice is hers and hers alone. And you'll damn well respect that because if you don't, the hell this family is getting ready to face will be all that much worse when you position yourself between two sisters."

Austin pushed away from the island, leaving his mug of coffee untouched. He threatened, "You out Simon I'll make it so you never see your sister again. And you know good and well I can make that happen."

Vanessa shrank back and closed her eyes.

What the fuck?

"What does that mean?" I growled at the man's back as he strode out of the kitchen.

He didn't stop when he replied, "She knows what that means."

My choices were to follow Austin to the door and possibly beat the fuck out of him while I demand he tell me, or go to Vanessa.

Easy.

I went to Vanessa.

She folded into my arms and unleashed the tears she'd been holding back.

Something else I was coming to understand. Vanessa was strong when she needed to be. She held herself together until the scene was over then she allowed herself to get sucked under by emotion.

Likely because that was who Malory and her parents needed her to be.

"Sweetheart," I murmured against her hair.

"I'm beyond disgusted," she cried. "My heart hurts and I'm irrationally mad—at everyone. Logically I know why Austin kept her secret but right now I hate him. And I'm mad Malory didn't tell me. And I hope Simon Rodman burns in hell for what he did. And I'm pissed at my dad for sending Malory away."

I wrapped her up tighter and asked, "What did that bullshit Austin said mean?"

"It's not bullshit. He gets overseas job offers all the time. He only turns them down because he knows it would hurt Mom and Dad if they moved away. They like us close. But Malory wouldn't fight it if he told her he wanted to take a job offer. She feels bad he always turns them down."

"You could still go visit," I pointed out.

"Malory will go along with whatever Austin says. So if they moved and he told her he didn't want me to visit, she wouldn't go against that."

Christ.

"Vanessa—"

"I know," she said and gave me a squeeze. "I know how that sounds. But until he just made that threat he's never tried to control her. We all know he can, because that's who she is, but we all know he loves her and he'd never do anything to hurt her. Believe me, when they first got together we were all worried. It took a while but he won us all over and he did that by proving he won't manipulate her. And I know this is going to sound...bad, but Malory needs someone who is going to be in charge. She works, she makes day-to-day decisions, but mostly she depends on him for the big stuff. And he's gentle with her. Almost to the point he babys her. If there's a chance something's going to upset her in the smallest of ways he'll step in. So really, I should've anticipated his visit this morning."

I understood shield those you love. I respected a husband who loved his wife. But some of that sounded unhealthy. Though it wasn't my place to say what was unhealthy in someone else's relationship as long as both parties got what they needed out of the arrangement.

"I should get ready for work."

"Maybe you should think about taking the day off," I suggested.

"Why? So I can pace my house and plot murder?"

"How about you not confess you're plotting murder and instead take the day to digest the last three days which have been hellish."

"How about you be my boyfriend Dalton and not Detective Neary and let me plot a very painful way to—"

Boyfriend.

I hadn't been that since I was sixteen.

"Sweetheart," I grunted.

"I can't take today off because I'm already taking tomorrow off so I can run last-minute errands for my parents' anniversary party."

Fucking hell.

"A party, by the way, I no longer want to attend since Simon and Tracy will be there along with their two douchebag sons. Obviously Austin will come up with a suitable excuse why Malory won't be there; likely she'll have the flu and he'll need to stay at her bedside to nurse her which will leave me to deal with everything. Not that that's new or surprising since I'm always the one who has to pick up the pieces."

So, I was right. Vanessa's strength came from years of conditioning.

"I'll be with you."

"You'll...be with me?"

I loosened my arms and tried to pull back so I could look at her but she pushed her forehead against my chest, refusing to look up.

"Nessa? Baby, I want to see you."

"No one..." she started. "It's always me."

"Baby."

"Give me this, Dalton."

I closed my arms back around her, slid one hand up her back, and curled my fingers around the back of her neck.

"It feels like my whole life I've been alone," she whispered so softly I dipped my head to hear her. "I don't think they mean to do it, but they're so careful not to upset her they don't think about me. I'm just expected to...I don't know...not rock the boat, to do what I can to smooth the way for everyone. To be the go-between, the dependable one, the one who will pick up the slack. No one's ever taken my side. And I know right now, with everything going on that sounds shitty. But there it is, the truth. You were right—I'm mad at my dad, but not for sending Malory away. I believe he thought that was his only option. I'm mad at him for overlooking me. They're all take. No give."

And I'd damn well done the same thing to her.

Not that I'd overlooked her. But I'd selfishly taken something from her without the intention of giving her back what she deserved.

"Vanessa—"

"But here you are at my side, holding me at my worst, promising to give me more."

She was killing me.

"I didn't—"

"But you are now and that's all that matters. For the first time since I was a child I don't feel alone."

I didn't know what to say to that.

Actually, I did.

Though what I had to communicate wasn't through words.

I shifted my hand from the back of her neck into her hair. Gently grabbing a handful, I pulled her head off my shoulder.

Then my mouth was on hers.

Three days.
It had been three days since I'd tasted her lips.
It felt like an eternity.
Now last night's promises were sealed.
With a kiss.

20

I WAS in my truck leaving my condo when I got Brady's text. With everything that had gone on last night I hadn't called him with the information about Utah. Information that now seemed moot. Though I needed to brief him on the latest.

But first I needed to check in on Vanessa. When I left her house she was getting in the shower. The woman was determined to go to work and no amount of pleading with her to stay home had worked. I finally gave up when she explained if she stayed home all she'd do was worry. She needed the distraction of work to get her thoughts in order. She also needed to figure out what she was going to tell Sullivan. Malory had promised to come back and explain. Austin had made it clear that wasn't going to happen. I'd suggested she should tell Sully the truth. She'd unhappily mumbled, "You're right, I should, but you know I can't."

And there it was—more evidence she'd been trained to do whatever she could to protect her sister. It wasn't my place to judge. I didn't have siblings but I understood loyalty and history. But I flat-out thought she was wrong about this. The relationship she was building with Sullivan was fragile and so was the trust. The boy needed honesty—period.

Before I could call Vanessa my phone rang and her name popped up on my truck's display.

I reached over, tapped the screen, and answered.

"Everything alright?"

"How do you feel about driving down to Jacksonville tonight after work?"

After two nights in a row with very little sleep, being woken up by an angry husband, knowing I was facing a day of interrogating a variety of people in various locations around town while spending the time between visits in a car with Phoenix, the last thing I wanted was to drive two hours down to Florida.

But I wasn't going to let Vanessa face Sullivan alone.

"I feel like you already have a plan."

"I was thinking, since he's always driving up here I'll call him and tell him we're going to go down there and take him out to dinner."

"He'll see right through that play, sweetheart," I warned.

"I know," she miserably agreed. "So I'll also tell him that Malory needs a few days to sort herself out."

He'd likely see through that, too, but I wasn't going to point that out.

"I should be done around five," I told her.

"So you'll go with me?"

She sounded surprised, which I didn't understand seeing as it'd been less than two hours since we'd talked in her kitchen. I thought I'd made myself clear.

Apparently, I hadn't.

"I told you I'm by your side," I reminded her.

"You did," she whispered.

"That means I'm by your side, baby. You want to go to Jacksonville tonight and have dinner with Sully, I'm with you. You feel the need to call him, explain things, and make arrangements to go down next week, I'm with you."

She went silent.

I understood that, too.

She had a lot going on and last night I'd added to that.

Something I'd thought about—what that would do to her dropping my shit on her lap while she was dealing with her family but it was too important to delay. She needed to know where I was at with her and she needed to know now, so I could take her back with having the understanding I was in it with her. Not thinking I would take off and leave her to deal with it alone. And I knew when I told her I wanted us to go back to what we had—she'd assume I was talking about the sex.

I wasn't.

I wanted to be able to hold her and have her know she was in my arms because I wanted to take care of her and not in a friendly-at-arms-length way. I wanted all access to her thoughts and emotions, and again not in a friendly way.

I wanted the intimacy.

"I hope this is real," she breathed.

I couldn't be pissed she was skeptical; it was my fault she doubted me. I'd fucked that up by not manning up when I should've.

"You've got my promise."

"Yeah."

"And we made a deal."

"We did."

"You call Sully, ask him about dinner, and let me know."

"Okay, honey."

Her soft 'honey' hit my chest and damn, I wished she was in front of me. But since she wasn't I'd have to show her how much I liked hearing her call me 'honey' in that soft, breathy voice tonight.

So it sucked when I had to circle the conversation around to something that would take the sweet out of her voice.

"I need to call Brady," I started. "We didn't get to talk about it much last night but he was waiting for my call to tell him the name of the camp Malory went to in Utah. I'm thinking since we have confirmation that might no longer be important—though maybe in the future it will be—so I'd like him to still look into it along with Simon Rodman."

"Do you..." Vanessa started but faded out.

"Do I what?"

"Do you think that's smart? I mean, you getting involved. He's a judge and Austin's right; he's powerful and you said you know him. Maybe—"

"I. Am. By. Your. Side," I enunciated each word. "By that I mean, I'm on your side. I have your back with this. And I don't give the first fuck how much power the man has. I also don't care what the law says, the man's a predator. Malory was sixteen. In some bizarre turn of events if the man had developed feelings for her he should've first waited until she was of age, then he should've legally untied himself from his wife, then he should've approached your father. And I say that having to swallow the bile that's clogging my throat. I know women fall in love with older men. I know in some cases that works. What does not work is a grown man who is married having a sexual relationship with a sixteen-year-old.

"I don't know where this is going to go. You don't know. Austin can say what he wants but the truth is your sister is unpredictable. She was also victimized. According to her husband she's twisted that into thinking she carries some sort of responsibility. One day, hopefully soon, she's going to come to the understanding she was taken advantage of and take *her* power back. And I think it's important we have everything we can get on Simon Rodman should we need to neutralize him and do it quickly."

"Okay, Dalton. I trust you to do what you think is best."

Thank fuck.

"Thank you, sweetheart."

"You're thanking me but you're the one calling in the favors and doing all the work."

"No, baby, thank you for trusting me."

I heard her suck in a breath before she told me, "The camp was called Change."

"Just Change?"

"Yes."

"Last thing, I need to talk to Phoenix about what's going on. Yesterday he was tweaked when he knew something big was going down but I wouldn't tell him. Now, with Rodman in play I need to tell him. The more people we have at our back the better."

I made the turn into the parking lot of the station, saw Phoenix folding out of his new SUV, and pulled to the other side of the parking lot so I'd have time to finish my call before my partner approached.

"You didn't tell him about Sullivan?"

"With what went down with you at work, I couldn't get you on the phone to talk to you. Not my place to tell your personal business without your permission."

I was shutting down my truck when she murmured, "You can tell him."

"Am I telling him to keep this to himself or—"

"I'll talk to Wren, though I'm not sure how much time I'll have today since yesterday was a day from technology hell and today we'll be playing catch up. But I'll ask her to lunch."

Phoenix was more than halfway across the lot with a look of irritation clear on his face.

"I'm at work, baby, gotta go. Text me after you connect with Sully."

"Okay, Dalton. Catch some bad guys but be safe doing it."

The way she said that was nowhere close to how my ex used to say goodbye when we were ringing off when I got to work. And not only because Layla would give a perfunctory 'I love you' that was more habit than meaning before she hung up. She'd done that all the way up until the end, even after I'd long since stopped saying or returning it. I wasn't one to spout empty platitudes by rote.

"Will do."

"Later."

I hit the end icon on the screen and nabbed my phone off the charging pad. Phoenix was at the side of my truck when I swung the door open.

"How pissed are you at me this morning?" I asked.

Phoenix took in my empty hands.

"No coffee?"

"I'll buy you one on our way to Outdoor Goods. But before that I'll tell you Vanessa and I are together."

Phoenix's study of me became critical.

I let him have that and continued, "I told her about Layla and my reasons for ending my marriage. I also explained my reluctance—"

"Reluctance?" Phoenix parroted.

I clenched my jaw.

"I admitted I'd retreated because I was afraid of falling in love with her and I was acting like a coward."

Phoenix nodded.

"And she forgave you for being an ass?"

"No, I had to convince her to take a chance on me. Then we shook on it."

"Shook on it?"

"Yup."

"Is that a code word for shacking?"

"I think you mean shagging," I corrected.

"Yeah, I'm an adult, thus I use adult words like fucking. I don't need code words. Though I should be brushing up on teenager acronyms. Half the time Griff texts me I need to Google his responses. What the hell does NBD mean?"

Was he serious?

"No big deal."

"Brother, it is when I can't translate my kid's texts."

"No, idiot, NBD means no big deal."

Phoenix's eyes narrowed.

"That little shit no-big-dealed me when I told him his mom was pissed he forgot to unload the dishwasher last night and he needed to do that as soon as he got home from school."

I wasn't sure if I wanted to laugh or if I was happy I didn't have children.

"Need to fill you in on one more thing before we head in. About yesterday..."

I gave Phoenix the abbreviated version of the last few days including what happened this morning.

"What do you know about this Austin guy?"

"Nothing beyond what Vanessa told me. He loves his wife and he's protective."

"What does he have to lose if this goes public?"

That was a good fucking question and one I hadn't thought of. Which was exactly why I'd needed to brief Phoenix. I had blinders when it came to this situation. My focus was Vanessa and getting her through as unharmed as I could.

"No idea but I'll ask Brady to look into him as well."

"One thing the husband's right about—Rodman's a powerful man and not just because he's a judge. He comes from old Savannah money. You know those condos that were built out on Bull River on your way to Tybee?"

I think everyone in the state of Georgia knew about the condos. There'd been a three-year battle between the landowners and a conservation group attempting to block the twenty-five acre, nine-story condominium complex which included a clubhouse, pool, and river access. A one-bedroom, nine-hundred-square-foot unit went for half a million. I knew that not because I was in the market for a half-million-dollar condo, riverfront or not. I knew because for six months before the construction was done, during the pre-sale period you couldn't watch TV or listen to the radio without hearing an advertisement for the luxury condos.

"I know the complex."

"The Rodman family owns that land."

How the hell did he know that?

"Let me get this straight. You don't know what NBD means but you're in the know about a piece of land two counties over."

Phoenix shrugged.

"I was looking for an investment and I read some news articles."

That was news.

"Did you buy one?"

"Fuck no. Investment or not I couldn't bring myself to pay over five hundred a square foot and a seven-hundred-dollar HOA fee."

"Do you know what HOA stands for?"

My joke was met with Phoenix's middle finger.

"Let's go check in with Brennon. I want my coffee."

"You mean your girly—"

"After the shit you've pulled for the last week," he cut me off. "I get a full month of the driver's seat and you keeping your trap shut about how I take my coffee."

Christ.

A full month of near-death experiences.

"Deal."

"Do we need to shake on it?" He smirked.

"Seeing as five minutes ago you asked me if that was a euphemism for fucking I'm not sure where you're going with that."

I thought Phoenix would hit me with a funny comeback. Therefore I was completely unprepared when he hit me with the opposite.

"Happy for you, Dalton."

"CHANGE OF PLANS," Brennon announced as soon as we crossed the threshold of his office.

My gaze went to the woman standing in the corner.

"Liza," I greeted.

Phoenix dropped his head and shook it. Even still, he was smiling.

"Damn, the vultures have arrived."

"Kent, always a pleasure," ATF Special Agent Liza Monroe returned. "Heard you took the plunge."

"You heard right."

"Sunny said she was too good for you."

Liza was one of the few people who Shiloh Kent liked. Or liked before she'd hooked up with her husband and her once ironic nickname turned into a not-so-ironic one when her not-so-sunny disposition turned warm and friendly. Special Agent Monroe was an acquired taste. You either got her sense of humor or you didn't. And if you didn't she gave zero fucks. Beyond that she was excellent at her job, and just like her humor you either got onboard or she railroaded over you. Fortunately for me and Phoenix she liked working with us.

"If you don't have plans tonight I'll call Wren. We'll get the family together, have a proper welcome home for you." Phoenix glanced over to me. "And you and Vanessa can use a break. Come over."

He wasn't wrong. Vanessa needed a night without drama.

The conversation moved back to why Liza was in town before I could tell my partner we had plans.

"Make that call," Liza started. "But first, let's get to business."

"Have a seat, boys."

Only Brennon could get away with calling big, hulking Phoenix a boy.

We took the chairs in front of Brennon's desk. Someone had rolled in a high-backed desk chair for Liza. She sat to the side of Phoenix and opened a file on the edge of the desk.

"Brennon filled me in. I've been over your notes—"

"Let's back up," I interrupted. "I take it the sale of the revolver went through."

Yesterday when we'd left work Billy the Kid hadn't been back to the gun store in North Carolina. We'd asked Clint to make an offer on the relic that would ensure "William Bonney" would cream his pants with excitement and unload the revolver. We'd also had a conversation with Frank Bristol. He'd called his wife, explained the situation before he passed the phone to me. At first Cara was shocked to learn that all of the safes that had been broken into had been purchased from Outdoor Goods. She had access to the list of customers who had made those purchases as did every employee in the store. It was her idea to set up a meeting with the store's owner. It was also her idea to have me and Phoenix use the back entrance to the offices to conceal the meeting—reading the situation correctly.

We didn't want whoever the employee was to know we'd cottoned on.

That meeting was scheduled for this morning.

"The revolver and your guy Clint worked this William Bonney guy. William offered Clint a collector's edition Desert Eagle."

Victim number three.

"Norton is in North Carolina now," Liza finished.

Norton Peters was Liza's partner. He was the beta to her alpha and it didn't matter the man had five years on the job longer than her. Norton followed Liza's lead.

I looked to Brennon for guidance. Liza being here meant the feds had taken over and we'd be moved into consultant capacity.

"Take Liza with you to meet with Trent Ackerman."

"We're leaving in ten," I told Liza and stood.

"Who's driving today?"

"Me," Phoenix answered.

Liza groaned then added, "Good thing my insurance policy's up to date."

Phoenix didn't rise to the bait. He rarely did unless he was in the mood to shovel it back.

TRENT ACKERMAN WAS EXACTLY as Cara Bristol had described him—no nonsense and business minded. His office was utilitarian. For a man who owned three sporting goods stores with a bent for fishing and hunting there wasn't a single game trophy on his walls. There was nothing but two large desks—both covered in file folders of different colors and thicknesses and a large desktop monitor on one of the desks—four filing cabinets, and a six-seater rectangular table where we were currently seated. The man worked in this space, he didn't spend time here or use it to impress visitors. He also dressed the part of an outdoorsman—canvas-style work pants, LOWA boots, and a flannel over a Henley. What he didn't look like was the multi-millionaire he was. Though right then after Phoenix explained in more detail than Cara had shared about the purpose of our visit, Trent Ackerman looked furious.

"Your source is correct," Trent confirmed. "When a safe with a digital lock is sold, the code is included with the owner's manual. The purchaser is encouraged to change the combo. However, the manufacturer has a master code. What you're suggesting would mean someone in my store has a contact at SafeCo and has access to those codes."

That was exactly what we were suggesting.

"Any idea of who that might be?" I asked.

Trent glanced around the table, stopping on Liza.

"I have no idea and I'd like to say no one who works for me would do such a thing." He paused for a moment to rub a hand over his bearded chin. "Something else for you to consider. SafeCo makes a great safe but there's a flaw in their design."

"What flaw?" Liza inquired.

"On all digital safes the keypad is removable. Battery replacement, keypad malfunction, code misplacement. Behind the keypad is a keylock. Higher end, more expensive safes that lock would take someone with extensive lock picking skills to break into them. SafeCo safes are fairly easy to pick if you know what you're doing. But the flaw is, that lock has a master key as well. Which in this case, seeing as the safes you're talking about were all different models, meaning each of those models would have different master codes."

"What does that mean?" Phoenix jumped in.

"A six-gun safe has a different master code than a twelve-gun safe and so on. But all SafeCo safes use the same master key for the lock behind the keypad. If someone got their hands on that, they could open any SafeCo safe and not need to bother with the master codes according to the model."

Holy fuck.

That wasn't a fucking flaw; that was grounds for recall.

"Cara told us that any employee can look up the customer information of who purchased any items in your store. Is that correct?" I asked.

Cara had made the introduction then had slipped out. I didn't want to throw the woman under the bus but we needed a better understanding of exactly which employees had what information.

"She's correct. And after she brought this situation to my attention I called a meeting with all three of my GMs to discuss new protocols. Unfortunately, times have changed, this proving we need to limit who has access to what. That meeting is set for this afternoon. If you'd like I can report to you what safety—"

"Your business procedures are not in question," Liza stopped him. "We appreciate your help and discretion. As part of that discretion we ask that you not inform your managers we were here today."

Trent's jaw clenched but without argument he dipped his chin.

"I'll ask Cara to put together a list of current employees and ones who have quit or been let go in the last couple of months. We have a low turnover so that will be short. If you'd like to share with me the names of the victims I will personally pull their receipts and find the employee who helped them, as well as the schedule of who else was working, and the security footage for the day they made their purchase and get that to you."

I waited for Liza to field that as this was now her case and Phoenix and I were there to help her investigation.

"I can get you a warrant by the end of the day," she offered.

Trent waved his hand in front of him as if to swipe her offer off the table.

"I don't need a warrant," Trent denied. "If one of my employees is breaking into homes or assisting someone who is and they're using their access to my customers' information I want the person responsible found. Again, I'd like to believe no one who works for me would do such a thing and this is all a coincidence but I think all of us at this table know it's not. You find the connection between one of my employees and someone who works at SafeCo and you have your person."

"We appreciate your help, Mr. Ackerman." Liza ended the meeting and stood.

Trent pushed his chair back, fished his wallet out of his back pocket, and handed Liza his card.

"Please call me direct if you have more questions."

Liza took the card, then handshakes and goodbyes were exchanged.

The three of us slipped out the back exit and were moving through the parking lot when Liza, who was walking next to Phoenix, snatched the keys out of his hand.

"What—"

"I'm driving," she interrupted. "I almost died four times on the way here and I might've tinkled a little, too."

"Tinkled?" Phoenix grunted.

"Urinated. Wet myself. Pee-peed in my pants," Liza singsonged. "You are literally the worst driver ever. Your license should be suspended indefinitely."

My phone vibrated, giving me the perfect opportunity to remove myself from a conversation that was going to devolve into an argument I wanted no part of.

I swiped the screen to answer Vanessa's call.

"Hey, sweetheart."

"Sullivan bailed," she announced.

Shit.

"Is he okay?"

"Yeah. We talked for about fifteen minutes. He didn't say it ugly but he admitted he was glad Malory backed out because he was thinking about doing the same. I told him we'd drive down to see him tonight and he asked if we'd come Sunday instead. He wants to spend some time with his friends."

Translation: he needed a break.

I didn't blame the guy.

"What'd you tell him about Sunday?"

"That I needed to check with you and I'd text him."

For the second time that morning I wished Vanessa was in front of me so I could kiss the ever-loving fuck out of her.

"Sunday's good with me. And since we're not going down to Jacksonville tonight, are you up to go to Phoenix's tonight?"

Without hesitation she answered, "Sure. I'll ask Wren what I can bring."

Shit.

"Maybe you should hold off on asking until Phoenix has the chance to call her and tell her he's called a family dinner that includes an old friend who's in town."

This time there was hesitation when she quietly asked, "She doesn't know she's having a dinner party?"

"Nope."

"Brave," she muttered.

She wasn't wrong.

Wren was sweet and generally go-with-the-flow but I figured Phoenix could push even the most patient person to their limits.

"You're crazy!" Liza yelled.

"Who's that?"

"The old friend I mentioned."

I turned back toward the car in time to watch Liza make a dash for the car. Phoenix dogging her heels.

"You're not driving," Phoenix denied.

"Um..."

"There was a break in a case we're working on. The feds got called in. Liza's with the ATF and in town taking over our investigation," I explained.

"I didn't think cops liked working with the feds," she noted.

"Did you see that on TV?"

"*CSI Miami,* so it has to be true," she teased.

Phoenix lunged and grabbed the keys from Liza. She opened her mouth, closed it, and opted to cross her arms over her chest and scowl.

"I have to go before I have to arrest a special agent for assault and battery on a police officer."

"That sounds...not good."

"It would be hilarious if we weren't in public."

"You're acting like a child," Liza told Phoenix like she hadn't been the one to instigate the whole situation.

"Is she talking to Phoenix?" Vanessa amusingly breathed.

"Yup. And when you meet her tonight you'll understand why the scene playing out in front of me is straight out of a *SNL* sketch, circa 1990."

I heard Vanessa laugh and I was smiling through it until she said, "I have to admit, Dalton Neary, if I wasn't already falling in love with you, you knowing *SNL* in the 90s had the best sketches would've had me fallin'."

Christ.

"Don't say shit like that when you're not in front of me."

Phoenix, now in possession of the keys, decided to end the standoff and get into the car. Liza glanced over at me, smiled, and called out, "Shotgun."

I was perfectly fine sitting in the back seat as long as I didn't have to sit in her wet spot and I didn't think she was joking about pissing her pants. Phoenix had taken a turn going thirty and I could swear I heard the tires chirp and I smelled rubber burning.

"Why not?" Vanessa asked as I made my way to the car.

"Because when you say shit like that I want to kiss you."

Liza had obviously heard me because she stopped opening the car door and jerked her gaze to mine.

"Now I really have to go, sweetheart. I'll call you after I get a chance to call Brady."

Liza's head tilted to the side and she studied me like I was an unknown, yet-to-be-discovered animal species.

"Okay. Bye."

The moment I pulled my phone away from my ear Liza launched in, "You, too?"

"Yup."

"Well, fuck me running, now I've lost both my wingmen."

Without waiting for me to respond she got into the car and slammed the door. But she did it smiling huge.

21

"GET THIS!" Wren snapped from the doorway to my office.

I knew exactly what I was supposed to get.

We'd had another crazy busy day catching up on all the work we hadn't been able to do yesterday.

So busy none of us had taken lunch.

I was feeling peckish.

Wren sounded hangry.

And by the sound of Caroline's last phone call having to deal with not so happy people who hadn't been able to get their questions answered yesterday she was over peopling for the day.

Good thing it was nearing the end of the day.

The bad news—we were nearing the end of the day and we'd been too busy for lunch so I hadn't had time to talk to Wren or call Dalton back after he texted me he'd spoken to Brady.

Thankfully my friend didn't make me play dumb.

"My husband's lucky he's so hot," she began to rant. "And sweet. And great with Griff. And good at other things or I'd be crazy annoyed right now."

I was fairly certain I knew what 'good at other things' meant if the perpetual smile on her face was anything to go by.

"Impromptu family dinner," I supplied.

Wren waved her hand and shook her head.

"Family's never annoying and Phoenix told me you and Dalton will be there."

I glossed right over me and Dalton being there hoping she wouldn't ask about him and me going to her house for dinner together because that would lead into a lengthy discussion about how that transpired and we didn't have time for that.

"Then why is he lucky he's a hot, sweet, good-at-a-lot-of-things husband?"

"He got Griff a dog. No. He got Griff a puppy."

Aww.

That was sweet.

"I take it he didn't talk to you about it."

"No. He did. I told him I wanted to wait until after Griff was done with the summer basketball league so he'd be home to take care of it. I thought we agreed, then today he texts with this."

Wren walked to my desk holding her phone in my direction so I could see the screen.

And on it was the cutest white fluffy ball with floppy ears. One was grayish, the other had more white than black. And if that wasn't cute enough, around one of its striking blue eyes there were patches of brown and black.

I wanted to dognap that puppy and cuddle it.

"Uh, Wren, honey, you can't be annoyed when that's the cutest puppy I've ever seen."

"That's the annoying part. I love her already and we don't get her for another week."

I could see how that'd be annoying.

"I'm naming her Poppy," she declared.

I pinched my lips thinking Phoenix and Griff might have other ideas.

"I thought it was Griff's puppy?"

Wren shrugged.

"That's the price for springing a puppy on me months earlier than we agreed. Besides, the two of them will try to name her AK-47 or something stupid. She's fluffy and cute, her name's going to be Poppy."

I had a feeling neither of her men were going to like the name Poppy but neither would deny her something she wanted. So the dog's name would be Poppy.

"Cute."

Wren pulled her phone back and changed the subject.

"Since I have seven extra people coming over for dinner tonight I'm dipping out early to hit the grocery store. If you're done for the day I'll walk you out. If not, Caroline's staying late and she can walk you to your car."

Oh, shit.

"Well..."

"No arguing, Vanessa."

Crap.

I no longer needed an escort but she didn't know that. Yesterday it hadn't been a problem because we were leaving at the same time so we walked out together and since Wren had been parked next to me in the parking lot I didn't have to explain she didn't need to get me to my car.

"About that. So, a lot has happened since we had dinner the other night."

"Obviously, you're coming to my house tonight *with* Dalton, and Phoenix let it slip that Dalton has removed his head out of his ass. Those were my husband's words, not mine."

Damn.

"Yes, but that happened last night. Before that we figured

out I don't have a stalker, I have a nephew who was following me while he plucked up the nerve to approach me to tell me that he was my nephew."

Wren's eyebrows hit her forehead.

"It's a long story. One you don't have time to listen to when you have to get to the store. But if you drop it now I promise to come early, help you cook, and do that filling you in."

"Okay...wait...a nephew?"

"Yes. He's eighteen."

"Holy crap. I have so many questions."

So did I. About a million of them. Unfortunately my sister hadn't replied to a single text I'd sent her today and Austin wasn't accepting my calls. That was both annoying and infuriating. I might be hurt my sister had kept something important from me and upset at Austin for not only keeping a secret I personally felt he should've told me but Malory was still my sister. I loved her and was worried about her. At the bare minimum I deserved a reply telling me she was okay.

"I'll tell you everything tonight. But since I don't have a stalker I no longer need an escort."

Thank God for that.

Wren being the great friend she was, didn't push.

"Okay. I'll wait until you come over to tell me but before I leave tell me about Dalton."

That might take longer than the Sully story.

"The last two days have been...taxing." *Understatement.* "Dalton hasn't left my side." *No, that wasn't right.* "Actually, he's been holding me together. Then last night after shit hit the fan." *Again, gross underestimation.* "He stayed over, told me he wanted to go back to how things had started. I told him flat out I wasn't up for a sex-only relationship. He told me about Layla and why he'd retreated, then he told me a bunch of other stuff that ended with him promising he'd prove I was the woman he'd been waiting for."

When I was done with my brief but succulent account Wren smiled.

It was totally smug.

"So I was right," she declared. "All he needed was the right woman to come along and he'd fall to his knees."

"You were right," I confirmed. "But I'm scared as hell."

"I'd ask you to repeat that since I love being right but I won't rub it in," she ungraciously granted. "Falling in love is scary. But it's also thrilling and fun and frustratingly exciting. And the end of that fall is so beautiful you'll look back and think to yourself you'd do it again and again, even the frustrating parts because you'll know it was all worth it."

I hoped she was right about that, too.

And she'd know since she and Phoenix had started off rocky. But for them the fall was just the beginning. Now they shared a beautiful life that was busy and chaotic and I knew because Wren said so often, she loved every minute of it. Phoenix had made all of those early frustrations worth it. Not only for her but for her boy, too.

"I want what you have," I admitted. "I want to pretend to be annoyed because Dalton did something sweet and have my face go soft when I complain to my friends about it. I want—"

"My face does what?" she interrupted.

"Every time you talk about him, especially when you're faking you're mad at him, your face changes. You get this look that radiates love."

"I love that you think that," she whispered. "I love that you get I'm just playing around when I tell you I'm annoyed when I'm really not. But just so you know, Vanessa, that's what you look like when you talk about Dalton and that started from the moment you told me about the hot guy you saw in the coffee shop. That's why I didn't want you to give up when I knew Dalton was going to pull away. Be smart, and by that I mean trust Dalton to protect your heart. Phoenix says the man is g... o...n...e... gone for you. Totally and completely head over heels. You're the game changer. You're the one. He was holding out because he hadn't met you."

I want the chance to prove you're the one I've been waiting for.

We'd shaken on it so there was no going back now.

"I fell in love with him over a weekend of sex. What's that say about me?"

"It says you're a smart, decisive woman who found what she'd been looking for and is smart enough not to waste time pretending she doesn't feel what she feels. The alternative to that would be who gives a fuck what it says about you. Like Adele says, you're a grown woman and you do what you want to do."

My lips twitched.

"This is a great song."

"It's a *legendary* song," she rightly corrected. "Now I'm going to the store then going home to make sure my son unloaded the dishwasher like I asked him to do last night but he didn't do. After I clean up the mess my head's gonna make when it explodes all over the place because I know the dishwasher will be full when I get home, I'm going to marinate the steaks we're having and settle in and wait for you to come over. In other words, hurry your ass over to my house."

"I'm almost done here."

Wren glanced at my still open laptop.

As my friend who wanted the details of my drama-filled week—and not because she wanted gossip but because Wren was the type of friend who wanted to make sure I was okay and if I wasn't she'd exhaust herself to help me get there.

As my boss who needed me to complete my latest assignment she needed me to stay and work.

So I helped her out by telling her, "I have two more emails to send then I'm done for the day. The last I talked to Dalton he said he'd be done with work at five. If he runs late I'll meet him at your house."

"Perfect. Dinner's at seven."

"What can I bring?" I asked as she made her way to the door.

"Nothing."

Normally I would weasel my way into bringing something but seeing as at that moment my life was all out of sorts I was giving myself a pass and going to their house empty-handed.

Well, not empty-handed...

I'd have Dalton's hand to hold and that would make my friend ridiculously happy.

Life hack: surround yourself with women who only want to see you happy and will lift you up and cheer you on like it's their job.

22

"...AND THAT'S EVERYTHING," I finished with a flourish and dropped my hand.

I was leaning my tush against one of Wren's kitchen cabinets, a glass of iced tea in one hand. I'd been using the other to gesture in the air while I'd told her the whole story of Sullivan and Malory and it was now resting at my side.

Phoenix, Dalton, and Griff were outside doing something in the backyard—which I couldn't see even though Wren had a huge window in front of her sink.

And Wren, she'd stopped slicing potatoes somewhere between Sully knocking on my front door and me explaining why I'd taken the DNA test. She'd been taking sips of her wine as she listened. That glass was now empty. She was also staring at it. And I didn't know what to make of her silence.

"So, what do you think?" I prompted.

Her head came up and she blinked.

"What do I think?"

"Yeah."

"I think my heart is shattered for your sister and her son."

Mine was, too. Which made me being angry with her all

that more painful. But I was human and couldn't help how I felt. And yes, part of that was me being selfish.

"Honey, I can hear you're mad—"

"Mad? That doesn't begin to touch how I feel."

"Do you want a glass of wine?"

I wanted a bottle of bourbon, which was why I wasn't going to drink.

"No."

"Do you want to go sit on the couch?"

"No. I want you to tell me I'm a selfish cow and I have no right to be furious about a situation that's not mine to be mad about."

Wren jerked her shoulders back and scowled.

"Why does that make you selfish?"

"Sullivan's not mine. He's Malory's. It happened to her, not me. Yet I'm so freaking pissed she didn't tell me but I don't have the right to be mad at her. It was her secret to keep, it was her trauma; she had to go through her pregnancy and giving him up on her own."

"Right. You're mad she went through all of that alone. Vanessa, she's your sister, you love her. Of course you're going to be upset you weren't able to be there for her when she needed you. But that's how she needed to do it. For whatever reason— right or wrong—she kept her secrets."

"But—"

"You're right, it happened to her. Sullivan was her secret to keep. Austin was right to not break his wife's confidence and tell you even when he knew you were in pain. Sucks, sister, but it's true. Austin's loyalty is with Malory as it should be. Him coming to your house first thing in the morning acting like a dick was out of line but only the last part when he threatened to take your sister from your life. The rest—his wife's pain has surfaced in a very real way. I'd bet in her mind she's back eighteen years ago being faced with a choice that had to be agonizing. Austin's going to react to that pain. If that was Phoenix and he'd left me in bed after what I'm sure was a horrible night I could see him doing the same thing, only a whole lot louder and meaner. You need to cut Austin some slack and move past it. Malory needs time and space to gather her thoughts. She loves you, she'll call you when she's ready. The rest, how you're feeling about all of it, those are *your* feelings. You have the right to feel what you feel."

"She had to be so scared," I whispered.

"I agree."

"That's the part I can't stop thinking about. My big sister scared and alone. The thought makes me physically violent. I want to beat Simon Rodman to death with his fucking gavel."

Wren's gaze skidded to the slider that went to her backyard.

"Maybe don't say that in front of Phoenix and Dalton or Shiloh when she gets here. I've heard cops frown on premeditated murder," she joked to take some of the heavy out of our conversation.

"I hate him, Wren."

"I know you do, honey. I hate him, too."

Life hack number two: find a friend who will hate your enemy just as fiercely as you do.

"Tell me about Sullivan," she urged.

I couldn't stop my smile.

Sullivan was the only good thing that had come out of this whole fiasco.

"He's sweet. He loves his parents. He was an excellent student. He's going to college in the fall. He's handsome, thoughtful, and I'm going to miss him when he leaves to go back to California."

I'd decided not to think about the part where I might lose

him altogether if he didn't want to carry on a friendship with me.

"He has a family and I'm so happy he loves them and they're good parents. I don't want to intrude on that ever. I was okay being his friend but last night he called me Aunt Vanessa and it hit me—I am his aunt, but still I'm not."

"I'm sorry, Nessa."

So was I.

I was sorry for a young man who was juggling some heavy stuff without the guidance of his parents.

Shit.

More secrets.

More lies.

Now I was part of keeping secrets that shouldn't be kept.

"I need to talk to him and implore him to tell his parents he found us," I murmured.

"I think you do."

"He loves them."

"So you've said."

"He's afraid of hurting them. But if he doesn't tell them and they find out it'll hurt them more."

If Sully didn't come clean his mom and dad would be where I was, hurt they could help him at a time in his life that was confusing and, on some level, scary. I didn't want that for them, especially not after they'd opened their hearts and lives up to the baby my sister couldn't keep. My family owed them everything.

"You love him."

It was crazy how Sullivan had entered my life only days ago but I absolutely loved him.

The kid wasn't mine and I adored him.

It was nearly instantaneous.

Malory had grown that child in her womb.

Given birth to him.

Loved him before she'd heard his first cry.

The reality of that slammed into me, making me dizzy with guilt.

She'd walked into my house to find the son she hadn't seen in almost nineteen years and I was mad about a damn secret.

Good Lord, I was a shit sister.

No, scratch that, I was a shit human being.

"Vanessa?" I heard Wren call.

"I love him," I confirmed.

"Where'd you just go?"

Where I should've gone when I witnessed my sister looking into her boy's eyes again.

"To the place I should've been all along. Where I thought I was but clearly wasn't."

"Where's that, honey?"

"At my sister's side."

Wren gave me a sad smile and nodded.

"And Sullivan's, too."

The doorbell rang.

Being the friend Wren was, she immediately offered, "If you need me to take whoever that is into the backyard to give you time, say the word."

God, I loved Wren with my whole heart.

"I'm good."

"You sure?"

See?

Wren was the best.

"Positive."

She pushed away from the counter, made her way around the island, paused long enough to grab my hand, and gave it a squeeze.

After that, pandemonium ensued.

Echo and Jackie were first to show. Then Shiloh and her husband Luke. And lastly Phoenix walked into the living room with the ATF agent Liza Monroe after he answered the doorbell when she'd rang.

Dalton had his arm around me talking to Echo when it happened.

I turned my gaze in the direction of the newcomer and blinked, then blinked again to make sure what I was seeing was real.

That was Special Agent Liza Monroe?

The woman who had shouted at Phoenix?

"Ohmigod," I whispered.

Right before I busted out laughing in a fit of uncontrollable hysterics.

All eyes came to me.

"Don't...don't..." I waved my hand in front of me. "Don't mind me."

"Why are you laughing?" Wren asked through her own laughter.

Life hack three: find friends who laugh with you even when they don't know why you're laughing.

"That's Liza."

Since everyone was already staring at me, I saw Wren's eyes get big.

"You know you're my bestie." Obviously I was talking to Wren. "But I think I'm gonna marry Liza."

"Come again?" Dalton asked from my side.

"I'm gonna marry her," I announced again. "Look at her. She looks like a fairy. She barely comes up to Phoenix's nipple and earlier she was shouting at him. Clearly she's rad and since I already have a bestie I've decided Liza needs to be my wife."

Liza smiled at me.

"Vanessa's going through a hard time right now." Wren

made an excuse for my odd behavior. "What she means to say is, hello, Liza, nice to meet you."

My gaze swung to Wren who was walking toward Liza with her hand out.

"Um. No, I meant what I said. You didn't hear it, Wren. Other than you and Sunny no one would be brave enough to raise their voice to Phoenix. But Sunny's his sister and you're his wife so you two don't count."

"Why'd you make her yell at you?" Wren looked up at her husband, but not nearly as far as Liza would.

"Me? Why would it be my fault she...wait, is this a woman thing?"

"Yes." All five of us women in the room answered in unison.

"I'm outta here," Griff mumbled.

"Oh, no, son," Phoenix denied. "You stay and learn how men deal with a hostile group of females."

I felt Dalton's body start shaking. I tipped my head at him to see him smiling.

"This should be good," he muttered under his breath.

"Pray tell what it is you're going to teach our boy," Wren snapped.

"Yes, baby."

When he didn't go on Wren prompted, "Well?"

"Yes, baby. That's the correct answer to *everything*."

The men chuckled.

I was taking that as their agreement.

"Or you could get driving lessons and people would stop bitching about your driving," Shiloh supplied.

"What's wrong with the way he drives?" Griff asked.

"Everything." That was Sunny.

"Death defying." That was Dalton.

"He rolls stop signs and thinks yellow is a suggestion." That was Echo.

"He doesn't know how to brake." That was Liza.

Wren sweetly smiled at her husband.

"Told you it wasn't just me."

"Yes, baby," Phoenix said through gritted teeth.

I glanced around at all the smiling people in Wren's living room.

They were new-to-me friends—save Liza. Yet, they'd welcomed me into their circle from the moment Wren had introduced me.

I leaned into Dalton and let that warmth envelop me.

Wren was right. I was going through some hard stuff. But I knew the man who held me in the curve of his arm would keep me upright. I also needed Wren. Phoenix and Brady had stepped up and helped in their own ways.

I let that settle, too.

Final life hack: find your people.

"VANESSA," Dalton wrenched his mouth from mine and growled.

I shifted my leg higher and cupped his erection over his shorts.

It was after dinner. After we'd sat around Wren and Phoenix's table and laughed ourselves sick. Okay, that was the women, Echo, and Luke who had laughed. Dalton and Phoenix mostly frowned as Liza dazzled us with stories about the two of them. By the time we'd said our goodnight I liked Liza more than I liked her when she'd first walked in. The woman was a spitfire. She was hilarious and I got the sense she didn't put up with anyone's shit. She reminded me a lot of Shiloh. A woman in a male-dominated field who had the grit and determination to earn, then demand, the respect of the men she worked with.

And I could tell Dalton and Phoenix respected her. Even though she was telling embarrassing stories about them, they were told with deep regard.

Dinner went great. The company was better.

As it turned out it was just what I needed—a night off from anything remotely heavy. Which meant it was likely Sullivan had needed that, too. So I only texted him once to tell him I was there for him in whatever form he needed me to be, including backing off completely if that was what he wanted. He texted back immediately and I learned something new about my nephew. He wasn't only smart, but he was emotionally intelligent and mature for his age.

This was his text: *I'm thinking things through. Thank you for giving me the space to do so. See you Sunday.*

I then texted Malory to tell her I love her and no matter what, I would have her back. Austin's, too, and I would wait for her to message me back. Unsurprisingly, I didn't get a response.

But since I was surrounded by laughter and good people I let her silence roll off of me and took hold of the boon that was being offered.

Now after a great night, I was in bed in nothing but a tee and pair of panties making out with Dalton.

Yet, he wasn't moving the festivities along as fast as I'd like.

"Baby," he groaned when I started sliding my hand up and down.

My movements had the unfortunate effect of Dalton moving his hand from my ass, a place where I liked it to be since he'd slid his hand under my panties and was cupping a bare cheek. I also liked it there because all it would take was a scant bit of adjusting and he could dip his long, thick fingers and they would hit where I needed.

But he was now moving in the wrong direction and I thought he should know.

"Wrong way, Detective," I grumbled when he pulled his hand out of my undies.

Those long, thick fingers circled my wrist and halted my fun.

"We're taking this slow," he horrifyingly returned.

I was ready *now*.

"Slow?"

"Slow," he confirmed and that confirmation was firm.

Like his swollen dick still under the palm of my hand.

"How slow?"

"Slow-slow."

It was dark in my room; he'd turned off the lights before he'd come to bed. That meant not only could I not see his expression but I'd been denied the pleasure of watching him undress.

I thought this was selfish on his part, however when he'd climbed in, claimed me, then commenced making out with me I quickly got over my dismay. This was only because I got to explore his warm, taut skin with my hands while his tongue was in my mouth.

"I don't know what that means."

"It means we're taking our time."

I wasn't sure how long we'd been in bed kissing and touching but I figured it'd been awhile and if not *awhile* it had definitely been long enough to get to some heavy groping.

Dalton pulled my hand away from his crotch, brought it up to his mouth—my hand that was, not his dick, that would be weird—and kissed my palm. That wasn't weird, that was sweet.

"I like the feel of you," he whispered.

That was even sweeter.

"I like kissing you. I like sleeping next to you. I like it better when you sleep in my arms. That's what we're doing. That's why we're taking it slow."

I seriously loved all of that. It made me warm and fuzzy inside.

But...was he serious?

"So no sex?"

"No sex."

"No handjobs?"

"No handjobs."

What!

"No sixty-nine?"

"No sixty-nine," he grunted like his denial was painful.

Hmm.

"So kissing, cuddling, and sleeping?"

"Yes."

"Now you're just being cruel," I complained. "You said you wanted to go back to what we had."

Dalton kissed my hand again before he placed it on his chest. I felt his hand travel up my arm, over my shoulder, and slide into my hair.

"We had more than sex," he told me and his fingers started drifting through my hair soothingly. "We had this. The closeness."

There was nothing to say to that because of course he was right. Likewise as sexually frustrating as it was lying in bed next to Dalton I loved he wanted more than the sexual part of what we'd shared over the weekend.

I cuddled in closer and savored the feel of him next to me.

"Night, sweetness."

"Night."

Dalton kissed the top of my head while I laid there thinking about which endearment I liked best: sweetheart, baby, or sweetness.

So in the quiet dark I thought of another life hack, one that had never been on my radar because I'd never had the opportunity to contemplate such a thing.

Incidentally, in case you were wondering, my favorites were ranked in order of occasion. Sweetheart, for everyday use. Sweetness, when he was being sweet and gentle. Baby, when it was growly and rough.

23

"SWEETHEART?"

"Hmm?" Vanessa hummed but didn't take her attention off my hands moving at my throat adjusting my tie.

"Are you gonna stand there and watch me tie my tie or are you going to grab your purse so we can leave?"

She was there picking me up for her parents' anniversary party. Correction, she was at my condo because I'd been called into work to meet with Liza and Phoenix. This took longer than anticipated so Vanessa was leaving her car here and I was driving us to the party.

"Is it weird I think you tying your tie is sexy?"

I didn't bother containing my smirk.

"No weirder than me fighting the urge to bend you over and fuck you in that dress."

That earned me a scowl.

"You play dirty, Dalton."

I finished with my tie, stepped into her space, and hooked her around the middle.

"Damn right I do."

"I want it noted this is cruel and unusual punishment for a crime I didn't commit."

She wasn't wrong. Two nights making out with her, stopping the proceedings far earlier than either of us wanted, was an exercise in self-control.

Torture.

Necessary, but nonetheless fucking torture.

"Sweetheart, you walked in here and threw down. So I got no choice but to play dirty."

"How'd I throw down?" She feigned innocence.

"Baby, the dress?"

Her lips twitched.

Yeah, she knew exactly what she was doing wearing that damn dress. Lots of cleavage but to class it up, making it suitable for a fortieth anniversary party, it was floor length. But when she moved just right there was a hidden slit. Later tonight I would find out just how high that slit went.

"And the shoes?"

She outright smiled.

I didn't need the red of her stilettos to poke out from the fabric as she walked to know she was wearing heels. Normally she had to tilt her head back and stand on her tiptoes to kiss me. Tonight we were damn near eye to eye.

The woman hadn't just thrown down, she'd instigated a challenge.

One I'd happily accept and best her at.

"When we get home I'm eating your pussy with you in that dress."

The smile remained but her eyes went hooded.

"And the shoes stay on when I bend you over and fuck you."

Vanessa swayed closer.

"But before I do that I want to see you on your knees in your sexy dress, those beautiful lips of yours wrapped around my dick as I fuck your throat."

"Honey—"

Her groan was cut off by a maniacal pounding on my door.

My blood ran cold.

No.

Fuck no.

Not now.

"Who in the world—"

"Sweetheart, go up to my room. Stay up there until—"

The front door banged open and in stumbled Layla.

"Oopies," she slurred.

Fucking hell.

I felt Vanessa stiffen.

Layla regained her balance and did her best to smile—it was sloppy, unattractive, and never failed to fill my veins with acid.

"Heya, Dalton."

Fuck.

Before I could say anything like get the fuck out of my house Layla caught sight of Vanessa.

"Who's she?"

"Baby, get your purse and nab my keys and wallet off the counter."

Vanessa stared at me for a moment. Unfortunately, this gave Layla's wine-drenched mind the opportunity to process what I'd said.

"*Baby*?" Layla scoffed.

I knew that tone.

It was the one she used every time she didn't get her way when she came here looking to play out this fucked scene. When her life had gone to shit for whatever reason it went to shit and she'd come by to remind me I'd ruined her life. It normally took until around the time I told her she wasn't staying with me before she turned up the bitch. She'd never seen a woman in my house or heard me call one baby so it stood to reason she'd skip the part where she cried and carried on about me divorcing her.

Same shit.

Over and over.

"Quiet," I barked. "Not another fucking word."

"What's she doing here?"

"We're not having this conversation when you're drunk, Layla. Or say, ever. We're *never* having this conversation."

"I'm your wife." The words were somewhat garbled but mostly angry. "I need a place to stay."

Saliva filled my mouth.

"Have you lost your mind?" I asked through clenched teeth, not actually needing an answer.

"Nice," she hissed and did her best to glare at me.

It was a Saturday going on five o'clock and she was already smashed.

"How'd you get here?"

"Are you going to arrest me, officer?" she spat.

I didn't bother answering my ex-wife, instead I turned to Vanessa.

The differences between the women couldn't have been more obvious.

They were worlds apart.

Vanessa is not Layla.

In the last week she'd been faced with some heavy shit. A young man walked into her life, turned it upside down, and she welcomed him into her heart. Her sister was falling apart. Her brother-in-law had been a dick to her.

Life had kicked her in the gut.

Yet she'd stood strong.

Layla had breezed through life.

Yet she'd crumbled.

And when I tried to help her pick up the pieces I became the enemy.

Layla drunkenly lurched forward, stumbled a few steps, and Vanessa jolted like she was going to jump and catch Layla if she should fall.

"Maybe she should sit down," Vanessa whispered.

Christ.

I clenched my jaw and took in my ex-wife teetering on her high-heeled boots—a testament to how drunk she was. The woman could likely run a 5K in a pair of four-inch slingbacks.

"She's not staying long enough to sit. Neither are we. Grab our stuff, sweetness, we're already running late."

"C'mon, Top," Layla cooed, losing the venom. "We need to talk."

This, too, was familiar.

The anger that was sparking flared.

"Here's what's going to happen, Layla. I'm walking out that door and when I do I'm calling dispatch. When a unit arrives, if you're still in my house you'll be arrested. If you're in your car, you'll be arrested. My advice—leave and do it with your phone out calling a taxi. More advice—when you come back to get your car do not knock on my door. If you do, I'm calling in and making a complaint."

"Top—"

"Don't fucking call me that!" I thundered. "Whatever bull-shit you have going on in your life is not my problem. It hasn't been for over a fucking decade. I keep telling you, Layla, you need to pull your shit together. For you, for your parents, for your brother, and lastly for your fucking husband. What I do not need or want or will allow is for you to bring this shit to my doorstep."

"But, Dalton—"

"He asked you to leave," Vanessa cut in bitingly.

Layla's gaze swung to Vanessa with a level of lucidity I hadn't seen in years, seeing as the only time I'd clapped eyes on my ex was when she came around banging on my door blitzed.

"I'm not speaking to you," she spat.

"You are now," Vanessa volleyed. "And Dalton asked you to leave. Not only that, he was clear with what was going to happen if you didn't."

"You don't know—"

"I know you're the woman who is right now drunk and standing in my man's living room after you barged in here."

Vanessa's verbal blow bounced around my living room missing its intended mark, but it hit me square in the chest.

"Your man?" Layla's attempt at a smirk failed horrendously. "He's mine."

Jesus fuck.

Time to shut this shit down.

Fortunately Vanessa did it for me and she did it in a way Layla's alcohol-drenched brain couldn't miss. Without a word she walked to the table, nabbed her purse, my wallet and keys, then came back to me, grabbed my hand, and walked me through the living room while keeping herself between me and Layla.

When we were at the door she craned her neck and made her point verbally.

"Next time you think to come back here and treat Dalton to this shit you should think long and hard because it'll be me you'll deal with."

"This shit? He ruined my life!" Layla screeched.

"No, Layla, you ruined your own damn life and while you were doing that you had a husband who loved you and tried to get you help. You ruined that, too, and threw him away. Now he's mine, and, sister, you need to hear this so pay attention, I will protect what's mine and to do that I've got no issue getting down in the mud with you. But you will never get past that door again."

Vanessa gave my hand a squeeze and asked, "Are we just leaving her in there with the door open?"

With my attention still firmly on my ex, conflicting emotions violently clashing in my chest, I did the only thing I could do—I nodded.

It took until we were at my truck for my lungs to fully fill with oxygen.

"Honey—"

I hooked Vanessa around the back of the neck, pulled her to me, but stopped before my lips hit hers.

"Thank you, baby," I muttered close to her mouth.

"For what?" I heard her ask but more than that I felt her arms go around me.

"For being you."

She was smiling when I kissed her.

That meant she neutralized the acid that had been churning in my gut.

A visit from Layla never failed to send me on a dark and twisted walk down memory lane.

Tonight was no different, but the memories were. Instead of reminiscing about drunken arguments and me begging my wife to get help.

My mind was filled with Vanessa.

24

DALTON HAD BEEN quiet the whole drive to the restaurant. That was, he'd been silent after he made a call to dispatch to report his drunk ex-wife was still in his living room and he asked the woman he called Molly to tell whoever went out there to lock his front door on their way out.

I understood his silence.

I wanted him to have what he needed even though I had about a bazillion questions about what had happened. I could deduce from what little conversation there was that was not the first time Layla had shown up at his house in that state.

The cruelty of that was inconceivable.

It also explained a lot.

Dalton might've been divorced for a long time but it would seem Layla kept dragging him back to the past.

I wanted him to have what he needed but we would be at the restaurant soon and I needed to know where his head was at.

"Before we get to Capone's..." I paused when his hand resting on my thigh squeezed.

Just because Dalton had spent the ride quiet didn't mean he

hadn't slid right back to being his normal affectionate self. Something I was beginning to learn; if I was within reach he was touching me—holding my hand, putting his arm around me, resting his hand on my leg.

"I was angry as fuck," he calmly said.

"Was? But you're not anymore?"

"No, now I'm just angry."

I wasn't sure I understood the difference but luckily Dalton continued.

Unluckily, what he had to say hurt my heart.

"About a week after we signed the divorce papers she called and said she wanted to talk. I blew her off. She waited a month, made another approach, told me she was learning about herself and wanted to share a few things. I agreed and stupidly met with her at my apartment. She was sober, but what she wanted to share was how happy she was without me, how much better off she was without me nagging her and bringing negativity into her life."

"I'm sorry, what?" I stopped him to ask.

A ghost of a smile pulled at his lips as he turned his hand over on my thigh. I glanced down at it and put mine on top of his, and when I did, his fingers threaded between mine.

"That's what she said."

"So she called you twice, made you believe she had something...I don't know...productive to tell you then perpetrated a sneak attack and was a bitch."

"Yup."

"What did you say?"

I hoped he told her to go fuck herself.

"Told her I was happy for her then showed her the door."

I had a bad feeling the story didn't end there.

"The next time she came around she'd just been fired. We argued, or more to the point she yelled, I listened, then I showed her the door. Finally I had to move. It was a glorious, peaceful year. Unfortunately, a friend of hers moved into the complex and she found me. She didn't delay resuming her visits."

Wait.

"You had to move."

"Yup. She didn't come around all the time, but anytime something went wrong in her life she was at my door screaming at me. Problems at work, her parents giving her a hard time about her drinking, a man dumping her, she missed a sale at Pottery Barn, didn't matter what it was, it was my fault. I ruined her life and she never misses an opportunity to swing by my place to tell me what an asshole I am. Tonight she was off her game. She hadn't gotten to the good stuff yet."

"You mentioned a husband," I gently asked.

"She's married. Has been for about three years. Don't know if her man knows she comes by my place and bitches about the state of their marriage but that's my fault, too. All their problems are because of me."

I bet they were.

"She's still in love with you."

"Baby—"

"She is," I insisted. "A woman doesn't stalk her ex-husband for over ten years if she's over him. And a woman doesn't seek out the man who ruined her life, she moves on and rejoices that man is out of her life. I'm not saying how she loves you is healthy but she does."

When Dalton didn't answer right away I glanced up from my study of our hands to see his jaw tight and his expression troubled.

"I thought losing me would be her rock bottom. That our divorce would be her wakeup call and she'd admit she had a problem and she'd get help."

"Honey."

"I wanted that for her. Not for me. By that time the girl I fell in love with was lost to me. But I wanted that for her, for her family. Obviously I viewed the deterioration of our marriage differently than she did."

Dalton's issues with commitment and relationship came into blinding focus.

"It's beautiful how much you loved her."

Dalton's fingers, which were threaded between mine, twitched. His gaze slid to mine for a moment before his attention went back to the road.

"Vanessa—"

I interrupted what I was sure was going to be his assurance he no longer loved her.

I didn't need him to tell me something I already knew.

"It is, Dalton. It's beautiful knowing you have that in you to give. How things ended and why, doesn't take away that beauty. You didn't ruin her life, honey; she did all that on her own by losing you. And my guess is when she's sober it eats at her. I can see how after all this time she's still not over losing you. I know I wouldn't be. My second guess is the man she married and what he gives her doesn't compare to the love you gave her and that eats at her, too. But her sickness doesn't allow her to admit she's where she is in her life because of her actions. So she goes to you, the man who she's loved since she was a teenager because you're her safe place. Layla hasn't hit rock bottom yet because she still has access to you. And I don't mean this ugly but tonight was the beginning of her wakeup call. Her rock bottom is closer than she realizes because tonight was the last time she barges into your house and forces you to participate in whatever sick game she's playing."

I hadn't noticed until I was done speaking how tightly he was holding my hand.

"Baby."

How he made one word sound so tortured I wasn't sure but I didn't like it.

"That's over for you."

The air in the cab went heavy; not exactly what I wanted for him after what Layla had done and with us almost at the restaurant where he'd meet my parents for the first time. Not to mention, Simon and his family would be there and I needed him to keep me on a very short leash so I didn't stab the asshole in the throat with a steak knife. Thankfully Capone's was an Italian restaurant and pasta was the main course so my access to knives would be limited.

"What do you need from me to help wash away Layla's visit?"

"Nothing."

"Dalton—"

"Nothing," he repeated and brought my hand to his mouth and kissed my knuckles. "You already washed it away. You did that back at my condo when you took my back then ushered me out using your body as a shield so she couldn't get to me. That's done. Totally and completely done and you made that so."

"Then why are you still angry?"

He pulled into the parking lot of the restaurant and maneuvered his bigass truck to the back where he'd have room to park his beast. This apparently took a lot of concentration because he didn't answer me until he pulled into a spot and put his truck into park.

Or maybe it was because he wanted all of my attention, which he got when he unbuckled his belt and shifted so his right elbow was resting on the center console.

Right then I wished truck manufacturers still made bench seats. Whoever thought it was a good idea to do away with the bench and add a huge junk compartment between the driver and the passenger was dumb. Kids across the world would never experience what it was like to fog up the windows while engaging in an epic make-out session parked on a country back road. Contrary to that, I was sure millions of parents were thrilled their children would not be partaking in a bench-seat make-out session that oftentimes included heavy petting and blow jobs.

"What are you glaring at?" Dalton inquired.

"I can't give you road head with that huge center divider."

"Come again?"

My eyes snapped to his smile.

God, he had a beautiful smile.

"You need to buy a truck with a bench seat so we can make out in it."

"Sweetheart, you got a bed and so do I and we both got couches. The kind of making out I want to do with you we should be using one of those, not court getting arrested on the side of the road while I got my tongue in your mouth and fingers in your pussy. Not to mention when I've got your lips wrapped around my dick I like to watch and I can't do that and drive at the same time."

I loved that he liked to watch me giving him pleasure.

"Fine." I gave in with an ungracious huff.

"That right there," he weirdly said. "That's you washing more of her away."

My breath caught and before I could get it back he continued, "I was angry as fuck my ex interrupted when I was otherwise happily engaged laying out this evening's plans. I was angry she was there to shovel her shit at me but you being there meant I was powerless to protect you from her bullshit. I'm not a man who likes to feel powerless—period. But especially not when my woman is going through some serious family issues and she's worried, stressed, and has only had one day in the last five to herself without someone intruding, laying their shit on her. I became less angry when you laid her out. So now I'm pissed, but I'm only pissed because instead of me making sure you're good to go in there and face your family we're sitting out here so you can ascertain where I'm at."

I already knew I'd made the right decision but right then, I knew without a shadow of a doubt giving Dalton a chance to prove he was exactly who I thought he was, was the only decision.

"I'm fine to go in there and face my parents."

He didn't look convinced.

"Honestly, Dalton, I'm fine. I know you'll be with me and I really love my parents. They're good people."

"I'm not worried about your parents. I'm worried about Simon and his family."

It probably made me a horrible person to wish ill on someone but I hoped Simon's car broke down on the way here and he was stranded on the side of the road for the next three hours.

"I promise not to kill him at my parents' anniversary party with ten other people in attendance," I vowed.

"That'd be appreciated."

By the look on Dalton's face he meant that.

"I'm kidding," I assured him. "Besides, we have plans tonight when we get home."

"Yeah, we do."

THE STAFF at Capone's had gone above and beyond decorating the private dining room.

The four vases of pale pink and white daisies looked beautiful sitting on the long table. More clusters of white daisies were artfully placed on what would become the buffet table. And pink daisies decorated the four hightop cocktail tables.

My parents looked blissfully happy working the room chatting with their friends. They'd met Dalton; both had instantly liked him. My mom had done a top-to-toe once-over and smiled. I couldn't blame her. Dalton looked f...i...n...e...*fine* in his suit. But that wasn't why my mom liked Dalton. No, it was her romantic heart, it was her belief in soulmates, it was her taking in a tall, handsome, police officer holding her daughter in the curve of his arm and making it known he belonged to me. My father being the kind of dad who loved his daughter, his first question upon seeing me after he told me how much he and Mom appreciated all my hard work planning the party was to ask if I'd cleaned out my garage yet.

Before last night my answer would've been no, but as soon as Dalton had gotten to my house he'd started working on cleaning while I'd cooked—well, 'cooked' might've been overstating me pulling some meat off a rotisserie chicken I'd picked up from the grocery store and layering it with some tortillas and cheese, and dumping a can of enchilada sauce into a casserole dish and throwing it in the oven.

Once the male bonding had commenced over Dalton cleaning out my garage so I could now park inside, it had turned to finances—because why wouldn't it, seeing as my father was a financial advisor? He was pleased to find out Dalton supplemented his pension with investments. This was when I tuned the rest of the conversation out. I'd learned from a young age as soon as the letters S and P were followed by the number five hundred that was my cue to find something else to do.

Which was what I did.

Mom and I had stepped away so the men could talk about boring things and my mother could fill me in on celebrity gossip which I found only a fraction more interesting than the stock market. But it was my mom's party and I was willing to do anything to keep her happy knowing her oldest daughter wasn't going to show.

An interesting side note: for the first thirty minutes we were there making sure everything had been set up, Malory wasn't mentioned.

I certainly wasn't going to bring her up but I'd thought my mom would at least tell me how sad she was that Malory wasn't going to be able to make it due to whatever fictitious illness she and Austin came up with.

So when Malory showed up right on time with a very unhappy Austin beside her I was shocked. Dalton politely ended his conversation with my father and claimed me.

Dalton and Austin had masterfully arranged my sister and me to be seated at the farthest end of the table away from Simon, Tracy, and their son James. Unfortunately it had been the polite son, Connor, who'd moved to Atlanta years ago who didn't show and not the asshole, James, who still kissed daddy's ass and was a whiny momma's boy.

We'd made it through cocktail hour and dinner. With dessert being set out, I was beginning to think we were going to get through the night without having to speak to Simon.

That was if my sister kept her cool.

Dalton leaned closer to whisper, "Sweetheart, you need to talk to her."

I glanced from my smiling parents to find Malory shooting daggers at Simon who was speaking to a man who worked with my father.

"Mal?" I quietly called.

Slowly. Agonizingly slowly she pulled her gaze from Simon to look at me.

Dinner conversation had been unbearably awkward. None of us brought up Sullivan or the huge fucking elephant that was sitting on my chest. Austin was unusually quiet. My sister jittery. Dalton did what he could to put them at ease but gave up when it was clear neither were interested in doing their part so his attention had shifted fully to me. Other than wanting to stand on my chair, clink my water glass to get the room's attention so I could out Simon as the motherfucker I thought he was, I'd been surprisingly calm.

"You're doing great," I told her.

"I hate him," she spat.

The emotion behind that statement and the fury I heard in her tone shocked me. I hadn't heard that firm, self-assured, resolve in her voice in years. Not since she was sent away.

I wasn't sure if I was elated or worried.

I thought it went without saying that I hated him, too, so I didn't bother agreeing with her.

"If this is too much for you, honey, you don't have to stay."

"I'm not bailing on you."

Dalton's thumb started to make slow, gentle circles on my leg, meaning he'd heard Malory.

"Mal—"

"It's time."

Oh, no!

"What's time?" I cautiously asked, hoping she wasn't about to stand on her chair, clink her glass, and blow up Simon's life.

I mean, part of me wanted her to stand up and take back her power. But until Dalton had all the information he needed from Brady I didn't think that was a good idea and Brady was still trying to dig up dirt we could use just in case Simon came after Malory or my dad.

"For me to stop leaning on my baby sister to take care of me."

That made Dalton's fingertips dig into my thigh.

"Mal—"

"You know I'm right."

She wasn't wrong but the timing of her revelation was worrisome.

"What I know is this week has been hard and it's brought up past trauma. I think we should find a time for just the two of us to sit down and talk."

"Austin knew," she started and glanced across the room to her husband talking to my mother and her tennis partner Lori. "He knew about Sullivan before I married him. It was only right. He needed to know why I was the way I was. Why I never wanted to have children. I made him promise to never tell you so you can't be mad at him."

"I'm not mad."

"But now that Sullivan knows, it's time."

I was seriously getting worried she was going to do something.

"Time for what?"

"To own it. To tell the truth. To stop keeping a secret that never should've been kept."

"Mal—"

"Jeez, Nessa, I'm not going to announce at Mom and Dad's anniversary party that Simon is my son's father."

I fought the urge to slap my hand over my sister's mouth and shush her.

"I want to go to Jacksonville with you tomorrow."

It took me a moment to remember in one of the many messages I'd left if I told her Dalton and I were going to Jacksonville to visit Sullivan.

"I know you need to ask Sullivan and if you and Dalton just want it to be you and him, I understand. But I want to see him when he's ready."

"Of course. I'll text him and ask."

Dalton stopped rubbing my leg and stretched his arm around my shoulder.

"Thank you for loving him."

My sister's whispered words floated around me.

Was this it?

Was this how I got my sister back?

Thirty minutes later I would find not only was my bold sister back but she was better than I'd remembered.

It happened when Malory and I were walking out of the bathroom.

Kismet.

Just not the good kind.

But the timing had been such it felt like the universe had stepped in and said, today's the day and bam there was Simon Rodman walking in front of the ladies' room door at the right exact moment Malory had opened it.

Bringing Malory and Simon face-to-face.

I stiffened and froze, wondering if I should yank my sister back into the bathroom and call Dalton to come get us, or shove her out of my way and claw his eyes out.

Malory had no such problem.

"Simon," she clipped.

"Mally, you look beautiful this evening."

Slimy fucker.

"Vanessa, lovely to see you as well. Is that Detective Neary as your date?"

I didn't get the chance to confirm.

"Time's up, Simon."

Oh, shit.

"I'm sorry, I don't understand what that means."

"Yes, you do," she said sweetly. "I told you when the day came and he found me, I'd tell him the truth."

Gone was the good-natured judge Simon pretended to be.

"You'd be wise to hold your tongue."

"He's eighteen, Simon. You can't use your money and power to take him from his family. Though since I've had almost nineteen years to think about it you were full of shit back then. You wouldn't have done a damn thing. Taking him would've meant you'd have to explain to your wife how you'd been carrying on an affair with an underage girl and got her pregnant. You would've had to explain to my father how you were having sex with his daughter. I was young and scared and because of that, stupid. I am no longer any of those things, Simon. Your time's up. You forced me to give my child up for adoption when I wanted to keep him but you will not force me to lie to him."

"You don't want to do that," Simon sneered.

"You don't want to know what happens if you fuck with my boy," she returned.

Someone cleared their throat. Simultaneously we all looked to the end of the short hallway leading out to the main dining room.

James.

Kismet.

"Go back and sit with your mother," Simon demanded.

James glared at his father, then at me, until finally he transferred his scowl to Malory. But it was more than a scowl, it was downright disturbing. My hand found my sister's. I held on tight while James gave her the death glare to end all death glares.

James had yet to decide if he was going to obey his father when Dalton hit our hallway party.

Dalton's scowl was much scarier than James's.

"What's happening?"

Dalton's question was aimed at me.

"Malory had a few things she needed to talk to Simon about," I told him in hopes he'd catch my meaning and end the standoff.

"Right. Conversation's over."

"Let's go, Malory," I muttered.

I gave her hand a tug.

Simon stepped closer.

Two things happened at once.

My sister stood taller and held her ground.

Dalton moved and when he did he stepped in front of my sister.

"Be smart, Detective," Simon sneered.

"That's my line," he returned. "And before you open your mouth and say something you'll regret, I was on a call when I walked back and the line's still open."

I couldn't see what was happening since my sister and Dalton were blocking my view. But I heard footsteps. After that my sister pulled me from the doorway into the hallway.

"I'm sorry—" Malory abruptly stopped and shook her head. "I don't know why I said that. I'm not sorry."

I wanted to do cartwheels, high-five, and dance around the hallway while shouting, 'my sister's back.' I settled on pulling Malory into a hug and holding onto her tighter than I had since we were kids.

"Love you, sissy."

"Love you back, sister."

Oh, yeah, this was the start of Malory Hale Newton coming back into herself.

25

VANESSA on her knees in that dress, with that slit I'd learned went all the way to her hip, in those red heels, my dick sliding in and out of her mouth while the taste of her orgasm was still on my tongue.

All of that, hot.

It became exponentially hotter when she took me to the back of her throat.

"Pop off, baby."

On a slow glide she pulled off.

"Up."

My hands went under her pits and I hauled her to her feet.

Face flushed. Lips puffy. Eyes hooded.

Christ. Beautiful.

"Dress off."

"You're hot when you're naked and bossy."

"Pleased you think so, but you telling me that isn't making that dress come off."

By the time her dress was off I was rolling a condom.

Top to toe, the woman was gorgeous.

I zeroed in on the front clasp of her black lace bra, reached up, and popped the clip and watched her heavy tits spill from their confines. I bent forward, pulled a nipple into my mouth, and drew deep. I moved to the other side, did the same before I stood, grabbed her hips, and turned her to face the bed.

Vanessa wiggled her bra free, tossed it to the side, slowly dragged her lacy black panties down over her thighs until they fell to the floor. She stepped out of them and bent to the bed, head turned eyes on me, her pretty wet pussy on offer.

I stepped closer, glided the head of my dick through her wet, my mind torn. Wanting to fuck her hard and fast but knowing after everything I put her through she deserved something different.

"Dalton, please."

"Nessa, baby—"

"*Please*, fuck me, honey."

I didn't know if it was the extreme need I heard or her sweet demand or both or my need to give her whatever she wanted, in whatever way she wanted it.

The head of my dick caught and I slid home.

Home.

That was what Vanessa was.

Then I was lost to her tight, wet heat pulsing around my cock.

Whatever control I thought I had was an illusion. There was no power exchange when I was inside of her; every inch of me belonged to her.

I watched her lids get heavy, her lips part, then the sweetest sound of all...

"Dalton," she groaned. "More."

My body responded to her plea. Driving my hips forward, I slammed deeper looking down at her round ass, watching my dick dip in and come out wet with her excitement.

"More?" I asked.

"*Yes.*"

One hand left her hip, slid up her back until my fingers curled around her shoulder. My other went between her legs, the tip of my middle finger found her clit, and she jolted.

"You're gonna come—"

"Yes," she groaned before I could get more out.

I tightened my grip on her shoulder, dipped my chin, and watched my girl take my fucking, doing that hard, watching intently, giving her more of my finger at her clit when I felt her pussy clench.

"Oh, God."

The power of my thrusts increased, rocking Vanessa forward, using my hold to pull her back, my dick getting ready to explode as she rippled tight.

"More," she rasped.

Fuck.

I let go of her shoulder, straightened, brought my hand down on her ass.

The crack of my palm meeting the soft flesh of her ass joined the sounds of our bodies connecting.

"Another?"

"*Yes.*"

I added a second handprint before I skimmed my palm over her ass, using my thumb to dip between her cheeks.

Circling her hole I asked, "Does my girl want dirty?"

"Yes."

My thumb slid down between her legs, gathering her wet. Using her excitement I gently pushed my thumb through the ring of tight muscles there.

"One day, I'm gonna take you here, too."

Vanessa's hips bucked.

Her cunt spasmed.

And finally she cried out her orgasm.

Free to take my own, I let go, driving my dick deep, fucking her ass with my thumb, staying at her clit.

Fucking phenomenal.

All of it.

Fuck.

I arched back, planted my dick to the root, and shot long and hard into the condom. The power of my climax ripped through me. My thumb came out of her ass, my hand went back to her hip, needing something to anchor me to her.

When she finally came back into focus those brown eyes were smiling.

I pulled out, helped her stand, but only so I could pick her up and set her on her bed.

"Be back."

I went to the bathroom, disposed of the condom, washed my hands, and did this quickly, not wanting to be away from her for long. When I got back to the bedroom she'd already taken off those sexy-as-fuck shoes and had the bedclothes pulled down. I hit the lights and crawled in next to her.

There was a lot we needed to talk about. She'd been in her head since that scene. She'd given me a brief rundown of what happened in the hallway at the restaurant. But when I'd tried to talk to her when we got back to her house she shut that shit down and told me I'd made promises that she'd expected me to make good on. I gave her that play. Now it sucked but I needed to know where she was at.

"Baby?" I called after she settled in, draping her arm over my chest, and her leg over my thigh.

"Hm."

"You okay?"

"Oh, yeah."

"I took you hard."

"Thank you," she sleepily mumbled and cuddled in closer.

Yep, the woman was phenomenal. She'd taken my fucking, begged for rough, got off with my thumb *in* her ass while my marks were *on* her ass, and she'd thanked me for it.

"Glad you're down with—"

"*Way* down with it," she corrected. "Feel free to do that again."

It was good she thought that, seeing as I'd been sliding into her ass a different way as soon as I was positive she was ready.

I continued gliding up and down her back when I told her, "We need to talk about what happened tonight."

"Ugh," she mumbled against my chest. "Way to harsh my mellow."

I smiled into the dark.

"Sorry, sweetheart."

I felt her inhale before she started.

"I think I have my sister back."

"Yeah?"

"When Simon got her in her face, she didn't back down. Then she called him out. I told you what she said to him. Maybe I should be worried because Simon didn't look happy but I'm proud of her. She needed to do that, so I'm glad she did. But it's James I'm worried about. I don't know how much he heard but I'm thinking all of it or at least most of it, if his bad impression of a villain attempting to cow his opponent with a hard stare is anything to go by."

"Austin's aware," I reminded her.

Which, after seeing the man go from being unhappy he was in a room with the man who'd had a sexual relationship with his then underage wife, and now not having to hide it from Vanessa, so he didn't—straight to furious I was worried he'd do something stupid.

"I missed my sister," she whispered. "I'm not happy about

the circumstances. I know she's hurting, but I'm happy she's coming back to me."

"Did Sully text you back?"

"Yeah, he's coming up here."

Smart play. He could leave if he wanted instead of having to kick people out of his place if it went to shit.

"He was okay meeting with Malory?"

"He said he was. I'm not sure how I feel about Austin not coming."

When we'd returned to the table Malory had told her husband she'd asked Vanessa if she could go with us to meet Sullivan. I couldn't say the man was relieved his wife was ready to face her boy but he was very supportive. He'd also explained he didn't feel it was a good idea for him to meet Sullivan the first time Malory sat down with him but wanted the chance to meet him before he went back to California.

"He's not throwing shade, sweetheart. Sullivan's overwhelmed enough, having Austin there might make Sully uncomfortable. He wants this meet to go well. Not just for Malory but for Sully, as well."

I needed to switch gears and get her back to being relaxed.

"Your parents looked really happy tonight. Great job with the party."

"Yeah. They're doing a big thing for their fiftieth; a two-month trip around the world. They've been saving for eons. They have a lot of friends but only a few they're close with so Malory and I thought we'd do something this year for them so they could celebrate with them. We decided small and intimate with only their inner circle."

Unfortunately that inner circle included a snake.

"This isn't going to end well," she predicted.

She wasn't wrong. I'd only spent a few hours with Jeff and Holly Hale but I didn't need more time to know they adored their daughters. Jeff was going to go ballistic and I didn't think Holly would be far off from that.

I felt her blow out a breath.

"I'm exhausted."

"Go to sleep, sweetness."

I heard her sigh and her arm went tight around my middle.

"Bossy."

I laid awake staring into the dark, sour in my gut, long after Vanessa's breaths evened out, thinking this was just the beginning.

The beginning of the end.

Hoping I was wrong but knowing I was right.

The worst was yet to come.

26

"I DIDN'T GET to tell you the other day when I was here but the porch and new garage doors look really good."

Who was this woman and what had she done with my sister?

Not that I was complaining.

I was the opposite of complaining.

I was ecstatic.

Ten minutes ago Malory had walked into my house with a confidence I hadn't seen in forever. It was different from the last time I'd seen it—there was no fun, wild child in step. It was a bold, sureness a woman should possess when she walked into a room.

It was beautiful.

I also hoped when Sullivan showed up she was able to keep this newfound poise.

"Thanks. Next up is my bedroom. The carpet in there is ugly."

Malory's gaze went in the direction of my bedroom and her lips twitched.

"So...Dalton," she prompted.

My eyes went to the same place as my sister's, which incidentally was where Dalton was right then getting dressed.

"He's the one."

"No doy," she drawled, sounding like a 1980's Valley Girl.

"Did you just 'no doy' me?"

Malory shrugged.

"It felt right, seeing as your answer warranted a no doy, since it was silly. Obviously I know he's the one, what I wanted to know was, well...everything."

I hadn't recovered from my sister no doy-ing me yet when the man in question strode into the kitchen.

"Malory," he greeted. "Sweetheart."

He moved around my sister and stopped to kiss my temple before he continued his voyage to the coffee pot.

I swear I heard my sister sigh.

"I was just asking Nessa how the two of you met."

That wasn't necessarily the truth but close enough. A stretch of the truth was better than freaking the man out by telling him I was in love with him and thought he was my soulmate.

"Vanessa's boss is my partner's wife," Dalton told her.

Thankfully leaving out the part about me thinking I had a stalker which was the catalyst for us getting together.

"Do you want kids?" Malory blurted out.

Jesus.

Rather than running for the hills Dalton chuckled and answered, "Absolutely."

"How many?" she pushed.

"Mal—"

"I'm an only child so at least two but I'd prefer three."

I could totally do three.

"Vanessa wants two," my sister helpfully supplied. "A girl and a boy."

"No, no, I could do three," I corrected because now that I was thinking about it I wanted three kids with Dalton. Boys, girls, didn't matter.

Dalton smiled at me over the rim of his mug.

"You're cruising into your mid-thirties. You need to get on that if you want three."

Was she crazy?

"I'm thirty-two, my eggs are hardly shriveling up," I countered. "And maybe this conversation is a little premature."

"Premature?" Dalton inquired.

"Just a little," I confirmed. "We've officially been together about five minutes."

"So?" my sister interjected. "Mom says when the universe speaks, it speaks. Five minutes, five months, five years. When you know, you know."

Yes, she was back.

This was my sister Malory.

She was unfiltered and diluted nothing—not her words, not her personality, not her spirit.

"I'm really happy to have you back, but maybe tone down the crazy until Dalton gets to know you. I really like him and it'd suck if he ran away because my sister's cray-cray."

Malory smiled.

Damn, she was beautiful.

"You really like me?"

I fought the no doy and went with, "Uh, yeah."

"You like me?"

"No, I *really* like you."

"Right," he muttered like he knew I was lying and I didn't *like* him so much as I *loved* him. "I *really* like you, too, baby."

Did he...

Did that mean...

Was he saying he loved me, too?

Holy Jesus.

Dalton's phone rang from my bedroom, cutting off the exchange.

"Could be Brady. I need to get that."

Mercifully Malory waited until Dalton was out of earshot before she announced, "You know what he means is he loves you."

"I think I do," I breathed.

"I like him. As in normal like, not love. But I do love him for you. Austin likes him, too."

Well, that was good news. The first time they'd met it hadn't gone well but last night, even though the night was tense, they seemed to get along.

"I hope you're not upset with Austin. He told me about what happened the morning he came by."

"I told you I wasn't." I winced and told the truth. "Okay, so I wasn't happy when I first found out he knew and I wasn't happy when he told me he was going to take you and move away. But after talking to Dalton I got it. He loves you. It wasn't my business until you made it my business. So no hard feelings. But if he tries to move you away, I'm kicking him in the balls and following you."

Mal gave me a sad smile.

"You know he'd never do that. He loves me too much to ever do something that would hurt me. I wasn't in a good way and he overreacted. He's worried Dalton's going to hold a grudge."

I waved my hand and told her, "Dalton gets it."

"I get what?"

"Why Austin barged in and acted like an overgrown ape," Malory answered.

Dalton's gaze came to me before he looked at Malory.

"He acted like a man who is deeply in love with his wife and would do anything to protect her including taking her from a place where he thought more harm would come to her. I understood where he was coming from and was only pissed because the woman I am deeply in love with was gutted. Like him, I will move to protect her from anyone who means her harm. All that is to say, yes, I got it. And it's water under the bridge as long as he doesn't pull that shit again and make my woman cry."

All the air from my lungs evacuated in one gust.

Then he went on like he hadn't changed the course of my life.

"Sucks, sweetheart, but that was Phoenix. There was another break-in last night. This time the intruder was caught on the homeowner's security cameras. They've got a name and last known address. Liza needs backup since the rest of her team isn't in place. Phoenix and I are on call, so we're her backup. Hopefully this won't take long but if I'm going to be more than a few hours I'll call you."

Was he serious?

"Um..."

"If this wasn't going to be fast, I'd have Phoenix call in one of the other guys."

"Um..."

"Fuck. I'll call Phoenix—"

"No. You go. Mal and I will be fine. You'll be back to see Sully before he goes back."

"If that's the case why are you looking at me like—"

"Like you just told my sister you were deeply in love with me, then rapped out your plans for the afternoon like you didn't just, oh, I don't know, essentially tell me you love me. That? Do I look like that?" I snapped.

"Yeah, baby, that's exactly what you look like," he said with a smile.

"You really need to work on your delivery, Detective."

"I'll work on it," he promised.

"Go to work, catch a bad guy, and be safe."

"Walk me to the door?"

His statement was framed as a question but the look on his face told me it was really a demand.

"Don't mind me, I'll just sit here and drink my coffee while the two of you suck face at the door."

On his way to my sister Dalton chuckled. He stopped doing that when he kissed her on the top of her head.

"You got this, Malory," he said softly.

"Thanks," she whispered back.

And just as softly he told her, "He doesn't have a resentful bone in his body. He's not looking to blame anyone for anything. He grew up surrounded by love. The only thing he wants to understand is where he comes from."

"But—"

"You gave him everything, Malory," he said quietly but firmly. "You gave him that family whether you wanted to or not. You gave him to two people who loved him and gave him a good life. Hold onto that; the knowledge your boy knows nothing but love."

If I wasn't already in love with Dalton that alone would've made me fall in love with him.

Malory sniffed and nodded.

I followed Dalton to the front door and didn't delay rolling to my toes and commenced showing him my gratitude until he growled into my mouth and took over the kiss.

When he broke the kiss, his lips went to my ear and he whispered there, "I am deeply in love with you, Vanessa Hale."

My belly fluttered. Too bad that was as far as the flutter got before the knock on the door interrupted.

"I swear to all things holy I'm taking you somewhere where no one knows us and we can go a solid week without someone pounding on a door."

I wanted that.

Badly.

"Sounds good to me."

Dalton let me go and answered the door, greeting Sullivan who was standing there looking nervous.

"Hey, bud." Then to me. "Give me a minute with Sully, yeah?"

God, I love this man.

He was going to pave the way for Malory.

"Yeah."

With a lip brush he said, "See you in a few hours."

Dalton stepped out onto the porch, closing the door behind him but not shutting it fully.

When I got back to the kitchen my sister was sliding off the stool, smoothing down her jeans.

"Do I look okay?"

I blinked and took in my very beautiful, always put-together sister.

She was nervous, I knew.

But about how she looked?

"Malory—"

"I didn't make a very good first impression," she mumbled. "And then I couldn't hack it and bailed on him. That was strike two. I want...I mean...I need this to go good for him. I don't want a strike three."

"Yeah, Mal, you look beautiful."

"I don't look like I'm trying too hard?"

God, my sister.

"No, you look like you're trying just enough. But really, Malory, Sully wouldn't care if you showed up in your hot pink and yellow polka-dot jammies just as long as *you* show up."

"Aunt Vanessa's right," Sullivan said from behind us. "Though that was oddly specific."

Aunt Vanessa.

That would never get old.

"Hey, Sully, how was the drive up?" I turned and asked.

"Boring," he answered me but kept his eyes glued on Malory.

My sister's exhale sounded as painful as her shoulders squaring as she shifted to face Sullivan.

It must've been the dreamer in me, the part my mother passed down, but I could actually feel the electricity spark in my kitchen. I didn't feel it the first time we were all together but now that the air was calm, I felt the tingle of something pass over me.

"Hi, Sullivan. I'm Malory."

Oh hell, I was going to lose it and start crying.

Sully smiled my sister's smile and played along.

"Nice to meet you, Malory."

If it wouldn't be totally creepy I'd find my phone and hit record.

"Are you hungry, Sully?" I asked.

"No. I stopped at TB on the way up here but I'll have a cup of coffee."

I walked around the island while muttering, "I'm worried about your nutrition, nephew. Do you eat anything besides Taco Bell?"

"Wait, there's something besides double decker tacos?"

"Great, you're going to be no help putting the soft versus hard shell argument to rest," I complained.

"If a double decker's not on offer, soft is the only way to go," he wrongly asserted.

"Told you so," Malory singsonged. "Hard shells break at the bend and you lose your meat."

"Or they crumble," Sully added.

"Great, now there's two of you to gang up on me," I

complained though I secretly loved they had something in common even if it was their preference in tacos.

I'd totally take it.

"How do you take your coffee?"

"Without grounds," he strangely said.

"Is that some fancy California style coffee you made when you worked at Starbies?"

"No, Auntie," he returned with his voice shaking with humor.

I was basking in the glory of Sully calling me auntie while simultaneously wondering if it was hurting Malory's feelings.

I stopped pondering this when Malory busted out into laughter. I went to the island and glanced down at my half full mug of coffee.

"What the hell is floating in my coffee?"

"Grounds." Sully's answer definitely held a tinge of 'no doy.'

"Shit," I mumbled.

"I'll make a new pot," Sully offered.

"Have at it." I waved my hand in the direction of the coffee maker.

I went to the other side of the island and took the stool next to the one my sister had claimed. Together we watched Sullivan move around my kitchen. A small, everyday thing, that normally would go unnoticed. But Malory was savoring every movement.

"Where are you going to college?" Mal inquired.

"Berkley. Both my parents—" Sully stiffened and didn't continue.

"Did your mom and dad go to Berkeley?" Mal prompted.

To her credit, if asking about his parents hurt her she'd covered it well.

"Yeah. My, um, dad studied architecture design and my mom was there getting her business degree."

"What are your plans? Do you want to be an architect like your dad?"

Please don't say law.

Please don't say law.

"No. Computer science. I like programming."

Thank you, God.

But also, hell yeah.

"I'm in web design," Mal told him.

"If you two start geekin' out about binary digits and CPUs I'm outta here," I groaned.

"I'm impressed you know what a binary digit is," my sister shamed me.

"Don't be. Our computer system went down at work the other day and I overheard the IT guys talking."

"How strong do you like your coffee?"

"On a scale of one to ten, an eleven," I answered.

"Same."

"That tracks."

"If that's a crack about the floating grounds, shove it."

Sullivan was filling the carafe with water.

Malory was smiling at him like he wasn't filling a carafe full of water but instead performing neurosurgery.

I was grinning at my sister.

In other words, none of us heard it until it was too late.

My front door slammed hard.

Malory moved first.

I was off the stool.

But neither of us were fast enough to stop James Rodman from walking into my kitchen and putting a gun to Sullivan's head.

"It's my lucky day," James snickered. "All three of you together."

"What are—"

James's face twisted into an ugly sneer, his wild eyes on Malory. "Don't speak to me, you whore."

"Whatever you're doing here, James—" I tried but he cut me off, too.

But even if he didn't do it with words the way his eyes went funny when he looked at Sullivan would've clogged my throat.

"So, you're my baby bro."

The words were innocuous but his tone was downright homicidal.

"Let's go," James barked and jerked his head toward the living room.

"James, please—"

Suddenly he moved. The barrel of the gun was no longer pointed at Sullivan's head and three loud gunshots exploded.

Debris rained down from the ceiling.

"The next one's in his head. All of you, *move*."

"Okay, James, I'll go with you." Malory scooted around me and dodged my hand when I tried to pull her back.

"Malory and I—"

"Move!" James shouted.

Sullivan's fear-filled eyes were on mine but his feet were taking him to Malory.

James was moving behind Sully when I saw them.

The three box cutters Dalton had brought in after he cleaned out my garage, making fun of me because they were hot pink, giving me shit after I explained I had three because I kept losing them. All three were lined up on the counter next to the fridge.

I tagged one on my way by and stuffed it into my bra.

It wasn't much, but it was something.

27

AS FAR AS executing a search warrant went, today's had been easy. Ashley Pender's instinct to protect her child trumped her boyfriend's criminal activity. Especially when that child was a toddler on her hip when she answered the door to three cops, then looked beyond the three on her porch and saw the street in front of her house was fully surrounded.

The woman opened the door and allowed Liza to search her while Phoenix and I went into the back bedroom to wake up Scott Miller. The fuckwit heard us enter, rolled to reach for the nightstand next to the bed, then promptly found himself no longer in bed but on the floor face down in a pair of baby-blue tighty-whities. Normally we'd let the suspect put on pants before we hauled his ass out cuffed to sit on the couch while we finished our search.

Scott, being a dumbfuck reaching for a gun meant he was sitting on his couch in his poor choice of color briefs.

"Neary. Kent," Liza called from the kitchen.

"You got him?" I asked Officer Perez.

She glanced down at Scott, snickered, then looked back at me with a smile.

"Absolutely."

Her 'absolutely' was two-fold. First, Scott was cuffed. Second, Maria Perez was a badass. I'd witnessed her taking down a man twice her size after she'd engaged in what could only be described as hand-to-hand combat. It wasn't until later I learned she had three black belts in various disciplines and was former Army Infantry with two deployments behind her. If Scott so much as sneezed Perez would be all over that.

I walked into the kitchen vaguely noted it was spotless, as was the rest of the house. It appeared Ashley Pender cared enough about her kid to live in a clean house. They also hadn't found any guns other than the one in the nightstand. So there was that.

Though they weren't done with the search yet.

"Ms. Pender works at Outdoor Goods, she's a cashier. Scott Miller's brother-in-law works at SafeCo in Alabama."

The connection.

Ashley didn't look up from her daughter bouncing on her lap, likely knowing she was going down along with Miller and these would be the last hours she'd get with her daughter for awhile.

The travesty of that was something I still couldn't get used to. Locking up criminals was the easy part; knowing the ripple effect of their crimes not so much.

"Ms. Pender has been forthcoming in her part. The stolen goods are in a safe in the garage."

The irony wasn't lost on me.

"Here's the combination." Liza held up a scrap of paper with numbers neatly penned.

I took the paper.

Then turned but stopped dead when I heard a radio call crackle from someone's radio.

"Roger sixty-one-oh-eight. Code seventy-four-forty, clear. Assistance needed at two-thirty-one Lyons Street."

Two-thirty-one Lyons Street.

"Sixty-one-oh-eight to dispatch. Incident two-eight-seven-seven, residence is empty. Possible discharge of weapon into the ceiling."

Code seventy-four-forty.

Shots fired.

Shots fired at Vanessa's house.

It was purely muscle memory that guided my hand to my radio.

"Eighty-ninety-eight responding code six. Incident two-eight-seven-seven. Residence belongs to Vanessa Hale. She, her sister Malory Newton, and Sullivan Wooten were in the residence when I left at..." I faltered as I sprinted through the crush of officers filling Ashley's living room. "Ten-oh-five."

I made it to the sedan, realized I didn't have the fucking keys, turned, and slammed into Phoenix.

I didn't bother wasting precious time arguing who was going to drive.

"Roger, eighty-ninety-eight."

Phoenix had the engine turned over by the time my ass hit the passenger seat.

"Explain," Phoenix demanded.

I pulled my phone out of my vest, unlocked the screen, and went to Vanessa's number.

As it was ringing I answered Phoenix. "Malory came over this morning to meet with Sullivan. When I left Sully had just gotten there. I talked to him a minute and left."

Voicemail.

Fuck.

"You think the kid lost it?"

No way.

"He was nervous about talking to Malory but no, I don't think so."

I tried Vanessa again.

Voicemail again.

I was scrolling through my contacts when Phoenix asked, "Malory?"

That was a fuck no.

"No."

I found Brady's number and waited.

"Yo—"

"Shots fired at Vanessa's house," I interrupted. "Vanessa, Malory, and Sullivan were in that house. I need Sullivan and Malory Newton's phone numbers. And while you're on it, it would be helpful if you run a trace on their locations."

I was always grateful for the help Triple Canopy provided, never more so than right now. Brady could get me what I needed faster than any of my colleagues could.

"On it. Give me ten minutes and you'll have what you need. Neighbors don't have security cameras," he finished with something I knew. "I'll hit traffic cameras in the area."

"Appreciate it."

"Out."

"Dalton—"

"I need a minute."

Phoenix gave me that minute which led to eight as he drove at a scarily high rate of speed. Unfortunately this gave me eight minutes to go to worst case scenarios. Being taken from the scene of the initial crime was never good. There was a gun in play and the person in possession of that gun had already demonstrated they'd use it.

"Wherever you are right now, shut that shit down," Phoenix growled.

"I should never have let Vanessa talk me into delaying the

install of the cameras and alarm once we knew she wasn't being stalked."

"Get that shit out of your head."

"I can't lose her."

"You're not going to lose her."

"She can't lose Sullivan or Malory."

"Don't go there, Dalton. You need to keep your shit together."

Phoenix made the turn onto Lyons Street.

Cop cars lined the street.

My stomach roiled as reality crashed around me.

NOTHING.

That was what we had.

Not a goddamned thing.

Sullivan's Nissan was at the curb.

Vanessa's cell phone was still on the nightstand in her bedroom. Malory's was in her purse on the sofa in the den. And Sullivan's wasn't found in the house but it was powered off.

No forced entry.

No traffic cameras in the area had caught Vanessa, Malory, or Sullivan. No vehicle speeding or driving erratic.

No neighbors saw anything.

Mrs. Thompson next door called in the shots but she was in the back of her house and by the time she made it to her front window she didn't see anything.

We had dick.

Just three bullet holes in Vanessa's kitchen ceiling and her street crawling with cops.

"Brady might—"

Phoenix was cut off when dispatch came over the radio.

"All available units to one-zero-two River Drive. Incident two-eight-ninety. Code seventy-four-forty. Please be advised reports indicated homeowner is Judge Simon Rodman."

I didn't bother responding to dispatch before I took off through Vanessa's house.

Thankfully Phoenix had his shit together.

"Twenty-eight-eighty-one responding incident two-eight-ninety. Code six. Please be advised there might be three hostages. Rodman is connected to Vanessa Hale. SWAT is advised."

FEAR GNAWED AT MY GUT. A fear I'd never known existed. The kind of fear a man feels when he's on the precipice of losing everything.

"Take a breath," Phoenix ordered.

There were not enough breaths I could take—not when Vanessa might be in there breathing her last.

I needed in that house.

"Come out with your hands up," Chip, the SWAT team's loud hailer, tried again.

Chip had no fucking clue who he was talking to. Just that someone was in the house and since the first unit had arrived they'd heard a gunshot.

Just one.

Vanessa. Malory. Sullivan.

One bullet had been fired.

"I have movement," Shiloh called out over the radio. "Window A one."

My gaze snapped to the bottom left window just in time to see the curtains move.

"Male. Light hair. Thirties," Shiloh continued.

I glanced farther to my left to see Shiloh looking through the scope of her M4.

"Charlie Team?" Merino, a member of SWAT, radioed. "Check in."

"Charlie Team in place," Valentine returned from the rear of the house. "No movement."

"Alpha Team, hold for entry," Team leader Oscala ordered.

Fucking finally they were going to move in.

28

IT WAS strange but I wasn't afraid.

I was angry.

Oh, yeah. To use Dalton's words from last night, I was angry as *fuck*.

I didn't have to be afraid when James Rodman had flown off his rocker. Or was that fell off his rocker and flew over the cuckoo's nest. However that went didn't matter because he'd done both.

Spoiled momma's boy had finally snapped.

If my first clue hadn't been kidnapping us at gunpoint, taking us to his father's house would've clued me in. And if I'd been dense enough to miss those clues—seeing Simon beaten to a pulp and tied to a chair would've done it.

I admit as much as I hated the man and had joked about wanting to stab him in the throat, I didn't actually want to be present when the man died.

But since Simon was taunting his out-of-his-mind son I feared I'd have a first-row seat to him biting the bullet—literally.

I could hear the police outside yelling for James to come out with his hands up. This was a relatively new development. At first I was happy to know the police were outside but now James was getting antsier and antsier, swinging the gun around, and I wasn't so sure yelling at him was a good idea.

"Tell me," James demanded, pacing the living room. "One of you, speak."

He waved the gun between Malory and Simon.

I wanted to get closer to my sister but I also wanted Sullivan as far away from Simon as possible. The living room was big but with the judge tied to a chair in the middle of the room like a bad movie we didn't have far to go. And I'd already tried to back Sully out of the room. That didn't go over well. There was now a bullet hole in the ceiling of the Rodman residence courtesy of Crazy James.

"What exactly would you like to know, son?" Simon asked, but with the cuts on his swollen lips his question came out garbled.

"Why?"

I'd actually like to know the answer to that as well but not like this.

"I know what you did, you fucking whore!" James yelled at Malory.

Sullivan made a low growling noise. I squeezed his hand in a silent plea for him not to bring attention to himself. I needed my nephew to remain quiet until I figured a way out of this mess or the police barged in.

Dalton would...nope...I couldn't think about him now.

If I did, I'd think about how he'd told me he was deeply in love with me and I hadn't gotten the chance to say it back. From there my mind would spiral into all the rest of the things I never got to do with or say to him.

I needed to keep my head in this room and figure out a way to get Sullivan and Malory out without James shooting one of us.

What was the saying? Never bring a knife to a gunfight.

Well, I had a box cutter in my bra. The blade would barely pierce the skin. I'd have to slash something important. Or get close enough to get the gun.

The police officer outside yelled again.

James walked to the window, glanced out, and drew the curtains closed.

"Time's up, Dad."

Shit.

My gaze went to my sister staring at James.

I knew that look.

I'd seen it twice in my life. Once when we were at the mall when we were kids and Malory socked a boy in the face for picking on a pimple-faced younger boy. She did not slap the guy, she'd closed-fist slugged him. The second time was when she saw a boy on our street kick a dog. She'd punched him, too, multiple times until he fell to his knees and then she kicked him and asked him how he liked it.

The only two times I'd ever seen her violent.

She had that look—it was more of a blank stare but her eyes tracked James's every move.

Suddenly I was scared.

Angry and scared.

Malory was going to do something.

"I hate you," James spat. "My whole life you told me I was a disappointment when you were nothing more than a dirty old man fucking a teenager." Simon swung the gun to point at Sullivan. "And then there he is, the bastard son."

I stepped in front of Sullivan and all hell broke loose.

With an unholy scream that sounded like Satan's battle cry, Malory charged James.

Their bodies collided. The gun exploded but I had no idea where the bullet went. Malory was on top of James, struggling.

Faced with the unbearable choice to get Sullivan out or help my sister I froze.

I became unstuck when Sullivan moved to Malory.

Malory.

Sullivan.

Malory.

It had to be my sister's boy.

Had to be.

If she survived and he didn't, she'd never, ever recover.

"No." I yanked Sully back. "C'mon!"

"I'm not leaving her."

Our conversation was cut off when the front window shattered.

The room started filling with smoke. Sullivan tackled me linebacker style. I hit the floor with a grunt, fought to catch my breath, but it was no use—my very heavy nephew was on top of me.

Footsteps pounded all around us. Some ran past us until a pair stopped next to me.

"Vanessa?" a man called my name.

"Yeah?" I wheezed.

"Up, both of you. Let's go."

Sullivan rolled off. I scrambled to my feet and scanned the room through the dissipating smoke. All I could see was a sea of police in black tactical gear. The fear I'd been able to hold at bay slammed into me. So much of it I shook with it.

I heard a high-pitched scream. This one was not my sister's battle cry but one of anguish.

Oh, God.

Malory.

"No!" I jumped to catch Sully but he was too fast.

"I need to get you out."

"You need to—"

"Thank fuck." The words were so rough they came out grated.

Dalton.

He was here.

"Sullivan—"

I didn't get to finish. Dalton's shoulder hit my stomach. His arm wrapped around the back of my thighs. I was up, then he was running.

"Sullivan!" I shouted.

"Valentine's got him."

If I thought the inside of the house had turned to chaos, outside was pandemonium. Two trucks that looked like they belonged in a war zone. Dozens of cop cars. Police officers everywhere.

All of this because James had gone mad.

Dalton put me down. His hands went to my hips to steady me.

"Malory—"

"Quiet."

The harsh snap of his demand shocked me. But it was stark fear on his face that had me holding my tongue.

"I'm not hurt."

Apparently that wasn't enough. Dalton's hands roamed. They started at my waist, traveled up my sides, over the curve of my breasts, to my armpits.

He paused there.

"Box cutter."

Dalton went back to his pat-down and didn't stop until his hands had touched every inch of me.

When he was done the fear hadn't left his eyes though I didn't get a chance to study it for more than a second before Dalton pulled me into his arms.

"Thank. *Fuck.*"

"Honey, I'm fine."

"Where's my sister?" I heard Malory shout.

Dalton didn't let me go but he did turn so I could put eyes on my sister.

She looked undone.

A disheveled mess.

But never more beautiful, standing in the front yard of the man who had taken advantage of her as a teenager, after that man's son had gone insane, holding the son's hand she'd self-lessly given up and in doing so gave him a beautiful life.

She'd won.

29

I LEARNED SOMETHING NEW.

No, rewind, I learned a lot of somethings.

The first was my sister was an absolute badass mama jama—but on that later.

The second thing I learned was after a home invasion, kidnapping, and hostage situation there was a lot of questioning. Hours of it.

The third, which went along with the second, was that there was a mountain of paperwork. I'd signed less paperwork purchasing a car.

The fourth was when Dalton said he was by my side, he meant he was by my side. He never left it. Not even when he needed to go to his desk to sign some paperwork. He'd brought me with him.

The fifth was Sullivan might've been a young man but he was *all* man. He stuck next to Malory. He didn't stop sticking when Austin came down to the station all wild-eyed and beside himself. This hadn't scared Sully or made him back away. He stood strong. I stood next to him when he called his parents. I already knew I loved my nephew but hearing him gently calm his mom down made me love him more. That call was made hours ago, meaning the Wootens were already on a plane headed to Georgia. They'd been in Chicago at a conference which meant their flight had already landed in Savannah and they were due at my parents' house imminently.

The sixth and final thing I learned sitting in my parents' back den with Dalton, Sullivan, Malory, and Austin was it was a very, very good thing Simon Rodman was currently in a hospital bed and James was behind bars. If not, my father would've put his former best friend into the ground.

Fury didn't touch what my father felt.

Though for Sullivan's sake he'd held his composure —mostly.

With the hard part over—mostly, we were still facing meeting the Wootens—Sully had learned what he'd set out to learn when he found me. It wasn't pretty, the history of it anyway, but Malory was forthcoming and honest.

The doorbell rang as we knew it would. Even still the room went wired. Whatever calm we'd managed to wrestle down flew out the window with that one sound.

My dad looked at Sullivan. "I know you're eager to see your mom and dad, but if you wouldn't mind I'd like to talk to them first."

Sullivan being the laidback kid—unless his birth mother was under attack, then he became something else altogether. I'd call it brave and fierce even though at the time he rushed to help Malory I thought it was crazy and dangerous, but that was neither here nor there. What was done was thankfully done. He was back to being his normal self.

So his nonchalant "Sure" didn't surprise me.

My dad stood, pulled my mother up beside him, then said, "Girls."

Oh, shit.

Malory immediately took to her feet.

Yep, my sister was back.

I was much slower which meant I brought up the rear of our party. My dad already had the door open and was inviting the Wootens into the house.

"Will. Pam. I'm Jeff, this is my wife Holly, and these are my daughters Malory and Vanessa."

I already knew from what Sullivan had told me that both of his parents were on the shorter side. Pam's red hair framed her very pretty face. Will's once-dark hair had a lot of silver streaks in it. Casually well-dressed, they made a handsome couple. They also looked scared out of their brains.

I wanted to hug them both.

But that would've made an already awkward situation weirder.

"Thank you."

That came from my sister. It was guttural and thick with so much emotion I flinched.

Pam stepped forward, offered her hand to my sister, and didn't let go once Malory took hold.

"Twelve years we tried," she whispered. "Then God gave us you. I always wondered if it was selfish, us being so happy knowing you had to give him up so we could have everything we wanted."

"Mrs. Wooten—"

"Pam," she corrected. "And there is no need to thank us for loving Sullivan. It is us who are forever grateful *you* were given to us. Without you, there is no Sullivan. Without *you,* Will and I wouldn't have a family."

I heard my mother sniff, or was that me?

"I know it's not my place to ask," my father started. "But I'm going to anyway. Holly and I have only had a short, few hours with him. Will you please stay awhile, have lunch with us, and let us get to know him a little before you take him."

"We discussed it on the way here. Pam and I would like the opportunity to get to know you." Will stopped, shifted his gaze to Malory, and went on, "All of you. Sullivan has always known he was adopted. We'd never planned on hiding that from him. We thought we'd give him this summer with his friends in Florida and when he got home we'd planned on offering to hire a private investigator to find his family. It would seem my son beat us to it. He was always impatient."

"Ambitious," Sully corrected.

I turned to see my nephew standing between Austin and Dalton.

Dalton shrugged.

Austin was looking at his wife with more love and pride than I'd ever seen. And that was saying a lot; Austin never hid how much he adored my sister.

"Yes, ambitious." Will beamed.

Sully broke away from his uncle and (hopefully) other uncle and made a beeline for his parents.

The rest of us stepped aside to give them space.

My mom sniffed again. This time I knew it was her since Dalton had claimed me, meaning I was in the curve of his arm, looking up at him, smiling.

After the sniff, my mom quietly murmured, "Let's give them a moment."

The six of us left the Wootens in the formal living room and made our way back to the kitchen.

My mom, always the hostess, went straight to the fridge.

"I can make sandwiches." She stopped and straightened from her perusal of the contents of the fridge. "No, a lasagna."

Lasagna was not only not lunchtime food but we'd had Italian the day before.

Thankfully, my father intervened.

"We'll order lunch in."

"Jeffery," she huffed like my dad had suggested we serve the Wootens poop for lunch. "We can't order in."

"Did someone say Taco Bell?" Sully asked with his parents trailing behind him.

"Please, sweet Jesus in heaven above, do not tell me you enjoy Taco Bell," my mom scolded. "I've fought with these girls since the first time their father introduced them to that crap. Do you know what's in that processed meat?"

Oh jeez.

Here we go.

"No clue," Sully admitted.

"We've tried," Pam put in. "But once he got his license we lost control over him hitting the drive-thru on his way to school, home from school, to and from work, so we gave up. Maybe you can explain to him how bad fast food is for a growing boy."

"Don't waste your time, Grams. Nothing beats processed meat between tortillas."

Grams.

Oh my God.

My mom sucked in a breath and I saw her cheeks tinge pink.

"Ordering something in sounds good to me. Less work, more time to get to know each other," Will put in.

Another round of introductions were made, this time to include Austin and Dalton. Austin, who was normally slow to be friendly, mostly because he was watching for signs Malory was overwhelmed or in distress, was shockingly welcoming to Pam and Will. He'd even kissed Pam on the cheek. Probably because he'd heard what she'd said to Malory.

Lunch was decided on—fried chicken and all the fixings,

which was fine with me since that meant I got double the crispy, fried bits Malory pulled off her chicken.

"Happy?" Dalton quietly asked as we walked to the den.

"Very."

"They seem like good people."

"Yes."

"This is going to work out."

God, I hoped he was right.

Totally unconventional, though maybe not. Families were made up of all sorts of situations. Blood, found, circumstantial, it didn't matter—as long as it was rooted in love.

And I knew my family had an abundance of it.

"Do you like sports?" my dad wasted no time asking as soon as we sat.

"I played soccer, baseball, and basketball until high school. But I stopped to focus on my studies and work."

I could tell Sully's answer impressed my father.

"Dad said that my grades and work ethic were more important but I really liked basketball."

Pam rolled her eyes but smiled at her son.

"You liked basketball because that pretty cheerleader Jodi cheered extra loud for you," she interjected.

Will put his arm around his wife.

"Nothing wrong with cheerleaders, Cherry; that's how I met you."

Cherry.

Cute.

"We were also in college, not middle school. And that girl was throwing herself at my son."

"Jodi, right." Sullivan snapped his fingers. "How could I forget her?"

The men chuckled.

My mom smiled a smile I'd seen thousands of times. It was

her 'I'm happy my family's laughing and happy' smile. Though since Malory had taken her turn I hadn't seen it very often. Seeing it now made me not join in with the laughter but on the inside I was smiling huge.

While we waited for lunch Sullivan was a good sport, answering all the questions my dad was throwing his way. Sometimes Pam or Will interjected or Malory or Austin would ask a question, but I sat quietly in the corner of the couch with Dalton, his arm around me, listening.

It happened when we were all sitting around what Mal and I called the Thanksgiving table. We weren't a formal family and ate at the small table in the breakfast nook. Except for holidays when Mom put out a spread and demanded we dress nicely and eat at the dining room table.

So there we were in not nice clothes but eating fried chicken at the Thanksgiving table celebrating (I thought) the blending of our families. And I thought it was going exceedingly well until Sullivan reached over and grabbed some of the crispy, fried bits I'd pulled off my chicken in preparation to mix with my mashed potatoes.

"Hey!" I snapped, stabbing at his hand with my fork.

I missed.

He shoved my crispy, fried bits into his mouth.

"What? You pulled them off. It's not like you were going to eat them."

"Don't start," my mother warned.

Too late.

"Something you need to know about me, sweet nephew, is that I save the crispy bits to mix with my mashed potatoes. It's the best part of the meal."

"Something about me, sweet auntie," Sully returned in the same sarcastic tone, "that's my favorite part of fried chicken and I have zero guilt stealing off your plate."

"You might not feel guilt but you're gonna feel pain when I stab you."

"A hundred times I've told you," my mother interrupted. "Do not threaten to stab people at the table." She paused, looked at Pam, and finished, "She's only violent when it comes to her food, I promise."

Pam sputtered a laugh.

My mother didn't lie.

"Oh, for God's sake, Nessa," Malory snorted. "Here."

She reached over and dropped half of her torn-off chicken skin onto my plate then the other half onto Sullivan's.

"I can see now this is not going to work," I mumbled.

"Seems it's working fine for me. Mom Number One..." Sully pointed his fork at his mom, "loves the crispy parts. She doesn't share. So if Bonus Mom wants to share with me, too bad for you."

The table went quiet.

I didn't think my mom or Malory were breathing and I thought that because I wasn't.

Bonus Mom.

That was cute. And sweet.

But...Pam.

I wasn't sure how she'd feel about hearing her son call his birth mother Bonus Mom.

Sullivan didn't seem to notice.

"Now if Grams or Gramps doesn't like ice cream and they want to share their scoops with me...*winning*."

The kid was funny, there was no doubt about it.

"I hate ice cream," my mother quickly lied.

And everyone knew it.

I felt Dalton's hand hit my thigh. Mine went under the table to cover his.

This was a mistake.

Sullivan swiped more food off my plate.

Little shit.

"Seriously?"

"What can I say, I'm a growing boy."

I skewered him with a dirty look.

"My son's right," Will said, then cleared his throat. "Seems this is working just *fine.*"

My gaze shot to my sister.

She was smiling huge.

Not at me but at her boy.

Yes, this was going to work out.

A blended family.

The Hales and the Wootens with Sullivan being the love that brought us together.

My eyes caught on my sister's hand when she wrapped her fingers around her water glass.

All of her fingernails were broken.

All of them.

Every single fingernail had broken when she clawed James's face and neck in an effort to save her son's life.

That brought me back to the first lesson I'd learned that day —my sister was a badass mama jama.

Life hack, or maybe life lesson: Never fuck with a woman's child unless you want your face clawed off.

30

NINE MONTHS LATER. *Springtime in Southern California*

"WELL? WHAT DO YOU THINK?" Sully asked.

I chewed, swallowed, then proclaimed, "I'm starting a petition to have In-N-Out open on the East Coast. Though Micky D's fries are better."

"Agreed," Sully said around a mouthful.

It was just us eating lunch in Sully's car parked outside In-N-Out.

Dalton, Will, and Austin went to Home Depot. Malory and Pam were at a home goods store. And Sully and I were supposed to be going to the paint store but we'd made a slight detour so my nephew could share his second fast food restaurant with me. I would never admit it out loud but I thought In-N-Out was way better than The Bell.

Sullivan was home on spring break. We'd come out for a visit whereupon Will had enlisted the men's help finishing off what used to be a shed into a tiny house for Sully who would be transferring to UCLA. He'd given Berkley a shot but he didn't want to be away from his mom and dad.

A lot had happened in the last nine months. The most annoying thing was Dalton had moved in with me. Okay, that wasn't the annoying part, that was the great part. The part that was annoying was I still didn't have my new kitchen because right after Dalton moved in, a wall socket had caught fire.

Don't be alarmed; it was a tiny fire, more than a spark but not enough to call the fire department and was quickly put out with an extinguisher. I wanted to pretend the fire hadn't happened and move to the kitchen and bedroom. Dalton, being a man, disagreed. Then he called my father and Austin for backup.

They won.

I lost.

Annoying.

The rest was awesome.

Dalton worked. I worked. We went out on dates. We hung out with our friends. He taught me how to play pool. My parents adored him—slightly annoying because my father sided with Dalton in all things house. My mother fawned over him—it was sweet. Malory loved him. And he and Austin had bonded. Their first and second meetings might've been full of drama but they were well past that and played basketball with Phoenix and Griff every weekend. The one visit Sully had made back to Georgia he'd joined the men. Malory and I went to watch and cheered them on. Malory was louder than I was.

My parents had spent the week between Christmas and New Year's in California. The Wootens had invited us all. Malory called Pam to explain Austin had booked them a trip to the Bahamas for their anniversary. Pam understood. Sully just went with the flow; he now had six new people in his life, each of us giving him varying forms of attention. Dalton and I decided to give my parents some alone time with their grandson. And that was something Will and Pam were happy Sully had now since both sets of their parents had passed, leaving Sully with no grandparents.

That was, until he had my parents.

There was a downside to this—they spoiled the kid rotten. My thrifty, save-for-a-rainy-day father actually flew him and my mother to California for Sully's nineteenth birthday. Malory and Austin went, too. I loved my nephew but I had a kitchen, bedroom, and new wiring for my house to pay for so I opted not to go but I sent a kickass present and FaceTimed.

The biggest thing that had happened was what the media had called, *The Scandal of the Decade*. Once the news outlets got ahold of the story—a superior court judge having an affair with an underage girl, getting her pregnant, then forcing her to give that child up for adoption made for some salacious head-lines. Tracy promptly distanced herself from her husband and immediately defended James as a victim in his father's horrible crimes. Thankfully, the jury didn't buy it and James was in jail and would be for years. Simon was forced off the bench before he'd left the hospital. He was disgraced but walking free. Though he never entered Sullivan's life. Nor had he contacted the Wootens or Malory. It was my understanding, reported by Dalton who went with him to visit Simon, my father made it clear that if he made trouble there'd be hell to pay. Apparently Dalton didn't like when I made fake homicidal threats but it was okay for a father of a daughter who had been violated to kill.

Side note: I agreed.

"Is your girlfriend coming over for dinner tonight?"

He'd met a girl up at Berkley who was from Malibu so about forty minutes away from the Wootens' depending on traffic. She was cute and sweet. I'd FaceTimed with her, too, when she was in Sully's dorm room—hand quotes—studying.

"Are you cray-cray? And have Mom Number One and Bonus Mom there? Um, no. I like Rebecca. I want her to stick around awhile, not run screaming into the night."

Man, I love this kid.

He was funny.

"I see your point. Bonus Mom can be—"

"Claw your face off."

I pinched my lips.

"Too soon?"

I busted out laughing.

We'd talked about that day. He and I knew he'd talked to Malory about it, too.

Right after it happened his parents watched him like a hawk but they'd reported he was fine and didn't have any underlying issues or fear.

"Maybe I should call her Mama Bear instead of Bonus Mom. Or Talon."

"She loves you," I said through my laughter.

"Yeah, she does."

I really, really loved my nephew.

"So no girlfriend tonight—"

"I didn't say that. I said she wasn't coming over for dinner."

I didn't want to know.

Sully was a good-looking boy. Nope, he was a young man and I could imagine if Pam didn't like that cheerleader cheering for her son loudly she'd probably have a heart attack if she saw the dreamy look Rebecca had a few times when we'd video chatted. I knew the look of a good make-out session.

I'd had plenty of those in the last nine months.

"Welp, we should go get that paint," I said and tossed my wrapper into the bag.

"Thank you."

"I should be thanking you for introducing me to the good-ness of a Double-Double with grilled onions and extra sauce."

"No, Auntie, *thank you*."

His tone was heavy with meaning and the air around us had changed.

It was time.

"I love my big sister. After she had you, when she came home something was missing. She was different. She never told us what it was. But I missed her. She was there physically but in all the other ways she was gone. When we were young, she was fun and loud and bold and brave and so funny she'd make me laugh until I peed my pants. But she lost her way, then she lost you, and she lost herself. I missed her. When you found us, she started to come back to herself. But that day when she stepped in front of that gun, she was back. But not fully, not until later that day when you and your parents sat at that table and openly accepted her. Then you called her Bonus Mom, and bam! Just like that, you breathed life back into her. I love you, Sully. I loved you the minute you told me I was your aunt. But when you showed my sister grace and understanding I fell in love with you. I couldn't be more proud to be your aunt, because you're a pretty rad kid. But also because you are the type of man who has it in him to forgive."

"They taught me that. My parents did. But I think she gave it to me."

He was killing me.

Yes, my sister forgave easily.

"I think you're right."

Sully snatched the last three of my fries out of the paper boat.

I rolled my eyes and threw the empty container into the bag.

"What? No threat of bodily harm?" he teased.

"Honestly?"

"No, lie to me, auntie."

"They weren't that great so I don't mind."

"Yeah, Micky D's are way better, but you gotta suffer through the fries to enjoy the Double-Double."

Yup.

I adored my nephew.

"I'VE NEVER BEEN to a beach at sunset," I told Dalton, looking out over the Pacific.

"Really?"

"Nope, only been to the beach on the East Coast."

"Florida?"

"Not the Gulf side."

Dalton tugged me to a stop.

"How do I not know this?"

I shrugged.

"I don't know."

"No, really. I know you can't be alone in the house without the TV or radio on. I know you put more toothpaste on your toothbrush halfway through brushing. You're a shit singer but you still sing and do it loudly and badly." That got him a scowl. "I know you have a compulsion to say 'bless you' every time you hear someone sneeze. You hate your feet being cold. You lift your feet up when I drive over railroad tracks."

"Okay, I get I'm a little nutty and you know it. So what's your point, buckaroo?"

I watched like I always watched when he busted out laughing.

Nine months of hearing and seeing him laugh and it never got old.

"My point is," he said through his laughter. "There's still a lot I don't know about you."

He knew all of the important stuff.

"It's probably going to take me a really long time to know all there is to know about Vanessa Hale." Dalton lifted my hand and kissed my palm. "Might even take the rest of my life."

"That is a very real possibility, Detective. I'm a complicated woman," I teased.

"You are the most uncomplicated woman I've ever met."

That was a nice thing to say.

"But while I'm on this journey of discovery, I want to take it with you as my wife."

I blinked slowly, trying to remember the last time I ate—lobster at Duke's, twenty minutes ago. So I couldn't be having hallucinations due to lack of nutrition. Ditto on the dehydration.

Was he...

"Marry me, sweetness?"

I said not a word as I stared at the man who had not left my side since the night he'd followed me home from the pool hall. The man who had loved me through one of the hardest times of my life and never uttered a single complaint. The man who put up with my bad singing and cold feet and he did it happily.

I didn't settle.

I'd waited for my knight.

"Yes," I whispered.

"Yeah?"

"Yes," I repeated.

Then I was no longer staring at the man I loved.

I was kissing him.

On a beach with the sun setting behind me.

It was the perfect ending to my fairy tale.

"VANESSA," Dalton growled.

My fiancé under me, my hands braced on his chest, I slid up slowly only to slam back down.

"You've got two seconds to stop eying your ring and get down to business."

I smiled but didn't take my eyes off my engagement ring. A perfect solitaire set in white gold that would one day have a band added to it.

"You're done," he grunted.

Dalton flipped me to my back, hooked his arm under the back of my knee, and drove in hard and deep.

"I love you," I panted through his strokes.

"Love you, baby."

And once again I was left with the question: Sweetheart, sweetness, or baby?

The growl, the sweet, or the gentle?

This time, sweetness won out, but only because that was what he called me when he proposed.

I felt his hand go between my legs.

His finger made magic there while his mouth worked my neck.

I'd been wrong.

This was the perfect ending to my fairy tale.

31

SOPHIE

"Sophie, are you listening to me?" my mother snapped.

Nope.

Not even a little bit.

Oftentimes I stopped listening to my mother three minutes into our conversations. This was because it took her approximately three minutes to get through the pleasantries before she started in on my lack of...fill in the blank. Motivation, ambition, drive...those were her favorites, but she had others that included the lack of a man in my life, or social life, or a country club membership—and yes, that was a real complaint. That was where a woman of my age should go to find a man.

My age being thirty-seven not sixty-seven so I was hardly getting ready to die an old maid.

Though if I didn't end this conversation soon I might die of boredom.

And, wow, that made me sound bitchy or like I was a horrible daughter. I wasn't; I loved my mother. But she was a mother, not a mom. Plus, she was a good mother, so really, I shouldn't complain—even mentally—that I wanted to poke my eardrums with ice picks when she started on a rant.

"Sorry, I'm at the grocery store."

"Grocery store?"

She sounded like I'd just told her I was at a female mud wrestling match and I was the main attraction.

"Yes, Mother. I need to eat."

"On a Friday night?"

"Yes, Mother, I tend to eat every night of the week."

"Bless. So much cheek."

The woman couldn't decide if she was a Southerner or British.

Side note: she wasn't either. She was born in England but moved to Kansas when she was five. That was where she met my father —not when she was five, when she was twenty. He was in the Army. According to her they had a whirlwind courtship, got married, and she followed him to Georgia when he PCSed. A year later I was born. She denies it, because a dignified woman didn't have sexual intercourse before marriage —insert eye roll—but her math didn't add up. She was pregnant with me before they'd made it to the altar. Not that it mattered because when his enlistment was up—which was two years after I was born—he took off to parts unknown, never to be heard from again. By then my mom had fallen in love with Georgia, or so she said, but really I think it was because she didn't get along with her very stuffy, stickler British parents. Now, that was not a dig on Brits. I'd been to England, I loved it there and the crap about the stiff upper lip stuff was total BS. The time I'd spent in London I found Londoners to be the opposite of everything I'd heard—most of it coming from my mother who was again five when she left and had only been back for visits since then.

So all of that to say, my mother was a complex and

confusing woman who loved me but damn, if she didn't ride my ass.

How her husband put up with her ranting I'd never know.

Now, Nathan, he didn't rant and drone on. He was neither confusing nor complex. Too bad she only met him seven years ago and got hitched to him two years ago. My childhood would've been much warmer.

"Excuse me."

That didn't come from my mother.

That came from someone next to me.

The voice was smooth like velvet but with a hint of grit.

"Sorry."

I quickly grabbed what I wanted and stepped away from the boxes of linguini I'd been rudely blocking while chatting with my mother.

Why I perused I'd never know. I always got the same brand. I liked what I liked and I didn't deviate.

One could say I lived a narrow life.

One could also say I had zero situational awareness as well. This became embarrassingly apparent when I promptly collided with a black-clad chest.

"Holy shit. I'm sorry." I quickly stepped back, hitting the display of Kraft grated cheese, knocking some of the thankfully plastic containers off the top only to step forward again and slam back into the man in an effort not to knock down the entire display.

"What's happening?" That was my mother.

"Are you alright?" That was the black-clad chest.

I pulled my forehead off the very hard, muscular chest, and tipped my eyes up to find the hottest man I'd ever seen in my life staring down at me.

"Someone kill me," I breathed.

"Do I need to call 9-1-1?" Again, my mother.

"No, Mother, please don't call the police. I'm fine but I have to go."

Without waiting for a response I pulled my phone away from my ear. On my way to shoving my phone into my pocket my hand brushed the man's forearm and hip.

"I promise I'm not trying to be weird and feel you up. I'm just afraid if I move I might do something else embarrassing like, say, trip and fall into the jars of spaghetti sauce. And red's not my color."

Oh my God.

What was wrong with me?

Red's not my color?

The man smiled.

It was dazzling and friendly and holy hot potato I wanted to ask him if I could take a picture. Not to do anything weird like pull it up later tonight while I was playing hide the dildo with my vibrator for extra stimulation—the plug-in kind, since I hadn't had a real penis in so long I'd forgone batteries.

What was better than one toy?

Two.

Two was always better.

But not two in the vagina at once...that was a little too kinky for me. Like double-penetration toy style.

What the hell is wrong with me? I screamed in my head.

"Sorry, God, I'm sorry."

I slowly backed away from the man. When I was far enough away I noticed he was in those black pants that police officers wore with the pockets on the sides and black combat boots.

Of course he was a hot cop.

He could have a whole IG page dedicated to his hotness.

"Nothing to be sorry about."

Before I made a bigger fool out of myself, I smiled and dashed away.

It wasn't until I paid for my pasta and garlic and I was safely in my car did I bust out laughing.

———

A WEEK LATER, it was again Friday night, and I was again going home alone to make dinner for me, myself, and I when it happened.

It went something like this...

"We meet again."

Oh, God, I knew that voice.

Only this time I was not in the grocery store, I was at the liquor store.

This could be dangerous.

"There are glass bottles all around me. I think perhaps it's safer if I stand still and let you grab what you want."

His hand went to my hip, his chest pressed against my back, and he reached around me to grab a bottle of red wine.

I might've moaned.

He might've heard it, if the way his fingers twitched on my hip was anything to go by.

"Thought you didn't like red," he said close to my ear.

His warm breath fanned over my neck. The smell of male sweat and outside and maybe a hint of tobacco invaded my senses. Then there was his voice.

Sweet baby Dolly, I was having a mini orgasm.

My sad, narrow, lonely life had come to this.

A sexy stranger giving me an orgasm in the wine aisle.

I might as well buy five cats, three birds, and start an alone-and-under-forty knitting club.

I had been reduced to voice orgasms.

My mother would say 'I told you so.'

"I'm Valentine," he said, still close.

"Sophie."

"Nice to meet you, Sophie."

Oh, yeah, totally having a vagina spasm.

"Nice to meet you."

That was as far as we got before all hell broke sideways.

And gunshots rang out all around us.

Read about Sophie and Valentine in **Playing with Danger** *coming soon.*

Finding Mercy

Claiming Tuesday

Adoring Delaney

Keeping Quinn

Taking Liberty

Triple Canopy

Damaged

Flawed

Imperfect

Tarnished

Tainted

Conquered

Shattered

Fractured

The Collective

Unbroken

Trust

Standalones

Romancing Rayne

Falling for the Delta Co-written with Susan Stoker

AUDIO

Are you an Audio Fan?

Check out Riley's titles in Audio on Audible and iTunes

Gemini Group

Narrated by: Joe Arden and Erin Mallon

Red Team

Narrated by: Jason Clarke and Carly Robins

Gold Team

Narrated by: Lee Samuels and Maxine Mitchell

The 707 Series

Narrated by: Troy Duran and C. J. Bloom

The Next Generation

Narrated by: Troy Duran and Devon Grace

Triple Canopy

Narrated by: Mackenzie Cartwright and Connor Crais

More audio coming soon!

BE A REBEL

Riley Edwards is a USA Today and WSJ bestselling author, wife, and military mom. Riley was born and raised in Los Angeles but now resides on the east coast with her fantastic husband and children.

Riley writes heart-stopping romance with sexy alpha heroes and even stronger heroines. Riley's favorite genres to write are romantic suspense and military romance.

Don't forget to sign up for Riley's newsletter and never miss another release, sale, or exclusive bonus material.

Rebels Newsletter

Facebook Fan Group

www.rileyedwardsromance.com

facebook.com/Novelist.Riley.Edwards

instagram.com/rileyedwardsromance

bookbub.com/authors/riley-edwards

amazon.com/author/rileyedwards

Made in the USA
Coppell, TX
08 March 2024

29918119R00193